WHAT READERS ARE SAYING...

ABOUT JOSLYN CHASE

"Author Joslyn Chase has now confirmed my first impressions of her being a formidable suspense writer bound to make readers sit up and take notice." ~ **Amazon reader**

"Joslyn Chase's storytelling prowess transcends mere excitement; it ventures into the realm of inspiration, reminding us of the power of narrative artistry." ~ **Conrad Bux, author of** *Killer Witness*

"Author Joslyn Chase expertly weaves high-stakes action with complex character development to please readers who want a fully-rounded novel." ~ **Reader's Favorite**

"As always in her writing, the settings and action scenes are vividly portrayed and the relationships between the characters are seamless and authentic. Ms Chase has a talent for bringing characters to life." ~ **ReadnGrow**

"There is a reason Chase is an award-winning author. Highly recommended." ~ **Justin Boote, author of *Badass***

"The author is a great storyteller." ~ **AstraDaemon**

"Joslyn Chase skillfully connects subplots, then injects a few surprises, then connects things again in an interesting cycle; weave, disassemble, repeat." ~ **Ron Keeler, Read 4 Fun**

"In the movie Field of Dreams, there is a now famous line, "If you build it, they will come." Apply this sentiment to Joslyn Chase—if she writes it, we will come and read it." ~ **William DeProspo, author of *Unlikely Outcome***

"Joslyn Chase paints intriguing pictures with vivid, colorful descriptions...you feel like you have a front row seat from which to watch as everything unfolds." ~ **Amazon reader**

Get your next Joslyn Chase book free!

But catch up on your sleep now.
Once you start reading,
it'll be *No Rest* for you!

Get the book free when you join
the growing group of readers who've discovered
the thrill of Chase!

Get started now at joslynchase.com or
simply scan the QR code below

ALSO BY JOSLYN CHASE

Nocturne in Ashes

Staccato Passage

Cincher's Waltz

Steadman's Blind

The Steadman Mysteries series

The Tal Bannerman Thriller series

The Cathryn Harcourt Mystery Shorts

The Historic Suspense series

The Tower

The Devil's Trumpet

Falling For The Lost Dutchman

No Rest

What Leads a Man to Murder

Death of a Muse

RAPID PURSUIT

14 Short Thrillers & Fast-Paced Suspense Stories

JOSLYN CHASE

PARAQUEL PRESS

RAPID PURSUIT

"A Band of Scheming Women" was first published in *Thrill Ride Magazine*, March 2024

"Still in the Family" was first published in *MCM, Passionate Crimes*, May 2021

"Kissed by the Snow Angel" was first published in *Steadman's Blind*, November 2019

"Death Makes a Dinner Date" was first published in *Alfred Hitchcock's Mystery Magazine*, July/August 2021

"Beyond the Horizon" was first published in *MCM, Black Widows*, May 2022

"Colder Than Gazpacho" was first published in *MCM, Betrayal*, February 2024

"A Study in Cashmere" was first published in *Short Fiction Break*, July 2020

"The Wolf & Lamb" was first published in *Alfred Hitchcock's Mystery Magazine*, May/June 2020

"Chamber of Vengeance" was first published in *Mystery Magazine*, October 2021

Publisher's Cataloging-in-PublicationData
Names: Chase, Joslyn.
Title: Rapid pursuit : 14 short thrillers & fast-paced suspense stories / JoslynChase.
Description:University Place, WA : ParaquelPress, 2025.
Identifiers: LCCN 2025900164 | ISBN9781952647338 (pbk.) | ISBN 9781952647321(ebook) | ISBN 9781952647468 (audiobook)
Subjects: LCSH:Suspense fiction. | BISAC: FICTION/ Thrillers / Suspense. | FICTION / Mystery& Detective / General. | FICTION / Thrillers / General.
Classification: LCC PS3603.H37 R37 2025| DDC 813 C--dc23
LC record available at https://lccn.loc.gov/2025900164

Contents

INTRODUCTION

Conflict is the heart of story.

In a short story, that conflict is often concentrated into a potent little package that delivers a punch. That's one of the charms inherent in short stories, and a superlative reason for reading them.

Everyone, everywhere, every day, is after something.

In pursuit of a goal.

In a story, as in real life, reaching the goal is rarely easy. Obstacles stand in the way. Other people compete for the same objective. We struggle internally with diverging desires.

The characters in the stories of this book are the same. They are all in pursuit of one aim or another. And, as the title suggests, they are fast at it.

Short stories are like gold nuggets—little treasures you can read and enjoy without a large investment of time. By their nature, they allow the writer to take greater risks, with the potential of a big return in story value for the reader.

Despite the smaller package they come in, short stories must deliver an emotional impact. Some of the most memorable reading experiences I've had came by way of a short story.

Off the top of my head, I remember the lasting emotional impact these stories left on me:

O Henry's "The Gift of the Magi"

"The Lottery," Shirley Jackson

Ernest Hemingway's "Indian Camp"

Stephen King's "Quitters, Inc."

"A Good Man is Hard to Find," Flannery O'Connor

Susan Glaspell's, "A Jury of Her Peers"

"Haircut," Ring Lardner

Jeffery Deaver's "The Weekender"

"Catch and Release," Lawrence Block

David Morrell's "The Abelard Sanction"

"The Veldt," Ray Bradbury

"Success of a Mission," Dennis Lynds

"She Fell Among Thieves," Robert Edmund Alter

Roald Dahl's "The Landlady"

"Don't Look Now," Daphne du Maurier

"The Necklace," Guy de Maupassant

I had to stop myself there because there are so many more to list.

Short stories are often sorely overlooked as a source for reading satisfaction and emotional sway. Many highly popular Hollywood hits are based on short stories, such as *Rear Window*, *Memento*, and *The Shawshank Redemption*.

With this book in your hands, you are wisely indulging in the advantages of the short story!

Many of the selections in *Rapid Pursuit* are companion pieces to my thriller novels. It is my hope that you will enjoy following the various characters to the novels they sprang from for more adventure, suspense, and impactful reading pleasure.

Thank you!

Author's Note

Fastpitch

I lived in Suffolk, not far from Virginia Beach, for several years and remember the tension hanging heavy with each passing hurricane season. My husband was a US Navy submariner, and when a hurricane threatened, he was part of the crew that had to take the submarine into the depths where it was safe from the storm.

Leaving me and the kids to weather it on our own.

During one such monster storm, I stepped out onto the porch and saw the sky had turned green. I packed up the kiddoes and headed inland, to my sister-in-law's in Kentucky. Just minutes ahead of the evacuation order that would clog the highways.

A few days later, we returned to devastation and began the long work of cleaning up the mess.

When Leah Cutter, the editor of *Mystery, Crime, and Mayhem* magazine invited me to submit a story with an extreme weather theme, I harked back to that experience and used it to create a fast-paced short thriller I hoped readers would love. "Fastpitch" was originally published in *MCM's* November 2024 issue.

So, hold on to your hat, turn the page, and let yourself get blown away!

FASTPITCH

Cold rain pelted down like gunfire, peppering the concrete landing beneath Jake Parkin's feet and sending him into a skid as he rushed around the corner toward the staircase. The pounding barrage blotted out the sounds he was used to hearing—the plaintive cries of hovering seagulls, the whir and crank of traffic on the avenue running alongside the high-rise apartment building where he worked as head of security.

A low ominous boom of thunder, like a cannon in the distance, rose above the rainsound as Jake gripped the glass door leading into the staircase vestibule, fighting the wind to get it open. He had fifteen floors to patrol and rarely used the elevator. The stairs helped keep him fit. Maybe not as toned as he'd been before retiring from the Virginia Beach Police Department, but reasonably ready to roll with whatever punches fell his way.

This afternoon, he had a more immediate reason for shunning the elevator.

Hurricane Pablo.

The tropical monster was sweeping toward the coast with a voracious hunger, heralded by a lash of wicked thunderstorms. The city's power grid was holding, but the juice could stop flowing at any moment and the last thing he wanted was to be trapped between floors in a heavy, metal box.

Many of the building's residents had followed the recommendation to evacuate but by Jake's reckoning, thirty-two people remained. Harvey Browning, the building's owner, had offered to let him off the hook.

"It's going to be a bad one, Jake. People have been warned. The smart ones are long gone."

Jake coughed into his hand. "Some of those still here are staying out of necessity," he said, thinking about Anna and her bed-ridden grandmother on the second floor. He watched his employer's ginger-colored eyebrows waggle up and down like boats on a choppy sea and knew the man was worried.

"I can't force you to stay under these circumstances. Get yourself clear, Jake. Stay safe. Then haul your butt back here and help me clean up the mess."

A moment passed, punctuated by the wind howling at the window. "I'll stay, sir," Jake said quietly. "I wouldn't feel right leaving my post at a time like this."

Browning nodded. "I figured that's how you'd feel about it. As for me, I'm grabbing the wife and high tailing it out of here. I wish you the best."

Now, six hours after he'd made that choice, Jake wondered if it was the right one.

He'd spent the intervening time checking and re-checking the security system and storm protection measures, reassuring nervous residents about the approaching hurricane. The building housed eight apartments on each level, with a luxury penthouse occupying the entire fifteenth floor.

The couple leasing the penthouse were currently basking on the French Riviera, so at least they were safely out of it, though damage to the apartment could potentially destroy a lot of expensive furnishings.

Or worse—breach the security system, putting the Franzen treasures at risk.

Jake had seen a copy of their insurance policy. He knew they kept jewels on the premises, rare and valuable coins, bullion. He'd be willing to bet they had a hefty stash of emergency cash, as well.

Testing every door, every junction box and connection, Jake walked his beat. Each apartment's entrance opened onto a common landing in the center of the building, open to the sky and circling the two elevators and sets of stairs.

He'd made his rounds, floor by floor, to the top of the building and back down again, getting soaked by the wind-blown pellets of rain. He stopped now at Apartment 203 and pressed the doorbell.

Anna's face as she peered out was wan and creased with worry. "Jake, you're sopping wet! Come in. I'll get you a towel."

Jake waved off the suggestion. "I'm okay. How are you and Juanita holding up?"

"I'm hanging in there, and grandma's in good spirits. Dr. Caldwell—he's the new therapist she's been seeing—prepared her for this eventuality. She's feeling strong."

"Glad to hear it. How are you feeling?"

She laughed. "Some of the good doctor's healing has rubbed off on me, I guess. I attend all grandma's sessions with her and..." She stopped, a rosy blush coming up on her cheeks. "He's been kind enough to give me some free counsel, as well."

Not a bit surprising. Anna, with her sweet, earnest face and obvious devotion to her grandmother, would elicit kindness in an eel. Jake touched her gently on the arm.

"Do you have enough flashlights and fresh batteries?" he asked. "What about bottled water?"

"We've got all that," Anna told him, a small smile easing the tension behind her eyes. "We'll fare better here on the second floor than those in the apartments above."

"Yes, count yourselves lucky," Jake said, packing some cheer into his voice. He refrained from pointing out the flaw in her reasoning, because she was right.

Unless the storm surge led to extensive flooding.

Originally from Puerto Rico, Anna Torres moved last year to Virginia Beach to be with her grandmother and help care for the ailing woman. The 28-year-old paramedic was known and loved among the residents for her warm and open spirit, bravery, and dedication to helping others.

Sentiments heartily shared by Jake.

With almost twenty years between their ages, Jake tried to squelch anything else he might feel for her. But it was becoming increasingly difficult to tamp down the admiration that grew as they spent time together on their local fastpitch softball league where she covered second base while he manned the pitcher's mound.

The after-game pizza dinners. The good-natured joking around while waiting in the dugout. The euphoric group hugs after a victorious game.

"Don't worry, Anna," he said, giving her hand a quick squeeze. "This'll blow over before you know it. In the meantime, I'll do all I can to keep everyone safe."

"I know you will."

Her words rang in his ears as she shut the door, leaving behind a bitter and mocking resonance. She believed him, trusting that he would do all he could to keep everyone safe.

But she didn't know about the man lying dead after the last disaster Jake had managed.

She didn't know about David.

Maxwell Kane braced his palms on the sill as he stared out the window, his back to the three-man crew waiting silently behind him. Two of them, Joiner and Conrad, didn't want to be here, had voiced their opinions on the violence of the storm and their desire to join the residents fleeing the city.

Lutz, the remaining member of the team, had impressed upon them the necessity of staying. Impressed it very firmly upon them, backing his argument with a description of what had happened to the fourth crewman as he'd attempted to run.

They would stay.

The rain continued, flung sideways by the turbulent winds and carrying the taste of salt from the Atlantic, just two blocks to the east. It spat against the window glass with monotonous severity. Kane turned, jaw set, and surveyed his men.

"There is no security on this earth; there is only opportunity," he said, quoting his favorite role model, General Douglas MacArthur. "This, gentlemen, is ours."

"Tailor-made, in fact," Lutz added. "With the Franzens out of the country and the building's security force pared down to one man, the pickings ought to be easy."

Kane felt a grim stab of satisfaction as he thought of that lone man standing between them and the Franzen treasure house. He wouldn't be standing for long.

"Let's not get ahead of ourselves," he cautioned. "Easy may not be the best word applied to our situation. But possible. Yes, gloriously possible."

He lifted his bottle of beer from the table, gone warm in the sullen humidity brought by the storm. "To Pablo," he said, tapping the amber glass against Lutz's own.

"To Pablo," the crewmen echoed, raising their bottles.

Back at his security post, Jake reviewed the emergency protocols for the building as he chewed on a roast beef sandwich that stuck dry in his throat. He considered tossing the whole thing in the trash but knew he'd need the energy to get through this storm. Instead, he washed it down with half a glass of gingerale and ignored the burn rising in his gut.

The TV screen mounted high on the wall to his left cast a blue glaze over the desk, tinting the spreadsheets and loosely organized stacks of paperwork scattered over its surface. A change in the shifting colors caught Jake's attention and he peered up at the screen, pointing the remote to raise the volume.

"...now classed as a Category 5 hurricane and predicted to strike land along the North Carolina and southern Virginia coastline sometime during the next hour."

Jake watched the news reporter's expensively-styled glossy dark hair pull away from its moorings and flap around her head like a flock of desperate bats. With the palm trees blowing sideways in the background, it made for dramatic television viewing.

"Despite orders to evacuate," the woman continued, shouting to be heard over the shriek of the gale, "some residents are opting to ride out the storm, stocking up on bottled water and non-perishable snacks, boarding up windows and sandbagging against the flood."

Something that looked like a barn door blew past behind her head and the camera angle shifted violently for a second or two before static claimed the screen. Jake switched it off.

Outside, the whiny pitch of the wind rose to a maniacal roar, shaking the building and sending a shiver along the fine hairs at the back of Jake's neck.

Pablo had arrived.

Maxwell Kane steered the white panel truck down the deserted avenue, tightly gripping the wheel as a long series of vicious gusts threatened to take control. There was virtually no traffic to deal with, but flotsam thrown by the storm littered the road, some of it stationary, requiring him to dodge around it.

And some of it still moving in jerky, unpredictable snatches. It gave Kane the willies, making him feel like prey stalked by a pack of moonstruck wolves.

He tightened his jaw and kept his eyes fastened on the rain-lashed street ahead. The apartment building's underground garage was blocked by a wall of sandbags in an attempt to keep the storm surge from flooding in.

Pulling the van to the curb, he set the brake and glared out the windshield. He'd planned this operation and waited for a big storm, counting on it to provide the cover and confusion he'd need to pull it off. But, capricious and volatile, the hurricane could work against him, as well.

A lot would depend on luck.

"The best luck of all is the luck you make for yourself," he growled under his breath, reaching once again for the wisdom of MacArthur. Kane had spent the last year grinding out the details, making his own luck. Things would fall his way.

He shifted his gaze to the rearview mirror, locking eyes first with Joiner and then with Conrad in the back. Turning to Lutz, he nodded.

"Let's move out."

As they'd been drilled to do, his crew grabbed their equipment and deployed, moving into position. Kane, Lutz, and Joiner slipped quickly inside the building, melting into the shadows, while Conrad made ready in the van parked far below the penthouse balcony.

Uniformed as maintenance workers carrying toolboxes and wheeling large protective packing crates, each had a vital function to perform in a short amount of time. Seventeen and a half minutes later, Kane joined Lutz in the foyer outside the penthouse apartment. He watched his lieutenant wipe a bead of sweat from his forehead.

"It's done," Lutz announced. "The entire alarm system is ours."

"And the elevators?" Kane asked.

"Locked down tight. No one is going anywhere."

Kane ran a diagnostic to confirm he had control of the building's security system. As the green light flashed on his tablet's screen, he heard the clang of metal on metal and looked up to see Joiner snap the padlock on the last looped chain blocking off all doors to the stairwells.

"Building is secure, sir," Conrad said, standing at attention.

"Excellent." Kane slipped the tablet into his pocket and turned to Lutz. "Time to advance. Get us in there," he commanded.

Jake watched in horrified frustration as the malfunctioning security network beeped and wailed. He'd cast in his two cents when Browning asked his opinion on the building's new protection system. He thought it relied too much on internet connections and not enough on old school redundancies.

The hurricane was wreaking havoc on it and the surveillance monitors had been the first to go. Jake felt like a blind man as, one by one, the screens winked out, going black. He fiddled with the control panel to no avail and tried rebooting the system without success.

Something was wrong.

Jake checked his weapon and holster. Zipping into a charcoal gray windbreaker, he raised the hood and exited the security office. Buffeted by frenzied gusts, he pushed his way toward the staircase vestibule and froze. The chill that feathered down his spine had nothing to do with the cold rain slapping against his bowed head.

A heavy chain snaked through the door handles, secured by a sturdy padlock.

Jake yanked the cell phone from his pocket, almost dropping it, and dialed 9-1-1. The call didn't go through.

He wasn't surprised. He knew cell towers were likely over-burdened or knocked out of commission by the storm. Jake also knew exactly what the chain and lock signified.

Burglars in the penthouse.

He thought about the Franzen's hefty insurance policy. Though it cut against the grain, he reasoned that maybe his best move was to hunker down in the office and let it happen. He had no way of knowing how many intruders were involved and it appeared as if they'd planned well. It was only material goods, after all. Property that the insurance company would pay to replace.

But what if it wasn't?

What if someone else tried to intervene, got in the way? What if the burglars decided shaking down one rich plum at the top of the tree wasn't enough?

Jake had pledged to protect everyone in the building. He could not just sit on his hands and hope no one got hurt. He knew, by wretched experience, how it felt to carry the guilt of a death he should have prevented, and he didn't want to add a single ounce to that burden.

Rubbing a hand across his forehead, he flicked rainwater off his face and gnashed his teeth, squinting up through the building's open central column at the fifteen stories rising above him.

He was going up.

Jake let himself into the maintenance room and surveyed the shelves, hoping something helpful would jump out at him. The air felt heavy on his skin—ominous, smothering, and briny. It cast over Jake the sensation of drowning and he gulped down a breath, savoring the swell of oxygen in his lungs.

He found a length of nylon rope and a box of large metal hooks the manager used for suspending heavy potted plants in the building's exterior walkways. Using three of the hooks along with a couple feet of sturdy flexi-wire and a bottle of no-nail super tack adhesive, Jake fashioned a grappling hook and fastened it to the rope. He knotted the rope at four-foot intervals.

The storm, as he stepped back outside, sounded like a hell-bound freight train full of shrieking passengers. He shuddered to think of the devastation it was leaving in its wake. Here, down low and inside the protected column of the well-built high-rise, the raging effects were mitigated. But each floor he ascended would bring him closer to the monster outside.

And the demons within.

The rain had slackened but still dripped down, bringing occasional debris with it, plucked from the littered sky. Jake gathered some essential items into a backpack and slung it over his shoulders, glad now that he'd forced down that roast beef sandwich. Something told him he'd be calling on all his energy reserves before the storm blew over.

Standing in the central courtyard, Jake swung the rope, propelling his makeshift grappling hook up and over the railing of the second floor. It caught and he tested it with his weight before using it to help him climb up and slip over the balustrade.

Releasing the hook, he took his contraption with him as he hurried to Anna's apartment and quickly explained the situation.

"Stay hidden," he warned her, "and keep your grandmother safe."

"But Jake, I should go with you. I'm a paramedic. There's no telling what you'll encounter up there. You may need me."

He gave her a quick smile. "I appreciate that, Anna, but Juanita needs you more. You have to be here for her."

A crease rose on Anna's forehead. Jake wanted to reach out and smooth it away. "You know I'm right," he said instead. "I have to go. Stay safe."

Hearing the door of her apartment snap shut behind him, Jake felt utterly alone. He was probably stupid for pushing ahead on his half-formed plan to defend and protect, yet he knew he couldn't do anything else.

Doubt pressed heavily on him as he leaned out over the second floor railing and tossed the hook up to the third floor landing. He was remembering the last time his plans had gone all wrong, forcing his retirement from the job he loved.

What if something like that happened again?

Despite the dark and violent frenzy happening outside the thick plate glass windows, the interior of the Franzen apartment looked like the layout of a glossy magazine. Kane felt a jab of malicious glee that went beyond the satisfaction of riches within his grasp. Such a perfectly put-together life deserved to be disrupted. Begged for it.

He was happy to oblige.

The three polyethylene packing crates lay open on the living room floor, ready to receive. Lutz had found the wall safe and was working his magic on the dials. Joiner began filling a crate with silver from the dining room, wrapping pieces of priceless Sevres porcelain and Capodimonte figurines. The place was like a museum filled with treasures.

Kane couldn't wait to see what the safe contained. Geoffrey Franzen collected coins and was quoted in *Forbes* as a big believer in stocking up on precious metals. His wife adored extravagant jewelry and Geoffrey was known as an indulgent husband.

Licking his lips, Kane peered over Lutz's shoulder, gauging his progress. He was about to urge him on when a voice sounded from the front hall.

"Geoffrey? I saw your door was open...Hope it's okay if I come in."

A high-pitched male voice. Finicky-sounding. "I thought you were still enjoying the sunshine in southern France. What a day you picked to come home!"

Joiner looked up from his wrapping, a question on his face. Kane shook his head. "I'll go," he mouthed. Drawing his pistol, he stalked into the penthouse apartment's entrance hall.

"Back out, the way you came," he commanded, holding the gun steady, aimed at the guy's head.

Geoffrey's neighbor stammered, his sweaty moon face going pale, mouth opening and closing soundlessly, like a fish. Raising his hands, he stepped backward on the marble tiles. Kane motioned with the gun for him to continue out the door.

Following, he backed the hapless neighbor up to the railing and sensed the guy was about to find his voice in a nasty scream. Before that could happen, Kane stepped forward and rapped him hard with the butt of his gun. The man crumpled.

"Joiner!" Kane called. "Help me out."

Together, they lifted the unconscious man.

"He got a good look at your face," Joiner said, scowling.

"True," Kane agreed. "But anything could happen in a storm like this."

Joiner met his eye. Nodded. "Yeah, anything."

Both of them grunting under the man's considerable weight, they heaved him over the rail.

From the corner of his eye, Jake saw something flash past, falling from above. It thudded onto the pavement below with a sound that sent an icy weight sinking in Jake's gut. He was nine stories up now, climbing the slippery rails floor by floor with his rope and homemade grappler, fighting the squall that threatened his every move.

Peering down into the courtyard below, he saw a dark human-shaped heap on the pavement and knew that some malevolent force—storm or otherwise—had claimed a victim. Despite his best efforts.

It was clear there was nothing he could do for the man on the ground, and there were others at risk, vulnerable and unaware of hazards beyond the storm. Jake pressed onward and upward.

The lights outside each apartment flickered and went out, casting a dark shadow over the courtyard and the tiers rising above it. Power to the building had failed.

Or been deliberately cut.

As Jake flung his leg over the rail of the tenth floor, he heard a long, drawn-out scream. The roar of the hurricane rose to an unbearable pitch, drowning out the rest of it. Jake leapt from the rail as a nearby apartment door burst open, almost blowing off its hinges.

A man and woman rushed out, clinging to each other, their faces etched with terror. Behind them, the interior of the apartment seemed to swirl and buckle, one entire wall blasted away by the ferocious gale.

Jake shoved the door closed, managing to latch it shut. Another couple erupted from the apartment next door, shouting something Jake couldn't hear over the howling storm. Wordlessly, he shepherded the Crowleys and Goodmans to the leeward side of the building and dug in his pocket for the master key, using it to open a vacant apartment.

Once inside the gloom-shrouded space with the door closed, he was able to make himself heard. "Stay in here," he told the foursome, "and keep the door locked."

"Shouldn't we go down to a lower level?" Gene Crowley asked. "Hurricane could blow the whole top off the building."

"I'm afraid we're dealing with more than just Pablo," Jake said.

Jill Goodman stared at him, her eyes wide and rimmed with smeared mascara. "What do you mean?"

Jake didn't want to scare them more than they already were. "Just stay in here together and lock the door."

"Jake's right," Crowley said. Giving his wife and the others a nudge toward the kitchen, he drew Jake aside. "I saw the rope hanging from the railing. What's going on, Jake? Why don't you want us going down?"

"The stairs are blocked, elevators useless. I'm using the rope to make my way to the penthouse."

"Blocked how? What are you talking about?"

"The building is under seige, Gene, and the hurricane's knocked out all communications. I'm sure the Franzens are the target. I'm hoping the intruders will limit their activities to the fifteenth floor."

"But you're going up there? To what end, Jake? To try stopping it?"

Jake shifted, impatient to get going. "That's not my primary objective. I'm concerned with the safety of the tenants. We've already—"

He broke off, but Gene Crowley picked it up. "We've already...what?"

"We've already lost one," Jake admitted. "There's a sight on the courtyard floor you won't want the ladies to see. Just stay here and keep your group safe."

Crowley's face was gray in the shadows, his eyes like sunken pools of darkness. "Okay, Jake. I see your point. I'll man the fort."

"Thank you."

Without another word, Jake left the apartment and hurried back to his grappling hook, half afraid the storm might have stolen it. But the hook and rope waited for him, and Jake used them to gain the eleventh floor and then the twelfth, checking each before proceeding.

Hurricane Pablo showed no sign of weakening or departing. It continued to rage and Jake felt the savagery of its bite more and more with each level he rose. Poised on his slender rope, high off the ground as the tempest buffeted him like a kite on a string, Jake fought his way from the twelfth floor to the thirteenth and then to the fourteenth.

His stomach knotted tighter than the rope as he threw his leg over the rail of the penthouse level, pulled himself up, and reached for his gun. With the stairway doors secured and the elevators out of commission, Jake figured the burglars would not be expecting him or anyone else.

He was wrong.

"Hello, Jake."

Shock rammed the breath from his lungs and Jake gasped, working to get it back. Squinting in the dark, he stared at the man in front of him and felt the fine hairs at the back of his neck rise to attention.

Maxwell Kane stood before him.

David's brother.

Kane allowed himself a smile, gratified at the look of stupid amazement stamped over Jake Parkin's features. Maybe the man had been trying hard to forget him, to forget how things went down that day.

Trying to forget how David had died from the bullet meant, instead, for him.

Maybe the man before him, panting like a dog, had put all his efforts into forgetting. But Kane had spent every day since that awful event remembering.

And anticipating.

Kane pointed his pistol at Jake, motioning for him to drop his own gun. After a moment's hesitation loaded with a dirty look, he did.

"Kick it over the side."

Another pause while Jake glared. Then, almost casually, the man nudged the gun under the railing with his boot. It disappeared into the gloom.

"Why don't we go inside," Kane suggested, pitching his voice like a thoughtful host inviting his guest in for lemonade. Once past the threshold, he shouted for Joiner who brought a dining chair into the living room and placed it beside the three crates, now nearly full and ready to be closed.

"Have a seat, Jake. We're just finishing up." He nodded to Joiner and watched him fasten Jake's wrists and ankles to the chair's appendages with sturdy cable ties.

"You may be wondering why I don't just shoot you now," he said.

Jake said nothing.

"Or maybe it's occurred to you that I could simply bludgeon you over the head with any number of handy instruments and blame it on Pablo."

Jake said nothing.

"Or shove you over the side like I did with your fat former resident."

Kane waited, but the man in the chair remained silent.

"I do none of these things, Jake, because any one of them would be too quick. Too painless. I want you to live with the torture of guilt for a good long while. I want you to suffer, as I have, for eternity."

Kane moved to the crate now filled with the contents of the wall safe. It had met, and exceeded, his expectations. Opening a velvet case, he lifted an exquisite emerald necklace and let the silken jewels slide across his fingers.

"Have you noticed the howl of the storm letting up? The eye of the hurricane is upon us. In this lull, we will lower these crates to the van below and make our escape. I do not think anyone will stop us."

Jake's silence and expressionless face fanned the flame burning in Kane's gut, fueling his desire to stab at the man, get beneath his skin.

"Oh, but there's one stop I have to make before I leave here," he said, squatting to put himself on Jake's level, not wanting to miss one scintilla of the pain and fear he meant to instill.

Reaching beneath the collar of his shirt, he pulled forth a lanyard with a laminated ID card attached. He showed it to Jake, reveling in the look of distressed alarm crossing the hated man's face.

"Dr. Caldwell needs to make a house call," he said.

Jake stared at the ID card dangling before him, recognizing the name. Understanding its significance.

Kane had been watching him, planning this moment with meticulous cunning. Somehow, the vindictive man had been masquerading as the therapist treating Juanita Torres and worming his way into the confidence of her unsuspecting granddaughter.

Preparing to betray them all.

Kane smirked, malicious and gloating with delight. "And here's the kicker, Jake. You'll enjoy hearing this—Anna imagines herself in love with you."

The words hit like a sucker punch to the gut—lightning fast, unexpected, releasing a blast of pain. Jake gritted his teeth, determined not to show how hard the blow had landed, and glared at the man in front of him.

Kane's eyes, cold and calculating, held his gaze. The corner of his mouth flickered in contempt. "I thought you should know that before I kill her. You can live with the agony of how things could have been, stew in the misery of losing the one who loved you."

A wave of anguish shimmered through Jake as he thought of Anna in the hands of this monster. But it was David's face that flashed in his memory, the look crossing his features as he'd fallen, struggling to speak and unable to utter anything beyond a burbling groan.

Whether David had deliberately shielded Jake or stepped inadvertently into the trajectory of the bullet fired from Kane's gun no one would ever know. But there was something Jake knew about David that his brother didn't.

Jake had believed he was being merciful and discreet by not divulging it, by sparing Kane the sting of knowing. If he'd let the whole story come out, would any of this be happening now?

Or would the rage and malice riveted on Jake be exponentially greater if Kane knew? If he'd understood that David was the confidential informant working with police to foil the meticulously mapped-out bank job?

Despite the fact that he had been the one to pull the trigger, Kane held Jake solely responsible for the death of the big brother he idolized. If Jake cracked that veneer, revealed David's betrayal, what would happen then?

He thought it could be the straw that would break Kane, stripping away the leash holding his fury in check, turning it loose.

It could be the last thing he ever said, but it would focus Kane's killing intent on Jake.

Away from Anna.

And once Jake was dead, Kane's reason for harming Anna would be too. His sense of self-preservation would kick in and he'd vanish along with his stolen riches.

Would it happen that way?

Jake thought it would. He opened his mouth to speak.

And the world went black.

It was the smell that woke him.

Jake swam up into consciousness, the strong odors of ozone and sea brine acting like smelling salts, pulling him to the surface. The roar and swirl of the storm hit him like an ocean wave and his eyes snapped open, staring about him in the dimness of the Franzen apartment.

Still strapped to the chair, Jake tugged at his bonds but they held tight. Kane and his crew were gone. The crates were gone. The balcony slider gaped wide open, letting in gusts of wind as the eye of the hurricane passed and the storm's violence began to rise again.

Rocking and scooting the chair, Jake inched toward the apartment's stone fireplace, hoping to find a projection within reach and jagged enough to saw through the cable tie holding his left wrist.

He had no luck there, but found an artsy brass-rimmed table nearby that offered a semi-sharp edge. Jake's efforts caused the tough plastic of the zip tie to tear into his flesh and the honed brass left its bite, as well.

Accompanied by the ghostly shrieks and wails of the strengthening gale, his forearm now slick with blood, Jake continued to work the tie back and forth, leaning into it, until at last the cable popped, falling away.

He flexed his wrist, feeling the pins and needles of returning circulation. With frantic haste, he hobbled the chair into the kitchen, grabbing a knife from the butcher block with his freed left hand.

The roar like a freight train in the distance grew louder as Jake cut through the remaining ties. He ran to the balcony and ventured to the rail, peering out into the gathering darkness. On the street below, he saw a white van and one of the crates. Presumably, the other two had already been loaded.

Debris fluttered and flitted along the road, but Jake saw no human movement. He went inside and closed the door.

He hoped to heaven he wasn't too late.

Grabbing a heavy Remington sculpture from the brass-rimmed table, Jake ran from the apartment to the chained stairwell door. He used the Remington to smash open the pad-lock and raced down the stairs, pausing on the second floor. The chain and lock disabling the door were on the outside, out of reach.

Agonizingly torn, Jake weighed the option of going down to the courtyard to search for his gun against the need to reach Anna and her grandmother as rapidly as possible.

He raised the Remington and heaved it against the glass of the door.

It bounced off, leaving only a small crack. Jake retrieved the sculpture and threw it again. And again.

Desperate with fear, unable to keep visions of what Kane might be doing to Anna and Juanita from flooding across his brain, Jake picked up the heavy bronze horse and hurled it with all his strength.

A spiderweb of cracks appeared and Jake kicked at it with his boot, clearing away enough of the glass for him to crabwalk through the gap. He sprinted to Anna's apartment. The door was locked, and he used the master key to let himself in, hands trembling, mind fizzing with urgency.

As he entered, he heard Juanita's voice but couldn't distinguish her words. The tone was fretful and bewildered, rather than frightened. It was Anna's voice, as she comforted her grandmother, that held fear and awareness. She understood they were in danger.

Thank heaven they were both still alive.

Jake drew a shaky breath and moved stealthily toward the hall closet door. The noise of the storm provided cover as he opened it and grasped the softball bat Anna kept there. He'd seen her stow it after their Saturday morning league games. After a second's hesitation, he grabbed the ball, as well.

The short entryway ended in a ninety-degree-angle turn into the dining room and the living room beyond that. Jake stood, his back against the wall as the sound of Pablo outside spiked intermittently, wiping out most of the tense exchange taking place. Risking a peek around the corner, Jake saw the women seated on the sofa with Maxwell Kane standing six feet in front of them, holding a gun.

He wasn't aiming the gun at Anna or Juanita. Just holding it casually at his side, knowing the threat of it would be enough for his purpose.

Which was what, exactly?

Jake fully believed Kane's announcement that he intended to kill Anna. Why hadn't he done it immediately?

Because he meant to do it in such a way to cause maximum pain to Jake. Which translated to maximum pain for Anna.

He meant to do something unbearable to her first.

The clamor of the storm washed over Jake, sounding like a crowd gone wild at a close-run ballgame. Biting his lip, he stepped around the corner and blasted the softball at Kane's gun hand as if the league championship—and something far more important—depended on that single pitch.

The ball struck Kane on the wrist and he dropped the gun, stepping back in surprise.

Jake rushed him, switching to the football tactics he hadn't used since college. They landed together in a heap on the floor, knocking over the coffee table.

"Take Juanita and get out of here," Jake shouted to Anna. He couldn't spare a glance to see if she'd heard and was complying. All his attention was on the man straining beneath him, trying to reach the gun three feet from his groping fingers.

Outside, Pablo was roaring and the seas were rising at his command. From the corner of his eye, Jake saw foamy waves licking against the window glass of the second-floor balcony.

Kane had given up on reaching the gun, instead aiming his clawed fingers at Jake's eyes. Jake grabbed his hand and twisted hard, feeling something snap as Kane growled and writhed beneath him.

They wrestled. Sweat dripped into Jake's eyes, stinging. He felt himself tiring and as he struggled to find his second wind, the floor suddenly sagged beneath them, dipping so they both slid along its surface toward the hole opening in the dissolving wall of the apartment.

Kane got a foot planted and levered himself over, flipping out from under Jake and ending up on top as they rolled along the slanting floor. He slammed a fist in Jake's face, smashing into the cheek bone. A gray haze crept into the corners of Jake's vision and Kane's hands went to his throat, squeezing.

But whatever Jake had done to his fingers made the stranglehold impossible to sustain. With a curse, Kane let go and Jake gasped in a breath as a piece of the apartment wall disappeared, sucked into the maw of the storm.

"Know this, Jake!" Kane shouted. "I'll find that girl and kill her. Like you killed David. No one in this world cared about me as much as he did."

Face twisted with fury and malice, Kane stared down, locking eyes with Jake. "You took him from me!"

Jake bucked, trying to shake Kane off him. "I'm sure you're right. David probably did care about you more than anyone else."

Grunting in rage, Kane dug an elbow into Jake's gut. Jake knocked it aside and huffed, "Maybe that's why he came to me and filled me in on all the little details of your heist. He wanted to stop you from doing something stupid."

Kane's eyes flew wide, and he grabbed Jake's face with his good hand, gouging in with the fingers. "You're lying! David would never!"

Jake bit at the hand and Kane pulled it away. "David did. How else would we have known all about your plans."

"You lying sack—"

The floor beneath them collapsed. The wall opened wide, a hungry mouth, sucking greedily. Salt spray slapped, cold and shocking the breath from Jake's lungs. He scrambled to grab hold of something solid and got a hand around a pipe as Kane slid off him and tumbled into the watery void, disappearing, his scream cut off like a butcher's cleaver coming down.

"Jake!"

Getting both hands on the pipe, Jake clawed his way up to firmer ground as turbulent salty water sloshed over him. Anna stood in the entryway of the apartment, her face chiseled thin by fear.

Fear for him.

"Get back, Anna."

Instead, she grabbed the softball bat he'd dropped and edged into the living room. Another piece of the floor fell away, almost knocking Jake from his clinging perch.

"Anna—it's not safe. Will you please get back?" he pleaded, scrabbling for a better hold.

For answer, she stretched herself flat on the floor and extended the bat, both hands wrapped tightly around it.

A million thoughts raced through Jake's mind. Things he wanted to do if he made it out of this alive. Things that might be possible which—before Pablo—had seemed impossible. The thrill tracing through his chest wasn't all due to the floor crumbling beneath him.

He grabbed the bat.

Harvey Browning, the building's owner, followed up on his promise to make Jake help him clean up the mess.

It took five and a half months to get it done.

Jake didn't mind. He liked the work, liked putting things right with his hands, liked the industrious feeling of seeing builders repairing, painters painting, and decorators laying carpet.

He liked the promise of something new and better coming to life.

And if he was honest, it felt just as good to know the life of Maxwell G. Kane was over. His body had washed up six miles down the coast after Pablo blew town. He wouldn't be coming after Anna.

Ever.

One chapter over. Another beginning.

Jake found himself humming contentedly as he walked into the newly refurbished two-bedroom apartment he shared with Anna and her grandmother. He kicked off his work shoes, leaving them on the entryway mat, and grabbed a soda from the fridge as he went to join the two of them on the balcony patio.

Passing through the living room, he stopped at the fireplace to admire the handsome stonework and polished mantelpiece. They were nice, but what really held his gaze was the two items lying, in pride of place, atop the shiny mantel.

A well-used softball and the scuffed-up bat that went with it.

He smiled and stepped into the sunshine.

Author's Note

Always Gonna Happen

While considering what kind of story to write for *Mystery, Crime, and Mayhem's Stolen Cars* issue, I decided to go a little madcap and have some real fun.

And boy, did I! This is one of those stories that keeps delightfully zigging and unexpectedly zagging and was a simple joy to write.

I hope you'll enjoy reading it as much as I enjoyed putting it on the page.

ALWAYS GONNA HAPPEN

Six months after Davy Larkins was shanked to death in the Monroe Correctional Complex for Men, he joined Sherman Tate on the outside, on the day of his release.

Sherman wasn't surprised to see him. They'd always been close, even when they weren't sharing a cell.

"Whatcha gonna do now, Sherm? You're out, free as a bird, with a whole new world of steel for the picking."

Sherman blinked. He rubbed his damp palms down the front of his denim work pants. "Oh no, Davy," he said. "No more car thugging for me. I aim to stay out this time."

Davy laughed. "Right."

Sherman locked his jaw and lifted his chin. He wanted Davy to know he was serious. Davy saw and changed his tone. "Can you do that, Sherm? You heard what the warden said when he was walking you to the gate."

"Yes, I heard it. I ain't deaf. He said stealing cars is all I know how to do and I'll be back in two shakes of a lamb's tail. But he's wrong, Davy. I can do it this time. I know I can."

"Sure, sure." Davy lifted an arm. "But what about that little beauty over there? Can you walk right by that without a second glance?"

Sherman stopped in his tracks, a low whistle rising up out of his throat. Davy was pointing to a sky blue Lancia Stratos, circa 1970, in pristine condition. A rare and beautiful beast. Salivary glands firing on overdrive, Sherman swallowed hard and clenched his fists.

"Watch me, Davy. Watch me pass it by, face forward, never looking back."

Sherman marched past. Every step felt like he was wearing cast-iron shoes, but he didn't stop until he turned the corner, and the Lancia was out of sight.

"Hot damn," Davy said. "You're really going straight."

"I really am," Sherman agreed.

And he meant it. Right up until the day the gods pulled back the clouds and dropped a fat juicy plum in his lap.

He and Davy were sharing a bag of greasy fries from a diner on the outskirts of downtown Seattle. Just walking and killing time before reporting in for work.

Sherman almost missed it, came so close to shuffling past without noticing, but Davy spotted it and clapped him on the back.

"There she is, Sherm," he said, pointing to the black Toyota Camry parked at the curb. "All fired up and waiting for you."

Sherman saw what he meant. The car was running, smooth motor humming, key in the ignition, doors unlocked.

And no one inside.

"It's meant to be, bro," Davy said. "Don't deny it, don't fight it. Just go." He cast his gaze around, eyes a little wild, a cunning grin curving his lips. "Go like the wind, Sherm."

Davy was right. There was no fighting it, not when it was so clearly ordained.

Sherman didn't remember opening the door, sliding into the seat, or peeling away from the curb. It was like a dream, not quite coherent. Not quite real.

Until the blare of sirens snapped him back to cold, hard, in-your-face reality.

Heart ratcheting up in his chest, Sherman turned to Davy. But the passenger seat was empty. He didn't know what to do, so he just kept driving, taking the turns at random.

Four blocks later, the whine of the sirens faded into the distance and Sherman's chest loosened up enough so he could pull in a full, deep breath.

He saw a sign for the I-90 entrance ramp and merged onto the freeway, heading east. As he pulled to the inside lane and passed a moving van, Davy climbed over the seat and sprawled against the door, giving Sherman a gleeful thumbs up.

"Whew! What a rush."

Sherman said nothing.

"Hey, don't feel bad, man. It was always gonna happen. Today just turned out to be the day."

"Shut up, Davy. What am I supposed to do now?"

"Do you want me to shut up, or tell you what you're supposed to do?"

Sherman thought. "Tell me."

Davy stared out the window for a long time. At last, he said, "I don't know. Just keep driving while we figure it out."

Sherman drove. He stayed mostly in the right-hand lane, obeying the speed limit and remembering to use his turn signal when called for. Traffic was heavy until they got past Issaquah where it thinned out, allowing him to get a good look at the vehicles behind him in the rearview mirror.

A cop car was coming up fast.

Vehicles leapt out of the passing lane to let the patrol car go by, and it was gaining on the little Camry at an alarming rate. As it drew within ten car lengths, the flashers flared on and a high-pitched wail raised the hairs on the back of Sherman's neck.

"What do I do, Davy?"

Davy gripped the dashboard. "Go down with the ship, Sherm. Don't pull over."

Sherman tightened his hands on the steering wheel and pressed his foot to the floor.

The police car zipped past, shaking the Camry in its wake.

Before Sherman could even heave a sigh of relief, a *ding* sounded from the instrument panel and the fuel light came on, burning like an angry red eye.

"End of the road, dude," Davy said, "but we knew it was always gonna happen. Let's get off the freeway and find a place to ditch this ride."

Hands shaking, heart still hammering in his chest, Sherman signaled and exited, guiding the car down the off-ramp. He turned right at the first intersection and took another right two miles down the road.

He had no idea where he was going, and he didn't think Davy knew either.

Tall pines lined both sides of the winding asphalt, swaying in the stiffening breeze. Afternoon was waning into evening and lights twinkled at sparse intervals as they passed small clusters of houses or shops.

Sherman drove until the engine started to cough. He turned off on a narrow dirt lane running beside an empty field and let the car coast to a stop.

"Fun while it lasted, wasn't it, bro?" Davy said.

Adrenaline still rushing in his veins, Sherman had to agree. "But what now?" he asked.

Davy raised a finger, like a teacher calling the class to attention. "Now, we wipe the car clean and get the hell out of here. Just leave it and find a bus station somewhere."

"Okay."

Using the tail of his shirt, Sherman wiped down all the surfaces he or Davy might have touched. He pushed the driver's seat all the way back so the cops wouldn't be able to tell how tall their car thief had been.

A gust of wind ruffled his hair as he climbed out of the car, and he shivered. "It's cold. I don't want to walk all over hill and dale without a jacket."

Davy peered in the windows of the back seat. "Check the trunk. Maybe there's something there you can wrap up in."

Sherman found the lever and popped the trunk. He lifted the lid.

Heart flopping in his chest, he stared down at the trunk's contents.

"Holy Mackerel!" Davy said. "Am I seeing what I think I'm seeing?"

Sherman reached out a hand and loosened the neck of one of the canvas drawstring bags. Bundled stacks of bills spilled out onto the floor of the trunk. A bolt of white-hot excitement shot through him.

Followed by a jolt of ice-cold fear.

"Where was this car when we found it?" he asked Davy.

Davy gripped his arm, still staring at the cash. "Somewhere on 31st Avenue, wasn't it?"

"I think it was. Right in front of—"

Davy gasped. "The bank! Dude, you grabbed the getaway car!"

Sherman's stomach twisted in his gut. "You're the one who—"

"Doesn't matter now, bro. You're deep in a crap hole. Not only are the cops after you..."

"The robbers are, too."

"Oh, yeah. They're sure to be pissed you stole their money *and* their ride after everything they did to get it. They'll hunt you and gut you like a ten point buck."

"What do I do, Davy?"

Davy blew out a long breath. "I hate to say it, but you can't take the cash. You'd be signing your death warrant."

"Well, I'm not just leaving it here."

"No, you're right. That would be a bad idea, too."

Shivering and miserable, Sherman hugged himself and listened to the wind rustling across the field. He opened his mouth to speak, but Davy cut him off.

"If you're thinking about turning it over to the authorities," he said, "you might as well just buy a one-way ticket back to Monroe."

"You got a better idea?"

"Matter of fact, I do, Sherm. You got a lighter?"

"You're going to burn the money?"

"Hell, no! We're going to hide the money and burn the car."

Sherman looked at the black Camry, regret knifing through him. He felt a fondness for the little car.

"Why do we have to burn it, Davy? We wiped it real clean. Let's just walk away."

"We wiped it clean when we thought the cops would be looking for a small-time car thief. For a bank robber, they'll pull this car into their fancy lab and go over it with a fine-tooth comb. They'll find your DNA, Sherm, and you'll go down."

Sherman kicked the rear tire. "Guess you're right, Davy."

"Course I am. Don't just stand there—go scrounge up some dried leaves."

Glad to give his shaking hands something to do, Sherman clambered through the strip of woodland next to the field, gathering handfuls of crackling leaves. As he scooped up a pile in front of a creaking oak tree, he saw a large hollow at the base of the trunk.

Big enough to hide the sacks of bills.

He and Davy stuffed the three bags of cash into the old dry cavity and found a large stone to cover the hole. They built a mound of dirt over and around it and scattered more dead leaves to hide their handiwork.

"That ought to do for now," Davy said. "Let's finish this and get out of here."

Back at the car, they stuffed the gas tank full of leaves and tinder and pushed a lit tree branch inside, fanning the blaze until it took hold and the Camry roared into flame.

Sherman stared, mesmerized by the flames and saddened by the Camry's pitiful demise.

"Don't let this get you down," Davy said. "It was always gonna happen."

They spent the rest of the night hiking in the dark, hitching rides, and waiting around at bus stops until dawn brought Sherman to the door of his crappy motel room.

He was so tired he hadn't even noticed Davy was no longer with him. Pushing his way inside, he collapsed on the bed and grabbed the remote, pointing it toward the TV. He thumbed through the channels and found a news report with footage of a plastic-faced blonde speaking into a mic on 31st Avenue in front of the bank.

Turning up the volume, he leaned back against a stack of pillows and listened to her account.

"...armed robbers were killed in the firefight with police, except for the driver who got away with the money before responders arrived at the scene. In a bizarre twist, the man believed to be the getaway driver was hit by a bus later last night and pronounced DOA at Harborview Medical Center."

"Looks like case closed, Judy. I understand that police believe all participants in the attempted robbery lost their lives during the crime."

"That's right, Jim. The only remaining mystery is what happened to the money."

"A mystery indeed. It appears the only one who knew took the answer to his grave."

Davy thunked down on the bed next to Sherman and gave his thigh a slap.

"Hot damn, Sherm! Looks like you're off scott-free. No one even knows you were there. Told you it was meant to be."

Sherman relaxed, flexing his shoulder blades against the pillows. "No one is looking for me," he marveled, delight spreading over him like butter on hotcakes. "I can go back and get the money."

Davy laughed, and Sherman joined in. When they'd finished a good long chuckle, Davy sprang up from the bed and tugged on Sherman's arm.

"Come on, man. Daylight's burning."

Sherman borrowed an old pickup truck from a buddy he'd known since high school. Abiding by every traffic law on the books, he drove down the I-90, watching for the exit he'd taken the night before and navigating the off-ramp like a Sunday driver, even with every nerve throbbing a drumbeat in his veins.

He passed the empty field. The burnt-out husk of the Camry was still in the lane beside it, blackened and deserted, with no sign that anyone had paid it the slightest attention. That was sometimes the way in these rural pockets, Sherman knew.

He cast his eye over the surroundings but saw only a single vehicle coming toward him in the opposite lane. It passed, and Sherman steered the pickup onto the shoulder, executing a three-point turn and heading back.

"Time to get to work," Davy said. "And let's be quick about it before we draw someone's interest."

Sherman had come prepared with gloves and a hand spade. Kneeling in front of the creaking oak, he scraped away the dirt and leaves, exposing the rock. Davy helped him dislodge it, grunting with the effort, and they stared at the bags of cash still resting right where they'd stuffed them in the dark of night.

"Yeah baby, we're rich!"

Davy tugged a bag from the hollow and Sherman reached in for the remaining two. Within minutes, they were back on the freeway, heading west, with the money stashed securely on the floorboard beneath Davy's feet.

Back in the motel room, Sherman placed the three bags in his bed. Sliding beneath the covers, he curled himself around them and slept for a solid eight hours while Davy kept watch.

Sherman's stomach woke him, growling angrily at his neglect. Giving the money bags an affectionate squeeze, he rolled out of bed and grabbed a quick shower. He transferred five twenty-dollar bills from one of the sacks to his wallet and stashed the rest of the cash inside the laundry hamper in his closet, covering them with a layer of dirty clothes.

"Let's get something to eat," he told Davy.

They went to his favorite diner around the corner and took a booth next to the counter. Feeling expansive, Sherman ordered a burger with the works, onion rings on the side and a strawberry malt.

As he dipped the rings in ranch dressing, enjoying the greasy goodness, two cops came through the door. Both swept a gaze over the tables and chairs, examining the customers.

Sherman froze.

He'd seen lawmen do this a dozen times before. It was routine for them to run a quick check with every new venue. He'd heard it called "situational awareness," and it amounted to mentally cataloguing the layout and the people within it. Not really a cause for concern.

Unless you were guilty of something.

"Take it easy, Sherm," Davy muttered.

Sherman swallowed the bit of battered onion sitting on his tongue. The policemen sauntered casually to the counter, taking a couple of stools not far from where he sat, greasy-fingered and uneasy. Sally, the waitress, poured coffee and pushed a saucer filled with creamer capsules between them.

Sherman left his burger half-eaten and slurped the rest of his strawberry shake, signaling Sally for the check. She brought it on a little brown plastic tray and Sherman pulled a twenty from his wallet, placing it on top.

"Keep the change," he told her.

Wiping his fingers on a paper napkin, he rose to leave. One of the cops stirred sugar into his coffee, saying, "Yeah, but here's the thing—those bills are marked. Some luckless son-of-a-gun is going to find that cash and think he's fallen into a bowl of cherries."

Sherman paused, helping himself to a toothpick from a dispenser on the counter, listening hard.

The other cop chuckled, blowing across the top of his coffee cup. "Poor sucker'll go on a spending spree and end up in a courtroom, charged as an accomplice in the robbery."

"Sure as bears take a dump in the woods. He should save himself the grief and just turn the money in."

A grunt. "Like that would happen."

Sherman caught Sally at the register, his twenty in her hand. He snatched it back. "Sorry," he mumbled, feeling his face go red. "Can I put that on a card instead?"

Outside the diner, Sherman pinched the bridge of his nose, hoping to ward off the headache pressing down on him.

Davy stood beside him, shuffling his feet on the sidewalk like he always did when agitated. "Nuts!" he said. "We should've just left the cash in the car and burned it all to hell in the first place."

Glumly, Sherman agreed. "Much as I hate to say it, that has to be our next course of action."

Davy sighed. "I guess it was always gonna happen."

He still had his buddy's pickup truck, so he shoved the bags of bills back onto the floorboards. With a vicious yank, he shifted into gear and drove to a nearby lakeside campground. The day was gray and overcast, the site deserted.

Sherman parked the truck in a spot with a stone-encircled fire pit. He gathered enough deadfall and kindling to make a fire and added handfuls of crumpled banknotes to get the whole thing started. He lit the paper, watching tongues of flame lick around the edges and flare to life.

It hurt.

Bundle by bundle, he fed the fire. It was full dark by the time he finished burning the last of the bills. Heart heavy, he trudged back to the pickup truck. Davy walked beside him but, for once, had nothing to say.

He drove to his buddy's and dropped off the truck. He had two choices now to get back to his motel room. Wait around and ride the bus.

Or steal a car.

He walked the street, making sure no one watched as he tried car doors, hoping to find one unlocked. He knew myriad ways to break into a car, but he considered finding one open like a sign.

"Yeah, and how did that work out for you last time?" Davy reminded him.

Sherman decided to take the bus. At the central station, he realized he didn't have the exact change required for the fare to get him home. He got in line for the change machine, watching the bustle of activity around him and taking note of the surveillance cameras placed in strategic positions.

Good thing he now had nothing to worry about.

He got his change and boarded the bus, feeding his two dollars into the slot beside the driver and taking a seat near the rear doors, next to Davy.

"Hey," Davy said. "Where'd you get the singles, wise guy? When you left the motel, all you had was twenties."

Sherman stared at Davy, a hard, heavy rock growing in his gut as he realized his monumentally stupid mistake.

"Aargh! There is no way I'm going back to Monroe for the sake of a crappy twenty-dollar bill!"

Jumping off the bus, Sherman let his gaze wander over the lot of parked cars. He chose a candy apple red BMW and worked his magic, sliding behind the wheel and firing the engine.

It felt good.

"Yeah, baby. Let's go!" shouted Davy.

Sherman shifted into drive and squealed out of the parking lot, leaving a stripe of rubber on the pavement behind him.

In his cell at the Monroe Correctional Complex for Men, Sherman stretched out on his bunk and stared at the ceiling. Davy sprawled beside him, humming tunelessly.

"Don't feel bad, Sherm. It was always gonna happen."

Sherman didn't feel bad. He felt rotten. Miserable. He really thought he could've done it that time. He could've stayed out.

"Hey, Squirm!"

One of the inmates, a guy called Trashcan because he ate whatever anyone else didn't want, was shouting and waving toward the prison rec room.

"You're on TV, gorgeous," he said. "They're playing your story. Again."

"Yeah, so what?" Sherman said.

Davy stirred on the bunk beside him. "Come on, Sherm. Let's go see what they're saying now."

Grumbling, Sherman pushed himself off the bed and followed Davy into the rec room. A morning talk show played on the TV while footage of the robbery rolled behind the discussion panel. Sherman's face flashed onto the screen, and someone cranked the volume up.

A woman interviewer was asking questions of the guest, a distinguished-looking gentleman in suit and tie. A lawyer, Sherman guessed.

"Funny thing is," the lawyer was saying, "there's only a five-year statute of limitations on bank robbery. All the guy had to do was sit on the cash for a few years and then he could have spent it at his leisure. No one would even be watching anymore for those bills to circulate."

The man said more, but Sherman couldn't hear him above the roar of blood in his ears and the hoots of derisive laughter from his fellow inmates. Mortified, trembling, he stared at Davy.

"I could have been rich," he said. "I could have stashed the cash and put in another five years washing dishes at Antonio's. And then, I could have been rich."

Davy stared back, sadness in his eyes. He shook his head. "No," he said. "You wouldn't have lasted five years with that money burning a hole in your laundry hamper. You'd have stolen your next car before the first year went up in smoke."

"No, I could have done it," Sherman insisted. "You're the one keeps telling me it was always gonna happen. Why not this, then? It could've happened."

Someone slapped Sherman on the back. Hard. Scornful and sarcastic comments flew so thick in the air around him that he barely heard Davy's response.

"Nah, Sherm," his friend told him. "It was never gonna happen."

AUTHOR'S NOTE

A BAND OF SCHEMING WOMEN

A Band of Scheming Women was originally published in *Thrill Ride Magazine: Sisters-in-Arms,* where it shared a Table of Contents with a marvelous lineup of thriller authors. To my delight, this story was also a finalist for the Derringer Award in 2025.

Before it was published, editor Matt Buchman invited me to include an introduction telling readers about what inspired the story. I'll repeat that here, for you.

I live in eastern Germany, only about ten miles from the Czech border. From home, and also from my office on the Vilseck Army installation, the sound of cannons going off and gunfire is a regular occurrence, since this is a major staging and training area for soldiers.

So, when considering the theme of sisters-in-arms, I naturally turned to the military. But I found myself not wanting to write about the current war in Ukraine. Instead, I fell back on research I'd recently done on the terrorist insurgent groups in Syria. I put together a team of military women and gave them a dicey situation to deal with.

I enjoyed their wild ride as I wrote the story—never quite sure what lay around every corner—and I hope readers will find a thrilling and satisfying adventure as they follow this band of scheming women.

A Band of Scheming Women

S taff Sergeant Dakota Ferguson held out her paper plate and accepted a charred patty from the Army unit's appointed burger flipper. The smell of the grilling meat made her mouth water, but the coating of dust which instantly settled on the greasy burger dampened her appetite a few degrees.

She only wished it could do the same for the scorching temperatures in southern Syria.

She tossed her head, liking how light it felt and the way her hair swished against her cheek. She'd taken a pair of shears to her long dark hair first thing after rising that morning, chopping and shaping until she felt free from the heavy, heat-binding locks.

Only after cutting it to ear level did she visit Sergeant Libby's quarters and ask her to fine-tune it into something passing as attractive.

Old school music from The Beach Boys played over speakers set on rickety stands, and a blow-up pool surrounded by lawn chairs dominated the center of the compound. The water in the pool was murky, full of sand and less appealing additives. A limp flamingo floated on the surface, its head hanging dejectedly to the side.

Despite the disheartening centerpiece, the beach party was in full swing, bikini-clad girls boogying, men sporting open Hawaiian shirts—or no shirt at all—joined in or watched from the sidelines. Shouts and laughter from the makeshift volleyball court occasionally rose to compete with the thumping music.

Dakota stood for a moment, just taking it in, breathing deeply and enjoying the respite from the constant strain of always being on high alert. Though the major terrorist groups, like ISIS and al-Qaeda, had been splintered and weakened, their factions were regrouping and gathering strength in the never-ending conflicts of the Middle East.

Nothing like a little job security to make a girl feel right at home.

She spotted a woman she liked, a trauma surgeon named Claire Carmona, sitting with her boyfriend at a picnic table partially shaded by a large beach umbrella. Sliding onto the bench beside them, she winced as her bare thighs met the solar-heated wooden surface.

"Yow! I just sacrificed a layer of skin to the sun god of this desert paradise."

"Ah," Claire said, "so you're the reason he's beaming down on us with such…" She paused, searching for the right word.

"Blistering abandon?" supplied Shane Lee, her boyfriend. He was a Signal Corps officer, and a good man to have around since he always seemed to have his finger on the pulse of the garrison.

Dakota took a bite of her burger, pleased to find it was only slightly gritty. She'd eaten worse. Swallowing, she said, "I hear they're playing a movie on the big screen tonight. Any idea what's showing?"

Before anyone had a chance to answer, a siren blared over the speakers, wailing up and down the scale, interspersed with a voice warning them of an imminent attack. Claire immediately rose and gave Shane a quick kiss. "Stay safe," she said as she rushed off to be with her patients in the hospital.

Shane shoved half a hotdog in his mouth and gave Dakota a thumbs up before hurrying away to the TOC, the Tactical Operations Center, where he'd be busy coordinating communications during and after the crisis.

Dakota considered taking her plate with her to the bunker, but abandoned the idea when a blast rang out behind her, shaking the ground and sending up a wave of dirt and sand.

A passing soldier handed her a flak jacket as she pushed to her feet. "Get under cover, Sergeant!" he shouted before running past to hand out more frag vests. Dakota's heart pounded painfully as she shrugged into the jacket and jogged for the bunker, the air around her filling with smoke and the sound of nearby explosions.

She hadn't taken a dozen steps when a high-pitched whine in her left ear made her cringe—then a flare of light accompanied a huge boom that knocked her off her feet. She rolled over, brushing sand out of her face, and saw she'd fallen just outside the hospital structure.

Crawling toward the door, she was met by a familiar face, a local man called Naji, who acted as an interpreter. He pulled her inside the large shed which housed part of the hospital unit. She sat slumped against the wall as the lights flickered and went out, leaving the corridor bathed in eerie sepia tones.

A moment of comparative silence passed, broken only by shouts from outside and the continuing blare from the siren. Then Dakota heard a whirring noise as the generator kicked in and the lights came back up. A medic rushed past, then turned and stared down at her.

Dakota felt a surge of relief at seeing Staff Sergeant Kiyana Quinn. They'd flown in together from the States and become fast friends. Kiyana's carefree short afro style had been the impetus behind Dakota's decision to cut her own hair. Kiyana knelt in front of her.

"Hey girl, what are you doing down there? Are you hurt?" she asked.

"No, I don't think so. Flak jacket did its job."

Kiyana frowned. Dakota tried not to flinch as the medic flashed a penlight into her eyes and ran practiced hands over her, checking for damage. "Feeling any pain?" she asked.

"Negative. I'm fine."

The siren abruptly changed its pitch. "There's the all-clear," Kiyana said, helping her up. "Come with me. I want to give you a more thorough exam."

Wobbly from shock but otherwise fine, she followed Kiyana through the door to the radiology room—from which Dakota heard a flood of fervent swearing. Looking in, she saw a jagged hole in the wall, dust and sand still filtering in on beams of late morning sunshine. A knot of medical personnel stared down at the remains of some kind of machine.

The hospital commander, Colonel Abraham Tate, rubbed a tired hand over his face. "That's it, then," he said. "The scanner's toast. Let's hope we can live without it in the aftermath of this attack."

"We've got two monitors down, as well, sir," a nurse informed him. "Can we transport patients to another MTF?"

"Negative. Lieutenant Gorman's bird got winged bringing in the latest casualties. He made it down but says it'll take ten hours just to get the parts to fix it. We'll have to muddle along the best we can." Turning, he straightened his shoulders and raised his voice. "Okay, people, we got incoming!"

Dakota stepped back against the wall as a pair of flight medics pushed past with a patient on a combat gurney. The long fabric of native garb hung over the side of the gurney and the man's head was swathed in cloth, the turban askew so that his face was half-covered.

She saw Claire running in from the far end of the corridor. "Tell me what you got," she shouted as she followed the medics into an exam room.

"Male, BP 100 over 40, GSW to the left arm."

Colonel Tate stood at the doorway, watching. Dakota peered in over his shoulder.

"What happened?" Tate asked the medics.

"Guy was riding in behind a convoy. They caught some fire and his driver lost control, shot in the face. Killed instantly. The jeep crashed in a ditch. Lucky we saw it happen and swooped in to pick him up."

The patient moaned, writhing on the gurney, his right hand making restless motions in the air. Claire pulled his headscarf away for a closer look and Dakota saw her face stiffen in shock.

"Lucky indeed," she said. "This man is an EHVI."

Colonel Tate stepped up beside the gurney and gave a low whistle. "Nizam Hadid," he said, confirming that the man in front of him was an Enemy High Value Individual. "One of our more prominent insurgents."

Dakota felt her eyes go wide. Kiyana, standing next to her, clasped her by the shoulder.

Colonel Tate looked at Claire. "Take good care of him," he said. "I guarantee this man has something we want."

The terrorist on the gurney gave a loud groan, muttering Arabic through gritted teeth. His eyes rolled wildly as he clutched at his chest.

"Patient is exhibiting pain in the upper right quadrant," Claire announced. Pushing aside his robe, she moved her fingers to his chest. With a howl, Hadid thrust her hand away, his protest manifest in any language.

"He doesn't like being treated by a woman doctor," Tate said. "What are your feelings about it, Major?"

Dakota smiled. She knew her friend's opinion on the subject.

"That's too damn bad," Claire said, locking eyes with the man on the stretcher. "I'm the surgeon on duty here. Look at his eyes and face, Colonel. That's some serious jaundice."

"Check his bilirubin level," Tate ordered a nurse. "And get a terp in here. We need to know every word this guy utters."

Along with half a dozen others, Dakota lingered in the corridor outside the curtained exam room. Kiyana stayed with her, poking her here and there to make sure she really was okay.

"Crazy days," Kiyana said, her voice tense and low. "If al-Zaanni knows we have his right-hand man, they'll be back here soon with more bombs."

Dakota swallowed hard. "Yeah. They have to save face, seal lips, and make a statement."

The interpreter who'd dragged her to safety approached at a run, swinging open the curtain as he went to the gurney.

Colonel Tate touched him on the arm. "Make sure he understands that Major Claire Carmona—a woman—will be the one treating him if he wants our help."

"Yes, sir," Naji said.

The two Arabs exchanged a flood of words, incomprehensible to Dakota who knew only a smattering Arabic. Hadid raised his head and glared at Claire for a full ten seconds before giving a frosty nod and dropping back onto the gurney with a groan.

After a few more exchanges in Arabic, Naji turned to the Colonel, his eyes solemn as he spoke. "I think you already know that this man is Nizam Hadid. He is the reason for the attack on our compound. He was on his way here to offer us vital information in exchange for his life."

Tate nodded, gesturing impatiently. "Can you elaborate? What information?"

Claire cleared her throat, adding, "What do you mean, in exchange for his life?"

"Hadid is ill," Naji said. "Dying. He needs..." he hesitated, searching for the English equivalent.

"A liver transplant," Claire finished for him.

"Yes! He will die very soon without it. He says he has valuable information about a planned attack on American soil, but he will only tell you if you save his life."

Colonel Tate snorted. "Why should we believe him?"

Naji relayed the question to Hadid. The terrorist made a croaking retort, half laugh, half moan, his eyes filled with bitterness.

"He says to consult your sources. He says al-Zaanni has been sending his people across your southern border for months, preparing for something big. They are nearly ready."

"Major Carmona?" the Colonel prompted, raising his eyebrows at Claire.

"Yes sir," she answered, understanding his tacit request. She hurried from the room and returned a moment later with Shane. She'd clearly put him in the picture.

"That tallies with what we know, sir," he reported.

Naji spoke up. "He swears on the Quran he is telling the truth. He will tell you the details when he has a new liver."

The colonel massaged his forehead, eyes closed, a pained look on his face. Seconds passed while everyone seemed to hold their breath. At last, Tate's eyes popped open, and he barked out an order to the man standing next to Dakota.

"Sergeant! Get Lieutenant Baker in here on the double."

"Yes, sir!"

The sergeant scrambled past Dakota and was gone. Tate scrubbed a hand across his stubbled chin. Dakota heard the rasp in the otherwise silent room.

"I hope to hell our scrounger can find us a liver," he muttered. "STAT."

Lieutenant Lila Baker twisted the ring on her finger, still not sure how she felt about wearing it. Still not sure what it meant.

The long-distance relationship was proving more difficult than she'd anticipated, and communication did not always happen smoothly. The ring from Mitch had arrived with a short, almost cryptic note and her attempts to reach him for a more thorough explanation had so far failed.

In the meantime, she wore the ring on her right hand and pondered over how she'd feel if he asked her to move it to her left.

Giving the ring one last twist, she refocused her attention on the task before her.

Lila had been raised by parents who loved the classics—Elvis, Robert B. Parker, and Golden Age Hollywood movies. From the time she was a little girl, *The Great Escape* had been her favorite, and of the many-splendored characters in the film, she loved James Garner's role best.

The Scrounger.

It had been a major influence in her decision to become a Logistics officer in the U.S. Army. She also loved languages and spoke several, with varying degrees of fluency.

Including Arabic.

She relished the challenges inherent in her job, and it had taken her less than two hours to track down a compatible liver for Hadid's transplant. But it came with a new set of obstacles. The liver was located just northwest of Palmyra, nearly a hundred miles distant.

And the route passed through an area of high conflict, held by the insurgents.

She'd found Colonel Tate in OR 4 and delivered the good news/bad news personally, feeling sorry for the poor fellows he sent to fetch the organ.

And then he'd blindsided her.

"Take Sergeant Quinn with you, Lieutenant," he ordered. "And get a move on. Al-Zaanni's not going to let him rest easy here for long." He jabbed his chin at the terrorist on the operating table where Major Claire Carmona was bandaging the bullet wound in his left arm.

"Sir?" Lila stammered. "Are you saying that—"

"Yes, I'm ordering you to deliver our...liver. Go!"

"But shouldn't we be sending out a squad of men, at the very least?"

Tate gave her a hard look and Lila bit her tongue.

"I'm sorry, sir. I didn't mean to question—"

"The insurgents will be expecting an armed group. Two civilian women delivering humanitarian supplies to the refugee camps is far more likely to escape their scrutiny. And if one of those women speaks Arabic and knows how to find a diamond in a sandbox, all the better."

"Oh," Lila said, understanding. "I think I can dress the part."

"I'm counting on it, Lieutenant. I've ordered TOC to work up some documents for both you and Staff Sergeant Quinn. They'll get you everything you need."

And so she found herself sitting next to Kiyana Quinn in a rusted-out jeep loaded with food and medical supplies, heading north through the Syrian desert. An awkward silence hung between them, and Lila didn't want to be the one to break it.

She knew the straight-laced nurse, Quinn, didn't like her. When they'd first met, Lila had made an unguarded crack about a black woman having an Irish name. Quinn hadn't been amused. Lila suspected the other woman regarded her as a pampered white-bread girl who'd probably attained her rank through connections rather than merit. It stung her to admit it was at least partially true.

Since then, it seemed to Lila that Quinn went looking for ways to one-up her—some blatant and others more subtle. Like tossing her duffle bag on top of Lila's things in the workout room or cutting in front of her in the lunch line.

And now, the two of them had only each other to rely upon as they crossed through hostile territory on a crucial mission they couldn't afford to fail.

Lila's stomach gurgled and her knees shook as Quinn steered the jeep over the rutted track, guiding them from one jarring bounce to another. All the while, she kept returning to one thought, holding it like a talisman in her troubled head.

What would James Garner do?

A flutter of air teased the back of Dakota's neck, left bare by her new haircut. She watched in amazement as the hospital personnel moved about, restoring the facility to almost its normal appearance, carrying on as if nothing had happened. A little surge of pride went through her. She liked being a part of this courageous group, doing something with her life that felt like it really mattered, like she was making a real contribution in defense of her country.

She moved along the corridor, looking for some way to assist, and couldn't help listening in when she heard Claire and

Colonel Tate pick up a discussion about the enemy patient's situation.

"An organ transplant—I can't do that kind of surgery here," Claire protested. "The place is like a slice of Swiss cheese. Half our equipment's shot."

"I know," Tate replied. "I've ordered my people to reach out to the coalition MTFs in the area. Failing that, maybe we can find a FOB that can accommodate you."

"Let me know asap."

In the course of her duties as Recon Specialist, Dakota had knowledge of the local MTFs, or Medical Treatment Facilities. She was also aware of two or three FOBs in the area—Forward Operating Bases, acting as strategic centers and secured positions for military operations. Some of them had reasonably advanced medical capabilities.

She took a tentative step into the OR.

"There's a FOB about fifty miles outside of Damascus that should have adequate facilities," she offered. "I can contact them."

"No need," Shane said, sweeping in from the TOC. He looked at Claire. "I've found you a surgical unit in an MTF just sixty klicks north of here. They're expecting you by nightfall."

"Great. But how do I get my patient from here to there when al-Zaanni's men are out there looking for him?" Claire raised an eyebrow, making it clear to her boyfriend that he'd just lost a few points.

"What about your women's clinic?" Dakota suggested.

She knew Claire and several women from the hospital offered their services at a makeshift clinic for local women, just outside the gate. Most Syrian women refused to show up at the official MTF because they were afraid of being dishonored if seen by men outside their own family.

"Explain," Tate said, turning his direct gaze on her.

Dakota felt her face go hot. "I mean, why not use the women's clinic as your departure point and dress like the locals? Draped in veils and an abaya, you'll look just like a patient leaving the women's clinic."

"What about him?" Claire asked, motioning toward the bed.

Dakota smiled. "Him too. Dress him properly and he'll look like a sick woman being transported home to the care of her family," she proposed.

Tate shook his head. "I can't see him agreeing to dress like a woman."

Claire smiled. She loaded a syringe with sedative and added it to the IV line. "I won't give him the chance to object."

"Good thinking," Tate said, dividing his compliment between the two of them.

"By the way, Scout," he added, nodding to Dakota. "Get your own abaya—you're going along. Your recon skills could make or break this mission, and I don't need to tell you how vital it is that we get that information out of this man."

Dakota clamped down on the protest rising to her lips. She should have seen that one coming.

Shane grinned. "Colonel, do you realize you've just put our fate in the hands of a band of scheming women?"

Tate regarded him gravely. "I do indeed, son. The hand that rocks the cradle—"

"Is the hand that's going to stitch a new liver into that wretched scumbag spawn of a fiendish camel," Claire finished.

She snapped off her latex gloves and threw them in the bin as she left the room, with Dakota on her heels.

Lila gritted her teeth and braced herself in the passenger seat of the rattling jeep. The unaccustomed ring she wore bit into her finger, and she repositioned it, trying not to think about how much Mitch would worry if he knew what she was doing. She noticed Quinn's jaw was tight, her elegant brown fingers almost white on the steering wheel, mirroring her own anxiety.

Their task of passing through hostile territory to secure the transplant organ and deliver it to Claire's OR was a daunting one, and like everyone else serving in the Middle East, she'd seen documentary footage of brutal murders committed by brigands and terrorists in the desert. They made the outlaws of the Wild West look like the Lollipop Guild.

She tried not to think about the kind of atrocities two women on their own might face. In keeping with their role of civilians delivering humanitarian supplies, they wore ordinary clothing, with headscarves as a token of respect. Such measures would only provide them limited protections.

Time and nature had conspired to make the ride beyond Palmyra a miserable one. The midafternoon sun hung persistently dead ahead, throwing up a glare that hurt the eyes and made forward progress over the pitted-out desert track precarious and unpleasant.

Still, they'd been lucky so far in their journey, unmolested by the few scattered groups of men they'd passed. At one checkpoint, a tall man in drab military garb had motioned for them to stop. Lila had almost melted with relief when he gave their papers a cursory glance and waved them on.

Shortly after that, she'd fielded a radio transmission from Shane, telling them where to take the liver—an easy forty klicks to the west. As if the first hundred weren't scary enough.

And now, the hospital where the organ awaited stood just ahead in the desert haze. Lila felt queasy from the release of tension. It had all been so uncomplicated.

Disturbingly so.

Quinn parked the jeep on the sand-covered tarmac outside the hospital's entrance. The glass of the double doors was cracked in at least three places, held in place by strips of yellowed cellophane. A single flowering plant in a terracotta pot stood on the stained tiles, scarlet blossoms hanging limp over the rim.

Inside, a brand of organized chaos reigned, but she and Quinn connected at last with the right people, signed the paperwork, and left the hospital with an ice-packed cooler containing the viable liver that would grant new life to one of the world's worst terrorists.

And—Lila fervently hoped—preserve the lives of thousands of Americans.

Back in the jeep, she asked for Quinn's opinion, as a medic. "How long before this thing is past its sell-by date?"

The other woman didn't answer right away and for a moment, she thought Quinn intended to ignore the question. Then, as if drawing upon her inner reserves, Quinn turned stiffly in her seat and regarded Lila with a plastic smile.

"Well, ma'am—see this built-in thermometer?" Quinn pointed to a dial registering just a hair above zero degrees. "That has to stay under 3.9 degrees Celsius to delay the breakdown of cells."

"Which means—"

"Which means, the liver has to be inside Hadid, with his blood flowing through it, by..." She glanced at her watch. "Midnight, to be safe."

"Okay, let's roll, Sergeant."

Quinn gave her a withering look and started the engine. "Did you really think you needed to give that order, Lieutenant?"

"It wasn't an order, Quinn. It was an attempt at conversation. You know—like between two civilized people."

With a snort, Quinn gunned the motor and pulled onto the washboard track leading out of town. They were heading west again, and the sun still beat against the windshield in a white-hot glare, but Lila felt a bud of hope blooming inside her, despite Quinn's glowering countenance.

They were on the home stretch. Nothing would go wrong now.

Or everything would.

As the last traces of the town's outskirts disappeared in the rearview mirror, a cloud of dust arose on the horizon. Two large canvas-covered trucks approached on the road ahead. A bad feeling stirred in Lila's chest as they drew near.

Quinn pressed harder on the accelerator, as if preparing to speed past. But rather than pulling slightly to the side to let them by, the trucks stopped in the road, forming a barrier across their path. Quinn cursed and slammed on the brakes, skidding the jeep to a halt.

Instantly, they were surrounded by solemn-faced men pointing rifles. They used the long barrels to motion Lila and Quinn out of the jeep while they poked through the blankets, food, and medical supplies in the back, jabbering away in Arabic the whole time.

Quinn scowled. "What are they saying?" she muttered.

Lila stepped closer to the medic and kept her voice low. "They're looking for Hadid."

"Clearly, we don't have him. What's taking so long?"

"They're discussing the merits of our supplies. They'll take some of it as the price for letting us pass."

"Baksheesh?"

"Yes."

Suddenly the flow of Arabic rose in pitch and excitement. Lila saw one of the men gesturing wildly toward the cooler on the floor of the front seat. Her heart sank. They would want to see inside, and once they got a look at the liver and understood its significance, she and Quinn were dead.

Not to mention Hadid and all that would follow in his footsteps.

She itched to grab the pistol holstered at the small of her back, felt trickles of sweat inching down toward it. But it would be like wielding a peashooter in a field of cannon.

Useless.

The Arab who'd found the cooler carried it to the man in charge of the raid. He bent and slowly placed it on the sand at Lila's feet, then rose and gave her an imperious glare.

"Open it!" he ordered in clipped Arabic syllables.

Lila continued to avert her gaze, looking at the man only obliquely, as a properly behaving woman should do, according to his custom. Checking to make sure her headscarf remained firmly in place, she tried desperately to swallow the lump in her throat, to calm the racketing hammer inside her ribcage.

And think.

But it was hard to think with the barrels of fifteen rifles trained on your heart.

Dakota swiped a hand across her brow, trying to keep the sweat from dripping into her eyes as she steered the battered pick-up truck along the sand-blown pavement. She was bathed in perspiration under the long robe and hijab she wore, glad once more that she'd shorn away her long, heavy hair.

She glanced at Claire, similarly attired on the bench seat next to her. The terrorist Nizam Hadid slumped between them. With a little help, they'd successfully spirited him into, and out of, the women's clinic. Under sedation, they'd shaved him clean and dressed him in traditional women's garments, including a niqab to cover his face.

For good measure, Claire had artfully arranged a cushion beneath his robe. He now looked like a devout and drowsy, unattractive pregnant Muslim woman.

Twenty minutes into their trek, he'd roused from his drugged sleep to discover what they'd done, raging so vigorously that

Dakota had fought to keep the jeep from ramming into a jagged ridge of rock rising from the desert floor while Claire settled him with another jab of sleepytime.

Now, with the insurgent snoring peacefully once again, she looked into the rearview mirror and frowned.

"There's a black SUV coming up behind us."

Claire shrugged, but there was a note of unease in her voice as she said, "Doesn't necessarily mean anything. It's not like there's a lot of turnoffs for it to branch onto or roadside places to stop."

"True," Dakota agreed. "But there's a town up ahead. I'm going to try shaking him."

"Sensible plan. Shane's got us on ATAK," Claire said, referring to the mobile tracking app TOC used for situational awareness. Its GPS operated independently of cellular and wi-fi networks. "He can guide us through a maze, if need be," she assured, confident in her man's abilities.

As they approached the town, the black SUV closed the distance and Dakota's hands grew slicker than ever on the steering wheel. She rubbed them, one at a time, on the skirt of her abaya.

The late afternoon light lent a hazy mystique to the shabby buildings of the town, softening the squalor, adding an artistic flair to the pervasive graffiti and grace to the stubby weeds growing everywhere.

Shane's voice crackled over the radio as they entered the town. "Take your first left, Dakota."

She did as he suggested, watching in the rearview as the SUV made the same turn.

"They're on us, Shane."

"Okay, up ahead on the right, you'll see a three-story structure. Turn right there and double back to the main road through town."

Following his instructions, Dakota bit her lip as their tail stayed right behind.

"You're nearing the town center," Shane said. "The streets get crazy in there. Lots of corners to hide you. Don't worry."

"I am worried, Shane," Dakota said, dismayed at the cluster of cars, people, and roving animals she saw on the road ahead. "There's also lots of traffic, pedestrians, and four-legged creatures making it impossible to move through here with any kind of speed."

As she spoke, she caught sight of a shepherd driving a flock of shaggy beasts right through the center of town. He herded them toward the road and Dakota saw he meant to cross them. She'd be stuck waiting, at the mercy of the black SUV.

Or she could make a move that would force the SUV to wait.

Jerking the wheel, she gunned the engine and skirted in front of the first crossing sheep, narrowly missing a man on a bicycle and a car in the oncoming lane. The stream of bleating sheep closed in behind her, effectively blocking the SUV's progress.

Her breath shuddered out in a shaky release of tension, but she knew the reprieve wouldn't last long.

"Okay, Shane," Claire said. "Dakota bought us a few spare seconds. Help us get lost."

Dakota focused hard, listening grimly to Shane's instructions, and following each point with determination. She kept a constant monitor on the rearview mirror, and just as her shoulders started to relax with the belief that they'd evaded their tail, she caught a glimpse of the SUV.

Without waiting for Shane's suggestion, she wrenched the wheel and tore onto a side road. Spotting a ramshackle garage standing open and empty, she darted into the space and slammed on the brakes. Springing out of the pickup, she ran to the door of the garage and gripped the handle to close it.

The door wouldn't budge.

"Help me!" she shouted as Claire burst out of the car. Together, they tugged desperately and at last, the door rumbled down, concealing them and the pickup from sight.

Heart pounding, hands shaking, Dakota pressed her ear to the hot metal of the garage door. She heard the growl of the SUV passing slowly outside.

And the change in pitch as it idled on the street in front of their hiding place.

Lila stared at the circle of armed and angry men surrounding her and Quinn. Her fingers plucked anxiously at the ring on her finger, and she swallowed hard. Quinn's eyes stretched wide and unblinking beneath her grimy forehead and Lila knew hers must look the same. She only hoped it lent her an air of innocence and not mere abject fear.

"That's our lunchbox," she said in Arabic, pointing to the cooler with her toe. "Just sandwiches and drinks."

"Open it!" the leader insisted, waving his rifle.

Lila dropped to a knee. "Okay, okay," she agreed, reaching for the cooler. "I would offer to share with you, but..."

She bit her lip and wrinkled her nose apologetically.

"But the sandwiches are ham. You know, *haram*. Forbidden. An abomination for faithful Muslims." She gave a regretful shrug and popped open the clasps on the cooler, poised to open the lid.

"I'm sorry to expose you to—"

"Stop!"

The leader motioned toward her hand where Mitch's ring sparkled on her finger, his eyes shiny with greed.

"Keep your sandwiches. Give me the ring."

Relief and dismay flooded over Lila in equal measure. The bandit's desire for the ring came as a saving grace. For her, for Quinn, and possibly for an entire nation.

But what did it mean for her relationship with Mitch?

She didn't have time to think about that now. The Arab held out his palm, an arrogant frown on his face as he waited for her to deliver the diamond into his hand. Clamping down on the emotions roiling in her chest, Lila twisted the ring from her finger and held it out, head bowed.

The leader snatched it in triumph. Giving her a disgusted glare, he kicked a bootful of sand over the cooler. With a sharp gesture, he sent forth a new spurt of shouted Arabic, ordering his men to take a hefty portion of the goods from the back of the jeep. In a flurry of motion, the men loaded their take, mounted their trucks, and departed, leaving a trail of dust behind them.

Lila brushed the sand from the cooler and refastened the clasps. Quinn gave her an appraising look but said nothing.

The temperature gauge now showed 1.6 degrees. Returning to the jeep, Lila radioed in a report while Quinn drove fast to make up for the time they'd lost.

Ten minutes later, they reached a fork in the road without a signpost to suggest which branch they should take. Lila contacted the TOC.

"Go left at the fork," Shane told her. "You're almost there, ladies. Well done."

Quinn turned left and steered along the narrow, rutted road. She hadn't said a word since the incident with the cooler, so Lila was surprised when she suddenly spoke.

"You saved our bacon back there, L.T." She paused. "Thank you."

"Don't you mean I saved our ham?" Lila smiled. It was the first time Quinn had called her L.T. and she considered it a step toward something like respect.

"I wish we did have a cooler full of ham sandwiches and cold drinks," Quinn moaned. "I'd trade in a heartbeat for that damn liver."

Lila raised an eyebrow. "Would you really?"

Quinn sighed. "No. Not really. Let's just get this done and over with."

"Roger that."

Suddenly the jeep shimmied and growled, shuddering as it bogged down in sand. Quinn tried finessing it out, but the tires only spun, sending twin rooster tails of sand spraying out behind them.

Much of the desert was hardpacked dirt beneath a light covering of grit, but there were depressions where the sand gathered in deep deceptive pools.

"The entire road's submerged, from here forward," Lila said, fighting off despair. They were so close.

Quinn got out and surveyed the quagmire of desert sand. "We'll have to dig the jeep out and turn it around," she said.

"Right. I'll ask Shane if we can get there another way."

Jumping out of the jeep, Lila went to the rear tires and knelt down, using her hands to scoop the sand away, clearing a path. For every scoop she took, more than half of it slithered back into place. It was maddening, and time was running out.

Quinn worked beside her, scraping away behind the other tire. At last, they'd cleared enough sand to see the bottoms of the tires.

Lila sat back on her heels and rubbed a grubby hand across her forehead. "Let's try using the floormats to add some traction," she said.

"If there are any floormats in this piece of junk," Quinn added.

A quick search turned up one floormat. Lila stared at the thick slab of rubber.

"Wonderful."

She took out her KA-BAR and began sawing the mat in half. It was tough going, and when the sweat gathered on her forehead and streamed into her eyes, Quinn took over and finished the job.

It felt like teamwork, not a competition.

"That'll have to do," Lila said. "Let's shove them as far under the tires as we can. Rubber side up."

Mats in place, Quinn put the jeep in reverse and hit the gas while Lila pushed from the front. The jeep whined and protested, but in the end it did what they asked of it, backing up and breaking free of the sand pit.

"Let's go!" Lila said, jumping into the passenger seat. Reaching Shane on the radio, she got directions for an alternate route and Quinn made the appropriate turns.

Once more, they were on their way and headed in the right direction. Lila checked the temperature dial on the cooler.

It pointed to 3.3 degrees.

Dakota held her breath, straining to hear any clues about what might be happening on the other side of the garage door. The space she and Claire crouched in was dark, the air stagnant and oppressive with heat, plastering the short hair under her hijab to her sweaty skin.

No windows. No way to see danger coming.

All they could do was wait and listen.

The engine noise from the black SUV continued to purr in idle. Dakota's imagination went wild, picturing a gang of terrorist thugs with rifles surrounding the garage, trapping them inside. She cringed, expecting the rickety door to roll up at any second, shifting this nightmare into a whole new gear.

And then a new noise invaded the darkness, sending a sharp thrill of terror straight to her gut.

The horn!

The pickup's horn honked—a couple of short beeps followed by a long blast.

Hadid was awake.

Scrambling in the inky blackness, she fumbled her way along the bed of the pickup, throwing open the door and leaping upon the figure leaning on the horn. Claire must have done the same from her side. They pulled Hadid away from the steering wheel.

Yet the sonorous sound continued.

Dakota gasped as she recognized the muezzin's call to prayer. They must be very near a mosque. The sound rose, rich and melodious, seeming to fill every corner of the hot garage. It was *Maghrib*, the sunset prayer.

Hadid continued to squirm beneath her hands, shouting indignantly.

"Be quiet, you fool!" she hissed into his ear. She knew only a few words of Arabic, but she spoke the one most likely to get his attention. "Al-Zaanni."

He stopped struggling, going tense and still. She could almost feel his fear seeping through her fingers.

The beautiful strains of the muezzin's call finished and faded, leaving once again the ominous sound of the idling car outside, only a thin sheet of metal separating them from certain destruction.

And then the sound of the motor shifted and dissipated as the SUV drove off. Dakota went limp, feeling drained and weak at the knees.

"Thank God," Claire said in a shaky voice.

"*Al-Ḥamdu lillāh,*" Hadid added, echoing her thanks in his own tongue.

Dakota said, "We need a new vehicle. Stay here and see what you can do for your patient, Claire. I'll go dig something up."

"Too bad we don't have our Scrounger with us."

"Copy that. Better Lila than me, but a woman's got to do..."

"What a woman's got to do. Good luck, Sergeant."

Moving quietly through the dusk, Dakota approached the house closest to the garage. It was a simple square structure made of cement and painted blue, with a tiny, covered porch in front. The door stood open to catch the evening breeze.

Dakota mounted the two cement steps to the porch. "*Marhaban,*" she called. "*Salam.*" Hello, I come in peace. About the only Arabic she had to work with.

She was relieved when a woman came to the door, flanked by two teenage boys, both who spoke a fair rendition of English. Through a combination of charades and broken sentences, she ascertained that the garage indeed belonged to the family and the father would return soon to park his car there.

When he arrived a few moments later, she arranged to borrow the car, leaving the pickup as collateral, and got a stack of fresh-baked flatbread into the bargain.

Once more on the road, with Hadid stretched across the back seat, subdued and keeping out of sight, Claire contacted Shane to report they were only a dozen miles from the surgical venue.

"No, I'm afraid you're not," he said. "The MTF is under attack. We believe al-Zaanni somehow got word you were headed there. We're routing you to a FOB with a small surgical unit, but you'll have to drive an extra fifteen klicks. Sending you the GPS coordinates now."

Dakota's fingers tightened on the steering wheel. The headlights swept out in front of the car, illuminating what seemed like an endless road. Her chest felt heavy as she worked to pull a breath deep into her lungs.

"Thanks, Shane," Claire said. "We expect to arrive by 8:30."

"Copy that. I've already rerouted Baker and Quinn. They should get there about the same time you do. With the liver." He paused. "Be careful, Claire."

"Always," she assured him, signing off.

Lila's neck muscles felt tight enough to snap from the constant tension as Quinn steered the jeep through the darkened desert. Clasping her hands in her lap, she rubbed her thumb over the bare spot where Mitch's ring once resided.

Was the ring's loss a sign that the two of them were not meant to be?

Or would they rise above this bump on the road to a lifetime of committed love? Would they tell the tale to their children and draw strength from it, knowing their bond could withstand any challenge?

It felt important to figure this out, but it didn't have to happen this very moment.

As they rode through the dark of evening, Lila heard, now and then in the distance, the *rat-a-tat* of gunfire and knew al-Zaanni's band of terrorists were out hunting for their traitor.

She hoped with every fiber of her soul that they hadn't found him.

At last, the jeep's headlights picked up the sign for the FOB. She relaxed back in her seat and let out a long, quivery breath, feeling her heartbeat gear down to a more sedate tempo.

They'd made it.

She peered at the temp gauge on the cooler. 3.6 degrees.

Claire would have to work fast to transplant the liver into Hadid before everything went south. Quinn pulled up outside the surgical facility and they rushed inside with the cooler.

A surge of relief flooded over Lila as she saw Claire in the OR, scrubbed and ready for surgery. Hadid was on the table, prepped and draped. His sleeping face, smooth but for a scatter of stubble, looked small and vulnerable without the burly beard. Dakota stood beside him.

"You're just in time," Claire said as they delivered the cooler. "Scrub in, Sergeant Quinn. I'm going to need your help in here."

Quinn went to the sink and Claire moved to the cooler to check on the liver. As she reached for it, the lights guttered and went out, leaving them in darkness and silence.

"What now?" Dakota said.

The radio crackled and Shane came on. "Hey guys, heads up," he said. "You may lose power."

"Way ahead of you, Shane," Claire said. "We're in the dark here."

"Sorry to hear that. We think al-Zaanni's men are sabotaging power stations across the grid to throw a wrench in our works. The good news is that means they probably don't know your specific location, so they're making a sweeping attack."

The lights flickered and came up as the generator kicked in and the FOB commander entered, a grim look on his face. "I come bearing the bad news," he said. "We're low on fuel for the generator. We've only got about twenty minutes worth of gas."

Lila gasped. "How is it possible that you have no fuel reserves?" she asked, unable to keep the criticism out of her voice.

The colonel regarded her dolefully. "You have no idea what we've been dealing with in recent weeks," he said mildly. "Most of the local supply stations are held by the insurgents. Those that aren't, have been systematically hit by saboteurs, and our supply convoys are ambushed when they cross the border."

Claire stared at him, dismayed. "I'll need a lot more than twenty-minute's worth, Colonel."

"I know. I sent some of my men out to requisition fuel and I'm sure they'll come through for us." He paused. "I hate to say it, but our sudden demand will probably tip them to your location. I've already sent most of my people out there to defend our perimeter."

Lila wobbled in her boots. This was the longest day she'd ever lived through. A sinking feeling seized her as she checked the temperature dial on the cooler.

3.8 degrees.

"We're losing the liver," she warned.

The colonel made an apologetic gesture. "We have no choice but to move forward. Start the surgery, Major, and we'll work on getting you the power you need."

Claire turned, her gaze taking in Lila and Dakota. "Scrounger? Scout?"

"We're on it," Lila said. Dakota was already halfway out the door—her wordless answer to Claire's plea.

"Stay on the compound," the FOB commander warned, following them down the hall. "Colonel Tate sent orders for you not to leave the premises. You're stuck here for now, I'm afraid."

Lila ran to catch up with Dakota, struggling to put her exhaustion aside and rally her energy reserves. They'd worked so hard and come so far.

And so much hung in the balance.

She'd be damned if it all went for nothing.

Dakota gritted her teeth, blocking out the sense of defeat threatening to take her down. Recon was her specialty, and she was itching to get outside the bounds of the FOB and scout the area. But she understood the reasons for Colonel Tate's orders, and she wasn't stupid enough to disobey them.

She'd have to confine herself to the compound.

Lifting her chin, she focused on the task at hand. Lila followed her out into the parking lot. She surveyed the dusty patch and saw only Quinn's jeep and the car they'd borrowed parked beside a pair of battered, rusty scooters.

"Anything left in the tank of your jeep, L.T?" she asked.

"Afraid not. We were running on empty just to get here."

"Yeah. Us too."

"The colonel's got men out combing the neighboring communities for fuel," Lila said. "I'm sure they'll bring back something soon."

"Yes," Dakota replied. "But in less than twenty minutes?" She looked around desperately, a crazy idea forming in her mind.

"Do you think you can scrounge me up a dryer hose?" she asked.

She watched the lieutenant's face light with hope. "Come hell or high water," she said, "I will get you a dryer hose." Her brow furrowed and she added, "What are you going to do with it?"

Dakota walked to one of the scooters and popped the tab on the storage compartment. It creaked open and, as she'd hoped, the key was inside. She inserted it and turned it a notch.

"Hallelujah," she said. "We got about half a tank."

"So what?" Lila said. "We won't get far on that. The FOB generator's got to be at least a 30-kilowatt model. It'll burn through that little half a tank in less than ten minutes."

"True. But it can run the motor on this baby for quite a bit longer. With a little luck, long enough for the power to come back up or the colonel's men to arrive with enough fuel to see us through."

Lila stared. "You're going to build your own generator," she said.

Dakota smiled. "That's the idea. We don't need to power the whole unit. We just need to produce enough to keep Claire's room up and running. Get me that hose."

She wheeled the scooter into the medical wing, guiding it down the hallway to the room next to Claire's OR and cleared space to work in. Before reclassifying as a cavalry scout, she'd been a helicopter mechanic and more than once had found those skills coming in handy.

Using a block, she braced the scooter's rear wheel off the floor, then found an orderly and asked him to bring her a toolbox.

Pirating parts off the other scooter and from some of the equipment in the room, she rewired a hub motor to create a simple generator which she mounted on a broken bicycle rack.

It took her fifteen minutes.

Only when she'd finished, did she consciously register the sound of distant gunfire. The soldiers guarding the perimeter were seeing some action.

No one had arrived with more fuel, and the FOB generator had begun faltering.

Lila ran in, carrying a wide-mouth flexible hose, cut jaggedly on either end.

"Sorry," she said. "It's the only one I could find. I checked the supply rooms first but came up empty. I had to cut this one off a dryer in the laundry room."

"It's fine. Hand me that duct tape."

Dakota attached the hose to the scooter's exhaust pipe and flung the other end out the open window.

"Let's hope this works."

The lights flickered. "Dakota!" Claire shouted from the OR. "Now would be a really bad time for me to lose the lights and electricity."

"Hold tight. We're almost there!"

Starting the scooter's motor, Dakota adjusted the idle speed and pushed her homemade generator up against the back wheel where it spun the hub and...

"It's working!" Quinn squealed from next door. "Go team."

Just then, a *boom* sounded from not too far away, rattling the instruments in their metal trays.

"They're lobbing mortars," Lila said. "How much longer on the surgery, Claire?"

Claire tossed them a harried glance, her eyes bloodshot and weary above the surgical mask she wore. "I'm just getting started," she said.

Dakota looked at Lila, who met her gaze. She looked worried.

"We need to buy her a lot more time," she whispered.

"Right. I'll scout, you scrounge."

Leaving a soldier named Carmichael in charge of keeping her homemade generator operating, Dakota ran a recon through the camp, gas can in hand. She siphoned fuel from gas tanks, cooking stoves, everywhere she could think of.

She delivered her collection to Carmichael. The scooter's motor continued to hum, supplying Claire's OR with the power she needed. But the hours stretched ahead, far outreaching their little store of fuel.

Moving with care, Dakota made her way to the back gate of the base. She stood behind the girders forming a zigzag barricade and peered into the blackness, listening to the intermittent chatter of gunfire and distant shouting.

She nodded to the soldiers manning the guard box, not sure why she'd come, considering the Colonel's orders not to leave the post. What could she do?

And then, motion in the darkness caught her eye and she watched two men in American camo, each clutching a red metal five-gallon gas can, burst from cover and run for the gate. One of them made it.

The other fell twenty meters short, amid a flurry of shots.

Without stopping to think, Dakota rushed past the barricade to help, joined by one of the guards and the soldier who'd delivered the can of gas. The *pockety-pock* of gunfire tore the night sky and dirt sprayed up around her where bullets hit the ground.

She grabbed the gas can and darted away as fuel sloshed inside. Only half full.

The two men lifted their fallen comrade and dragged him through the gate. He'd taken three to the vest and one to the helmet. Enough to knock him down and out, but nothing making him bleed.

Back at the medical unit, Dakota met up with Lila. Her friend wielded a chain saw in her arms.

Dakota raised an eyebrow. "Where'd you find the saw?" she asked.

"I found two saws," Lila corrected, "each with a full tank. But I'm sorry to say I'm not the one who thought of it. Lieutenant Jordan suggested I try the rescue saws from victim extraction kits."

"Brilliant!"

"Oh yeah," Lila agreed. "Every little bit gets us that much closer to the end of a successful surgery."

Dakota shifted her gaze to the little makeshift generator sputtering away on pilfered portions of gasoline.

"I hope we can all hold out for as long as it takes," she said.

They did.

Lila stood outside the tactical command post, listening to radio transmissions as reinforcement soldiers arrived from the south, driving off the insurgent forces and securing the base. She sagged against the door jamb, languid with a delicious and curiously soothing brand of fatigue.

She'd laughed when the colonel's search party came through with a truck full of gas, just as Claire cut the thread on the last suture. Dakota's souped-up scooter, aided by her own foraged dryer hose and the bits of fuel mined from a myriad of sources, had endured to the end. Claire and Quinn had done the rest.

All from the hands of a band of scheming women.

The hospital had sustained minimal damage from the enemy mortars, which was good because medics hauled in a dozen injured soldiers from the perimeter. Men and women who'd held the terrorists at bay, defending the little FOB and the high value target which lay inside.

No one got any rest except Nizam Hadid, who slept peacefully through it all.

As the sun rose on a new day, Lila watched Colonel Tate's group arrive in a dusty flurry of trucks and jeeps. She went out to meet them, not caring that her hair was a mess, her hands ragged and raw from scraping sand, every inch of exposed skin grubby with a film of desert grit.

"I understand the surgery was a success," Tate said, closing the distance between them with his long strides. "How long 'til he's out of sedation?"

"Claire said he should be coming around any moment now, but he'll be sore and groggy."

"Not my concern," Tate said. "We've come through with our part of the bargain, now it's his turn."

Lila grimaced, not liking the suspicion that rose in her mind.

"What if it was all a bluff?" she asked.

"It was no bluff," the Colonel assured her, his face grim. "DHS confirms the activity on our southern border. There's a lot of buzz about something going on. I intend to get the details from our patient. Now."

"Hadid got what he needed from us," Lila said. "What if he refuses to talk?"

"We put that liver in him, and we can damn well yank it out again. He'll talk."

By noon, the vital details of al-Zaanni's plans had passed into the hands of the Commander-in-Chief and the Secretary of Defense who were formulating plans of their own and putting them into action to rout the terrorists and foil the heinous attack slated for the American people.

Lila had faith those plans would succeed.

She settled into the bunk she'd been allotted with a satisfying sense of disaster averted. Tracing her thumb along her naked ring finger, she let her thoughts linger over the image of Mitch's face, the touch of his lips, the comfort of his hand tucked securely around hers.

Realizing how much she missed him, how much she wanted to build a future with him in it, she turned on her side and snuggled into the pillow.

Arabian bandits and long distances wouldn't stand in her way. Tomorrow, come hell or highwater, she'd find a way to call Mitch and let him know.

A thin wall separated the room she shared with Claire from the one assigned to Quinn and Dakota. A gentle snoring penetrated the partition.

Her teammates—the women who'd shouldered the heavy threat of death with her over the last twenty-four hours—were already snoozing. Lila smiled and closed her eyes.

And was asleep before her lashes touched her cheeks.

Author's Note

Still in the Family

Crimes of passion can cover a lot of territory. Some people may be driven to commit dastardly crimes by an obsessive passion for another person, a burning ambition, a treasured belief, a long-held ideology, or good old-fashioned lucre. To name a few possible motivations.

I mulled over a number of ideas for *Mystery, Crime, and Mayhem's* issue devoted to such crimes, hoping to come up with a twist on the idea—a crime and an outcome of the sort readers wouldn't expect.

I think I hit the target.

"Still in the Family" was first published in *Mystery, Crime, and Mayhem: Passionate Crimes,* May 2021.

I had a lot of fun writing this one, and I hope you'll have a great time reading it!

STILL IN THE FAMILY

B leeding red paint.

That's how Charlotte felt about the watercolor, as if it was a living thing, bleeding out truth and beauty in equal measure. As always, she found herself caught up in the fine grain of ancient paper, the richness of pigments formed from tiny insect bodies ground to powder and mixed in a liquid medium to bloom and grow into the mass of scarlet poppies before her.

A click of heels on the polished floor snapped Charlotte from her reverie. She straightened her spine, leaning forward from her seat on the hard wooden bench, not letting her gaze wander to the newcomer in the room. She knew it wouldn't be Lena, might even be someone nice to talk to, but she preferred to maintain an icy distance within these walls.

These walls. Where she took her first steps, had her first birthday party. Where she'd labored over schoolwork and tossed through sleepless nights of teenage angst. These walls had embraced her through happy times and tragedy, held her up after the death of her mother, seen her through the fretful days of her father's illness and the sad weeks that followed his passing. These walls had been her home for most of her life, and now she was only a guest within them.

Not, however, a welcome guest.

Meyerhof Manor, in the Bavarian Oberpfalz, opened its doors to the visiting public on Tuesdays and Thursdays, 10 a.m. to 4 p.m. Every Thursday afternoon, Charlotte paid the entrance fee and walked straight to the painting, head held high. It belonged to her. Everyone knew it had passed down through countless generations of her family since Albrecht Dürer originally gifted it to a distant ancestor at the turn of the sixteenth century.

Charlotte's father had meant it to pass to her, but had somehow neglected to stipulate that in a proper legal document. In fact, the illness that struck him so unexpectedly and dispatched him so precipitously had given him no chance to set his affairs in order. Lena ended up taking everything.

Charlotte shifted on the bench and the smell of lemon oil furniture polish floated up to her. She stood, swiping at the seat of her pants. Once or twice after visiting, she'd noticed faint grease stains from the housemaid's overzealous use of the oily stuff. She took a last look at the painting, *her painting,* and turned to go, dropping her ticket stub into a waste bin as she walked by.

Lena may have stripped her of her rightful inheritance, but Charlotte took consolation in the fact that debts stacked up over the decades were eating away at the estate and Lena had inherited those, too. She knew it galled her father's widow to be reduced to charging admission so strangers could wander her home, and it was a certainty that Charlotte's presence there every week further irritated her.

Thus, Charlotte strived to never miss a Thursday.

All told, there were only two things Charlotte wished she could get from Lena. She wanted a confession that Lena had caused her father's illness and subsequent death. In her heart, Charlotte felt it was so, but she had no evidence, absolutely no foundation for the belief other than her deep antipathy toward the woman. She accepted this with reluctance, resigned to go without this satisfaction, and set her heart on her second desire.

She wanted that painting.

"So, how is the old Dämonin?" Emilie asked, stirring sugar into her coffee.

Charlotte sniffed at the fragrant vapor wafting from the well-sweetened cup and smiled. She liked the way Emilie always referred to her wicked stepmother as the She-Demon. She took a tentative sip at her own cup but the tea was still too hot to drink. Dabbing her lip with a pink paper napkin, she leaned back and studied the painted mural decorating the wall of the Bäckerei. It showed an oafish baker in wooden shoes peering into a brick oven filled with golden bread.

"I wouldn't know," she replied. "I never see her there, but sometimes I think I can feel her watching me. I hope I'm right about that. I hope her skin crawls with shame at the sight of me."

"If she was anything nearing a decent human being, it would," Emilie said, breaking off a piece of apple strudel and placing it on her tongue. "I'll bet she gets reports about you from the guard."

"Elias? I've nothing to fear from him. He hates her as much as I do."

"Not possible." Emilie took another bite of strudel. "What's he got against her?"

"My father hired Elias years ago as an assistant estate manager and always treated him like family. When Lena took over, she demoted him to watchman."

Emilie shrugged. "It could have been worse."

"Oh, it was worse," Charlotte said, putting down the quark-tasche she'd been about to bite into. "Elias's daughter got sick.

Leukemia. Lena put up all kinds of obstacles over the medical coverage and kicked up a fuss whenever he asked to spend time with his dying daughter." Charlotte ground her teeth and took a gulp of hot tea, feeling the burn spread through her chest. "At least she gave him a week off for the funeral."

Emilie's eyes widened. A moment of silence passed while Charlotte's pulse gradually slowed to normal. She looked down and saw that she'd torn her cheese pastry into shreds. "I've spent more hours agonizing over that woman's evils than I care to number."

Emilie reached for her hand, squeezed it hard. "You'll feel better if you do something about it," she said. "Make some kind of stand against her."

"I know this. I've thought about it long and hard, Emilie. She's wily, and she puts on a good face. Most people don't see beyond that to the black soul beneath, but some day she will answer to God and I can only pity her for that."

"Because you're a good sort, Charlotte," Emilie said, regarding her with a sorrowful eye. "But is that enough to give you peace of mind here and now?"

Charlotte scraped the twists of pastry into the waxed bakery bag. "No." She screwed up the bag, holding it tight in her fists. "But I have an idea what I can do about that."

Thursday afternoon. Charlotte bought her ticket at the door and stepped into the great hall, watching dust motes dance on the sunbeams slanting in from a row of high windows. The warmth of the spring day followed her into the room, intensifying the smell of old wood paneling and library paste but in spite of it, Charlotte shivered a little.

Taking a deep breath, she let it out in a long whistling sigh as she walked the runner of carpet that led to the gallery. *Her* painting, the Dürer watercolor, hung in the corner of a small alcove, overshadowed by a Rembrandt purchased in the eighteenth century by a distant forefather. The Rembrandt held pride of place in the center of the room, directly opposite the wide doorway. During her visits, Charlotte had noticed the tiny security camera placed unobtrusively above the door to monitor the most valuable Rembrandt and the comings and goings of visitors to the alcove. The little Dürer was out of its range.

Pausing outside the doorway, Charlotte noticed a woman in a long lavender cardigan inside the alcove. Preferring to have the room to herself, she passed the opening and stopped in front of a series of sketches executed by one of her long-ago relatives. They depicted hunting scenes and pastoral landscapes filled with painstaking detail, tiny curling leaves and intricately textured fabrics. Charlotte couldn't imagine having the time or the patience to devote to such a task, but the result was beautiful.

The slow and steady clomp of unhurried footsteps sounded behind her and Charlotte turned to see Elias, the guard, approaching on his rounds. He raised his hand in a brief wave and she gave him a wistful smile, sad to see how gaunt he'd grown, how gray the strands of hair beneath his cap. As he approached, the woman in the lavender cardigan passed out of the alcove and Charlotte peered in to see the small room empty of visitors. She entered, passing beneath the camera's eye, and settled onto her usual seat. Crossing her feet, she tucked them beneath the bench and studied the scene before her with satisfaction.

The guard came to stand beside her. Charlotte said, "Do you know how much I love my painting, Elias?"

"I have an inkling. You're here every week to pay homage. I'm sure it reminds you of your father."

"It does." Charlotte paused. She glanced at the camera above the door, wondering if it picked up sound, decided it didn't. She took a breath. "I've spent a lot of time staring at my painting, but for all that, I've never noticed what a handsome frame surrounds it."

"Indeed," the guard responded. "It suits such a pretty picture to have a lovely frame." He gave a heavy sigh. "I'm glad to see you well, Miss Charlotte, but my employer discourages me speaking with the guests. I'll move on."

He tipped his cap and left the room. Charlotte returned her gaze to the wall in front of her, listening carefully for the sound of anyone else approaching. One minute passed, and then two, before she skirted beneath the camera and left the alcove.

Heart hammering inside her chest like a manic sewing machine, she moved quickly toward the exit. A scant meter or so before she reached the door which led into the side garden, a voice cried out, "Halt! Stop that woman, she's a thief!"

Charlotte turned, her mouth dropping open in surprise. Pounding footsteps echoed as Elias crossed the hall and grabbed her by the arm. A few guests stared, ready to be entertained by the drama before them, delighted to be getting more than their ticket's worth.

A figure descended the staircase and passed through the red velvet ropes that set the private rooms apart. A tall woman, dressed in a navy pantsuit, every dark hair styled into submission, face perfectly made up. A discreet trace of expensive perfume followed in her wake.

Charlotte lifted her chin as Lena approached. Elias tugged at her arm. "I wish you hadn't done it, Miss Charlotte," he murmured in a voice just loud enough to carry. "I know your father wanted you to have the painting, but this is not the way."

"What's happened?" Lena demanded, her ruby-stained lips thinning into a strained line across her face.

"It's the Dürer watercolor," Elias replied. "She's taken it."

Charlotte's stomach dropped. "What? I have not!"

Lena marched to the alcove and Elias dragged Charlotte along behind her. The other visitors crowded in, not wanting to miss the excitement. Charlotte nearly smacked into Lena's ramrod back as the woman halted suddenly inside the doorway. Craning her neck to the side, Charlotte stared at the wall which had housed the Dürer as long as she could remember.

It contained only an empty frame.

"It wasn't me," Charlotte said. "I didn't take the painting."

"Search her," Lena commanded.

Elias hesitated. "Shouldn't we call—"

"Search her!"

Charlotte glared and threw wide her arms in a taunting invitation. "Go ahead. I'm not hiding anything."

Again, Elias balked but gave in under Lena's imperious pointing finger. He opened Charlotte's handbag. "Sorry about this," he said as he sifted through her personal items, looking for the rolled or folded painting. Next, he searched her pockets and even frisked the legs of her pants in case she'd tucked the missing Dürer inside her socks.

"She doesn't have it," he informed Lena. "And she's not carrying any kind of tool for cutting it from its frame."

Charlotte smoothed her jacket where Elias had rumpled it. "I told you I didn't take the painting. You've got no reason to keep me here."

She saw the muscles tighten in Lena's jaw. The woman pulled a mobile phone from her pocket and began tapping it with red-lacquered fingernails. "I'm calling the police." She nodded toward Elias. "Hold on to her."

A pair of policemen arrived within ten minutes. They instructed Elias to lock the doors and cordon off the visitors for later questioning.

"What happened here?" asked the senior officer, a small man with a pug nose and large brown eyes. His features were crowded toward the center of his face, making him look like a ferret.

Lena stepped forward, jutting out a hip and making a gesture like a game show hostess presenting the prize. "This girl has stolen a valuable painting."

"I haven't," Charlotte said, shaking her head.

The policeman turned to Elias. "What did you see happen?"

Elias's brow furrowed. He looked uncomfortable and Charlotte saw his Adam's apple bob as he swallowed and began speaking. "Miss Charlotte made her usual Thursday visit to the painting. I saw her come in as I was making my rounds and I stopped to say hello."

"Where did this conversation take place?"

Elias nodded toward the bench. "There, in front of the painting."

"And the painting was present at that time?"

"Oh yes, we both admired it. We only spoke for a moment and I left the room. It couldn't have been more than three minutes later that Miss Charlotte came out. I was again passing the alcove and when I looked in to make sure everything was all right, I saw the painting was missing from its frame. Miss Charlotte was rushing toward the door and I thought she must have taken it." He shook his head. "But I've searched her and she doesn't have it."

"She must have hidden it somewhere in this room," Lena said.

"We'll search it thoroughly," said the man in charge. Charlotte watched as the two officers poked into every nook and cranny, behind every piece of artwork, and got down on hands and knees to examine the undersides of the benches.

"Nothing here," said the senior man. He directed his sergeant to search the area outside the room. "Pay special attention around the exit," he admonished. Turning to Elias, he added, "Could she have passed the painting to an accomplice? Was someone waiting outside, perhaps?"

"She never made it out the door," Elias answered. "And to the best of my recollection, she didn't pass anyone on her way to the exit."

"Very good, we'll question and search the others in any case. Sit tight," he told them, "I'm going to do that now."

An hour passed while Charlotte, Lena, and Elias sat on the benches in the alcove, avoiding each other's gaze. At last, Lena spoke.

"I believe you have a soft spot for Charlotte," she said to Elias. "Maybe *you're* the one who stole the painting for her." She strode to the doorway and raised her voice. "Officer, I think you should search my guard. He may be the accomplice we're looking for."

Elias gave her a wounded look. "After all my years of faithful service," he said, "this is how you treat me. I suppose I should have expected it."

He rose and held his hands out to the side, subjecting himself to a systematic search by the senior policeman, who found nothing of note. The man's ferret features scrunched into a frown. "I'll admit, I'm baffled. What happened to the painting?"

He seemed to be directing his question to Charlotte. She shrugged. "All I know is that I didn't take it."

He sighed. "All right," he said, indicating Charlotte and Elias. "I'm afraid you'll both have to come down to the station for further questioning."

Twelve hours later, after intensive interrogation that led the police nowhere, Charlotte and Elias were released to go their separate ways.

Charlotte didn't return to Meyerhof Manor. With the Dürer gone, there was no point. Lena was free of her, and she was free of Lena.

Really.

Finally and wonderfully free.

She thought of her father, missing him with that old familiar ache, like a thread pulling on her heart. Missing him, but not missing his worldly goods. The only part of that she'd ever wanted was the painting.

She rolled down the window of the taxi, letting the salt breeze lift her hair, and surveyed the scenery with contentment. The road wound through the Mediterranean coast outside Marbella, giving her glimpses of the turquoise sea and the heavenly smell of sun-warmed sand. She'd looked forward to this vacation for three long months. As the taxi pulled up outside the rented villa, Charlotte's heart leaped with excitement.

She over-tipped the driver, who smiled and deposited her luggage on the doorstep. Not bothering to smother the huge smile that spread across her face, Charlotte punched in the code the agent had given her and entered the villa's foyer.

She wheeled her suitcase across the terra cotta tile and hung her camera case on the coat rack, next to a lavender cardigan. She grabbed hold of the soft knitted fabric and breathed. Lemon furniture oil.

Emilie had arrived the day before. Charlotte walked to the back of the house and saw her friend, splayed out in a scarlet bathing suit, iced drink to hand. In the deck chair beside her, lounged Elias, already looking a little burned.

Emilie raised her drink. "It's about time you arrived."

Charlotte ran to her, gave hugs all around. "You know we had to travel separately and you two deserved a few extra days in the sun. I'm forever in your debt."

"No worries," said Elias. "We pulled it off, didn't we?" He'd cut his hair and looked fitter than last she'd seen him. "The police might believe you took the painting but since you didn't, they can't prove it."

"Not a soul suspects it was actually me," Emilie said gleefully.

"Besides," Elias added, "the police don't have the resources to watch us forever."

"No, they don't," Charlotte said. "I feel closure. It's done. It's gloriously done."

She laughed and raised her face to the sun's caress. Slowly, she sobered and couldn't keep the wistful tone out of her voice when she asked, "Can I see it?"

"Of course you can see it," Emilie said. "It's yours. It always has been."

The three of them linked arms and went inside to look at the centuries-old Dürer, gifted long ago to a distant forefather.

And still in the family.

Author's Note

Kissed by the Snow Angel

Have you ever laid down in the snow, kicked your arms and legs, and made a snow angel? Kind of fun, wasn't it?

The snow angel in this story isn't like the benevolent ones you and I have created.

It's lethal.

I originally wrote "Kissed by the Snow Angel" as a special bonus for readers who pre-ordered my thriller novel, *Steadman's Blind.* In the book, Chief Steadman and his partner, Deputy Frost, find themselves traveling a twisted, crazy road to reach the scene of a triple homicide. And that's just the beginning.

I enjoyed getting to know them so much that I started a whole series based on their cases. Readers love them too, and Amor Towles chose "Cold Hands, Warm Heart," from the series as one of *The Best Mystery Stories of the Year* in 2023.

If you'd like to spend more time with Steadman and Frost, check out the Steadman Mysteries series.

And now, I invite you to curl up with a warm blanket and have some fun with my snow angel story.

KISSED BY THE SNOW ANGEL

"Why do I get the feeling, Chief, that Michigan's middle finger is flipping us off?"

Chief Deputy Randall Steadman shook his head and gave a rueful laugh. "It *is* the Mitten State, Frost—and with good reason."

He stared out the thick plate glass at the snow globe world beyond, thick flakes whirling as if shaken by a furious hand. Gusts of wind, so powerful they shook the window, howled in the tumult like a banshee set on revenge. He turned away and regarded the deputy sharing his table, noting the young man's dejected posture. This was his first out-of-state law enforcement conference. Too bad it was a bust.

"Doesn't seem fair," Steadman said, "to get more snow dumped on us in western Washington than we've seen in twenty years, only to travel a couple thousand miles to get dumped on again."

He stirred the sluggish coffee in front of him, breaking up a slimy layer which had formed on its surface. He pushed it away. "I could live with that," he said, "but the storm is interfering with cell reception and it's my wife's birthday. Bad enough I can't be with her—I'm determined to at least get a call through."

"Sorry, Chief. I didn't know it was Vivi's birthday. Wish her a good one from me, will you?"

The deputy leaned back from the table, balancing his chair on two legs. Steadman gritted his teeth. He hated when people did that but found it was worthless asking them not to. Habits were tough to break. He concentrated instead on unwrapping a mint, sucking on it to erase the coat of sour coffee scum on his tongue.

"I'm betting they'll cancel the rest of the conference," he said.

Frost's chair thumped down. "Bat scat!" he said, using his favorite peculiar curse word. "They had a psychologist from the Marshal's Service lined up to talk about behavioral analysis. I was really looking forward to that. Not to mention, the skiing. Guess that's not going to happen."

The harsh blizzard conditions and high winds called for all hands on deck, and the local lawmen were engaged in saving lives and maintaining safety conditions. Many of the out-of-town guests were being tasked to support their efforts, further depleting attendees for the conference. Steadman had offered his assistance, but so far there'd been no takers.

He crunched down on the mint. "At this rate, we may have to ski home, partner. No flights going out. We're stuck here for the foreseeable future."

He thumbed the button to wake his phone. The screen lit, but there was still no signal. He slumped, kneading the candy wrapper between his fingers. Faint murmurs of conversation rose from the few occupied tables in the conference room, sounding to Steadman like the drone of a fly trapped inside a window. He sighed.

A loud *snick* crossed the empty air as the big double doors swung open and the local sheriff entered and scanned the room before making his way to Steadman's table. They'd met yesterday at the conference's kick-off mixer. Sheriff Calloway.

"Word got around that you offered to help," he said as he reached Steadman, "and we could sure use it. Just got a report of a missing person and there's no one left to send."

"Well, seeing as how you've reached the bottom of the barrel..." Steadman began.

The man didn't crack a smile. "I didn't mean it that way, Chief, and please pardon me when I say there's no time for chit chat. Things are really bad out there. The missing man is Lance Medford, works for a pharmaceutical testing lab not far from here. He was in the building, and then he wasn't. Probably went out for a smoke and got disoriented, but it's got to be checked into. Will you and your deputy lend a hand?"

Steadman noticed Frost's posture improve. He figured both of them would benefit from a chance to get out of the stale hotel and contribute what they could to the stricken community.

"Of course, Sheriff Calloway. We'd be glad to."

"Sorry to say I don't have a vehicle to spare, but I've got a high-powered flashlight and an extra radio. The lab's only half a mile down the road. Did you bring sturdy boots with you?"

They had. And lots of extra socks. Something past experience had drilled into them.

"Great," said Calloway, handing Steadman a printed page with preliminary details, including the lab address and name of the person who made the initial call. Will Parsons. "Come with me and I'll get you equipped the best I can."

The three of them headed to the hotel's security office and Calloway handed Steadman a heavy-duty flashlight, a small hand-held radio, and a pair of ski masks.

"Bundle up warm," he said. "Conditions out there are no joke. With the wind chill factor, body temperature can drop into the danger zone in under ten minutes. Get to the lab, get inside, get the story. Search for the man, if warranted, but don't put yourselves in danger. Frankly, if he hasn't already made it to safety, there's nothing we can do for him now."

Steadman swallowed. His week in Michigan had moved from theoretical to hands-on in the course of a few short hours. "Understood," he said.

"If I guess right, the guy's probably back at the lab by now, getting reamed by his boss. But check it out, and if you need backup, radio in."

"Got it," Steadman said. He and Frost hurried to their rooms to change into warmer gear and Steadman was glad they'd come ready for some snow time. This wasn't the sort of thing they'd had in mind, but it was nice to be flexible.

Stepping out into the elements took his breath away. Frigid air attacked him with buffeting force, nearly knocking him from his feet. He nodded to Frost and saw that the eyes peering through the cutout in the ski mask held as much eagerness as trepidation. The two of them had faced extreme conditions while working together before and come through it well.

Steadman hoped that record would hold.

He shone the flashlight's powerful beam against the gloom and pushed into the wind like a swimmer fighting the current. He was a jogger, covering four or five miles on most days, and half a mile had sounded like an easy distance. But the freezing temperature, slippery snow, and gale force winds sapped his energy faster than he would have believed possible.

"Let's kick it into high gear and get out of this mess," he shouted to Frost.

They picked up their pace, shuffling quickly along the icy surface of the road. Flurries of crystallized flakes pelted Steadman's parka as the wind shrieked and wailed, threatening to suck him into the void one moment, and in the next moment nearly shoving him headlong into the drifts. He tasted snow melting on his tongue like shaved ice without the sweetness. The intensity of it gave him a headache.

"There it is." Frost's snow-caked arm motioned toward an industrial-looking building about thirty yards distant.

"Good eye," said Steadman. Flying snow reduced visibility and they might have missed the signpost, pushing right on past. He felt a surge of desire for a warm room away from the cutting wind. They trudged through the small parking lot and Steadman counted five cars hunkered down under shells of undisturbed snow.

The thick-paned double entry doors were locked and Steadman saw no movement beyond them to indicate anyone on the premises. He found a button attached to a speaker beside the door and pressed it.

"Deputies Steadman and Frost," he shouted into the speaker. "We're responding to the report of a missing person."

There might have been a buzz, but it was lost amid the screams of the wind. Frost pulled on the door and it opened. Steadman almost pushed him into the vestibule, fighting the gale to pull the door shut behind them, dropping the windy howling to a subdued moan. The sudden silence fell like a blanket. Only the sound of their panting filled the darkness as they waited for something to happen, the cone of Steadman's torch pointed at the floor. Dirty boot prints covered the tiles, pointing in every direction as if the wearers had danced a polka there.

Light flooded from beyond, and Steadman saw they were in a glassed-in area with another set of doors. A man approached. He slid a card through a reader and the lock clicked, allowing them entrance.

"Thank you," Steadman said, removing his gloves and stamping his feet on the mat. "Are you Will Parsons?"

"Yes, I am. I'm the one who called about Lance."

"Is he still missing?" asked Frost.

Will hesitated. "No," he said, shaking his head. Relief melted through Steadman. He didn't want to go out searching in that hazardous squall, and he hated to think of anyone out there, lost in that mess.

"No," Will continued. "We found him."

"Where was he?" Steadman asked.

Will tipped his head toward the doors. "Out there. Still is. We didn't want to move him until…"

Steadman's stomach dipped inside him. Oh no. "You mean—"

"I'm afraid so, sir. He's dead."

Steadman clenched his teeth as the chill blasted him again, renewing the headache that had been on the wane. Once more, he and Frost battled the driving wind and snow, carrying an empty stretcher between them which Will Parsons had supplied from the first aid room at the lab. The man walked in front, leading them to Lance Medford's body, and Steadman wondered if there was any chance he might still be alive. One glance at the blue, frozen face and the idea fled his mind. The man had clearly been dead for some time.

Steadman switched on the radio and got a squeal of static. His efforts to get through to dispatch went nowhere.

"I assumed this thing would be tuned to the proper frequency," he grumbled to Frost. "I don't know which one they use here."

He fiddled with the dial until he heard a clear transmission, then broke in and identified himself. His recipient gave his own call sign in a scratchy, wavering voice and asked how he could help.

"We've got a situation here," Steadman said, "and I need to reach the paramedics and the sheriff. Do you happen to know the frequency for—"

"Oh sure, I can tell you all that. Hal Cooper's my name. I cover emergencies for local radio and newspapers, so I know the whole network."

The man's warbling tone suggested he was an octogenarian. At least. Steadman pictured a retired military officer or fireman, someone still yearning for excitement and keeping his hand in by writing articles for small time publications.

"That's great, Hal," he said. "Please give me the frequencies for an ambulance and Sheriff Calloway."

"Will do, son, but I smell a story. Promise you'll get back to me with the details."

"I'm not sure how much I can—"

"Just note my channel and contact me when you can. Here's the information you're after."

He gave Steadman the frequencies, and asked him to repeat them back. "Don't forget me, now," the old man said and signed off.

Steadman tuned the radio and reached emergency dispatch, asking them to send out a team of paramedics and requesting they meet him at the lab. He was informed it might be a while before anyone showed up. Live people in need of help trumped the dead.

"Copy that," he said, signing off. He turned to their guide. "Stand back, if you would, Mr. Parsons, and train the light on us please."

Steadman held out an admonishing arm and nodded to Frost. They each used their cell phones to document the scene and the position of the body, and Steadman took several close-up shots from various angles. Wind whipped torrents of snow around them, obscuring the view and making it necessary to repeat many of the photos. Steadman knew they had to work quickly, but he insisted on examining the body in situ before they moved it. The heavy gloves encumbered his hands as he searched the victim's pockets for a cell phone, without success.

"All right," he said, "let's get him on the stretcher and back to the lab."

They lifted the victim onto the orange canvas of the stretcher and Steadman took another series of photos before he and Frost hefted the load and carried Lance Medford's remains back to the lab. After seeing the body situated in a half-empty storeroom and covered with a sheet, Steadman excused himself and found a quiet corner of the building. He radioed Sheriff Calloway.

The sheriff wasted no time on what he called chit chat. "Did you find the man, Steadman?"

"We found him, Sheriff. Frozen to death at the side of the road, about a block from the lab."

"What was the fool man doing? Do you know?"

"We haven't questioned anyone yet."

"Well, can you do that? Will you and your deputy stay and take statements? I'll get there as soon as I can."

"Yes, Sheriff, but I have to tell you I think we're dealing with a suspicious death here."

There was a pause. "Oh hell, Steadman, that's the last thing we need. What makes you think so?"

"The victim had no cell phone on him, which strikes me as odd, and though we found him lying in a pile of snow, there was no snowpack in the treads of his boots. I don't think he walked there."

"Seems thin, Chief. Anything else?"

"When I opened his parka to check for a cell phone, there was snow on the *inside*."

"Well, sure. It's rough out there. Half a dozen ways snow could have got up inside his coat." Steadman heard a loud sigh from the sheriff's end of the connection. "Look, Chief, I don't think there's a basis for suspicious death. Let's treat this as an accident unless, and until, something changes. Take statements from everyone on site and sit tight 'til I get there. Got it?"

"Yes, sir. It's your town."

"That it is, Steadman. Thank you for recognizing that, and for stepping in where you're needed. Just..." Steadman heard shouts in the background on the sheriff's end, followed by a slamming noise. The sheriff spoke again, tension in his voice. "Just don't overstep, Chief. I gotta go."

Static buzzed on the line before the radio let out a squawk and went still. Steadman gripped it hard, staring at lime-painted cinder block walls as the silence congealed around him.

Steadman ventured through the dim corridors, straining to discern where the murmur of voices was coming from. Following the sound, he found the others in a room with scattered tables and sofas. Vague images flashed across a large flat-screen in one corner, but the audio was turned down and no one was watching. Steadman picked up the remote control and switched off the screen.

"All right folks," he said, asking for their attention and getting it as four heads swiveled in his direction. Frost stood near the door as if on guard, and a look of relief spread over his face as Steadman took the lead.

"I'd like to meet you all," Steadman continued, "and hear a little about why you're here."

He looked at Will Parsons, noting that the man had changed out of the jeans and boots he wore while leading them to the site where Lance's body lay. He now wore dark blue sweats and sneakers, apparel that suggested he wanted to be comfortable, but the tension in his shoulders and the way he ran his hands through his ginger-colored hair suggested he was far from it. Steadman gestured in his direction.

"Let's start with you," he said.

"I'm the lab chief," Will said, shifting his position on the couch. "Which means I'm in charge of all the research that goes on here."

"Which is what?" Steadman asked.

"Our company is developing a number of drugs to treat various ailments. Right now we're excited about a breakthrough drug for the treatment of Alzheimer's Disease. We're just wrapping up trials and anticipate FDA approval by next month."

Steadman raised an eyebrow. "That's a big deal," he said. Four heads nodded.

"And what was your relationship to Lance Medford?"

Parallel lines rose on Will's forehead. He opened his mouth to speak, then closed it and looked away, fighting to hold on to his composure. When he did speak, his voice was husky. "Lance was my best friend. We've known each other since high school."

Steadman waited a respectful moment before asking, "Did you, or he, begin working here first?"

"I did. Lance hit some hard times when the retail concern he worked for shut down and he lost his job. His wife left him and took their kid. I helped him get hired on here and it's worked out great. Until now."

"What was his position here?"

"He was the lab manager. Kept things running smoothly—paperwork properly filed, reports made in a timely fashion, correspondence with government agencies, test subjects, suppliers. That sort of thing."

"Sounds like a critical link to what you do here. Was he qualified?"

Will shrugged. "Sure. He had an MBA."

"From...?"

Will shifted again, crossing his legs. "He attended Cathcart College."

"Okay." Steadman was pleased to see Frost taking notes, his pencil moving furiously over the pages of a pocket notebook. "Why don't you go next," he said, facing the woman on the couch beside Will.

"I'm Beth Parsons," she said. "Will is my husband."

Steadman was surprised. Though seated together, he hadn't noticed any sign of affection between the two. As if reading his mind, Will Parsons reached out to squeeze his wife's hand and draw her a little closer.

"And do you work here as well?" Steadman asked.

"Yes. I'm a researcher and analyst."

"And how long have you known Lance Medford?"

"Since before Will and I married. About six years."

"Can you tell me a little about him? What kind of man was he?"

She covered her mouth with a shaking hand, pressing fingers against her lips. Will's hold on her tightened as her large brown eyes went luminous with a sheen of tears. She blinked them away and took a deep breath.

"Lance Medford was a nice man, an honorable man." Her voice cracked, and the tremulous hand went back to her lips.

Steadman nodded and turned away, directing his attention to a quiet blonde woman, thin to the point of scrawny, and clearly upset. She'd been biting at her lip and wringing her hands since he'd walked in the room.

"How about you?" he said. "What's your name and position here?"

"I'm Janet Ralston. Junior researcher. I compile results and prepare them for analysis."

"And your relationship with Lance?"

A tinge of pink stained the woman's cheeks as she gripped and regripped her hands. "We were dating."

"How seriously?"

Her watery gray eyes sought his and her voice sounded bleak, drained of hope. "It might have gone somewhere," she said. "Now I'll never know."

"I'm sorry," Steadman replied. He paused a moment, then turned to the remaining member of the group, a man with a deeply tanned complexion that looked like it came out of a bottle. "And you are...?"

"Hector Arnez. My company has invested a great deal into the Alzheimer drug and I've been spending a lot of time here, following the progress of the trials. Will called me when Lance went missing and I came over to see if I could help."

"What exactly happened?" Steadman asked, looking at Will.

"The three of us were on shift when the storm hit and Dale Quinlan—he's the regional manager—sent orders for us to stay here and maintain the security of the lab. He wanted one of us on watch at all times."

"What about the regular security personnel?"

"They don't come in until the facility closes for the day, but with the hazardous road conditions, Quinlan wanted them to stay home and us to stay here. We wrapped up our work in the lab at 3:00 and Lance took the first watch, walking the halls and monitoring the video feeds while the rest of us hung out here in the lounge."

Steadman nodded. Frost's pencil moved behind the notepad.

"About 5:30, Beth made us some sandwiches and I brought one to Lance, except I couldn't find him. I figured he was walking the rounds or in the bathroom, so I waited. But when he didn't show, I got worried. We all searched the building and came up empty. That's when I called for help."

"Why would he go outside? Was he a smoker?" Steadman asked, remembering the sheriff's theory about getting disoriented in the swirling snow.

"No, he wasn't. I have no idea why he would have left the building. It makes no sense at all."

"You mentioned video feeds. We're going to need to see those, as well as the logs for the swipe cards."

"I can access that log for you right now," Will said.

A low counter spanned the far end of the room, decked with a row of computer monitors. Will sat in one of the wheeled chairs and rolled himself to a keyboard, tapping the keys. Steadman stood behind, along with Frost, and watched the monitor come to life. A few more pecks, and the log popped up.

"This is where we all swiped in for our morning shift," Will said, pointing out a series of entries between 6:30 and 7:00 that morning. "And this is when Lance must have left," he continued, indicating an exit logged at 3:26.

He moved the cursor down the screen. "That's odd," he said. "This shows someone swiping out at 3:39 and swiping back in again at 4:05."

"Who was it?" Steadman asked.

"I don't know. I don't recognize that card number. Let's see..." He punched some keys and brought up a new screen, popping the unknown number into a search box. The resulting name was Mandy Martinez.

"Who is Mandy Martinez?" Steadman asked.

"She's a genetic consultant we've used in the past, but she retired and moved to Florida months ago."

Frost's pencil stopped moving. "It sounds like someone got ahold of her card and used it to leave and return to the lab this afternoon," he said.

Steadman cleared his throat. "We need to see that surveillance video."

A loud buzzer announced the arrival of the paramedics. Steadman went with Will to let them in, leaving Frost to keep an eye on the others. In the store room, the paramedic team leader, a big-boned woman with a long, graying ponytail, examined the body and officially declared Lance Medford dead, noting down the time and other particulars.

"What's your thought on cause of death?" Steadman asked. "Anything stand out to you as unusual?"

She stroked a finger down her nose and gave him a considering look. "Not that I saw, but the ME may pick up on something. No apparent injuries, other than possible frostbite. I'd say his appearance is consistent with death by hypothermia. Nothing hinky here, Chief. The poor man just got kissed by the snow angel."

Kissed by the snow angel. Taken into the bosom of a cold and early grave. Steadman didn't believe the man had walked out of that lab for a rendezvous with death.

Someone had pushed him into the angel's arms.

He watched the paramedics transfer the body to a gurney, rolling it to the exit while he followed. He saw them out the door, noting that conditions outside were worse than ever, before turning to the front desk where Beth waited to speak with him.

"I've got that CCTV footage you wanted," she said.

He joined her behind the desk and watched the grainy black and white video. The angle he was interested in showed an interior shot of the glass doors where he and Frost had first come in. Nothing was happening, so Beth fast forwarded until someone appeared on the screen. She slowed it down, and Steadman saw a figure pause before the exit to swipe a card before pushing through the door and out into the swirling mess. A flurry of snowflakes chased around the vestibule, blown by a furious wind, then fell as if struck dead when the door closed.

"That was Lance on his way out," Beth said.

Steadman wondered if her pun had been intentional but decided not to comment. The figure wore the same coat and clothing as the corpse and though his face had not been clearly discernible in the video, the footage did seem to confirm the swipe log. The time stamps matched.

Beth fast forwarded again and Steadman peered hard at the screen, watching for anything that struck him odd. No one else appeared until Will brought Lance's sandwich to the front desk at 5:37. After that, it was quiet again until Will and Beth walked out into the snow to search for their missing co-worker, at 5:59, while Janet stayed behind to hold down the fort.

"The swipe log says someone left and re-entered between 3:39 and 4:05. Go back to there," Steadman said.

Beth replayed the section, but no one appeared in the video.

"It's been tampered with," said Steadman. "Who has access to this?"

Beth stared at him. "We all do." Her brow crinkled. "You think one of us had something to do with Lance's death, but you're wrong. We were all here together. None of us could have followed Lance into that storm."

Steadman watched the rise and fall of her chest, noticing her growing agitation. "You were together the whole time? Without interruption?"

She faltered. "I think so." She frowned, hugging herself. "No, I'm sure of it. We were."

Steadman had his doubts. Everyone seemed inclined to pass the death off as a tragic and unexplained accident, but he was certain there was more to it.

"Does your husband know about your affair with Hector Arnez?" Steadman asked. He was fishing, based on a single glance he'd caught between Beth and Hector, but he saw by her face that he'd hooked something solid. Her eyes grew wide with alarm.

"No," she said, her face flooding with a wash of scarlet. "And he's not going to. It's over."

"What about Lance? Did he know?"

She was unable to hold his gaze. Looking away, she crossed her arms over her chest and remained silent.

"I think he did know," Steadman continued, "and he meant to tell Will, his best friend, about it."

"I promised him I'd end it, and I have. I didn't murder Lance to stop his tongue, if that's what you're suggesting."

Steadman stood. "I'm heading back to the lounge. Are you coming?"

"No. In spite of the day's upset, we're trying to maintain protocols. I'm on guard duty."

He nodded and set off down the hall, pulling his cell phone from his pocket and staring at it in disgust. Still no signal. He thought of Vivi at home, waiting for his call, worrying about him as she watched news coverage of the extreme weather conditions. Was she alone, or had she arranged something with friends? Had she got the package he sent?

He halted his footsteps and stared at the barren lime green wall, barraged with a sudden longing to be home, watching his wife tear open the wrapping paper on his gift, a hand-made sweater she'd admired at a shop during a recent week-end trip to Port Townsend. He'd miss seeing those delicate hands caressing the wool, the light in her Nordic blue eyes as she turned to thank him. Her kiss.

He sighed and started his feet moving again. It couldn't be helped, and he knew she understood. A lawman couldn't ask for a better wife. Shoving the useless phone back into his pocket, he stepped into the lounge.

Tension hung in the air, thick as the frosting on that birthday cake he was missing. Janet Ralston sat in a chair, her knees drawn up and held against her chest by a pair of skinny arms in a long-sleeved T-shirt, eyes staring ahead in an unfocused gaze. At one of the small round tables, Hector read from a tablet while sipping from a mug. Steadman guessed chamomile tea. The herbal smell of brewing leaves wafted over him, meant to be soothing, but the wary shifting in Hector's eyes belied that effect. Will sprawled on a sofa, his face turned toward the television screen, but Steadman doubted he saw anything there. As before, the sound was turned down.

Frost sat in a hard-backed chair, but rose to meet Steadman as he crossed to the kitchenette to help himself to coffee. And to poke around. He opened all the cabinets and saw nothing he wouldn't expect until he came to the last, which contained an assortment of liquor. And none of the bottles was dusty.

"I noticed that, too," said Frost. "And take a peek at the wastebasket."

Steadman saw wadded napkins, a soggy coffee filter stained brown with ground beans, and a discarded box from a bottle of Benadryl. He looked at Frost.

"Kind of funny," Frost said, "that we just heard that update on the latest date rape drugs, and liquid Benadryl mixed with alcohol is a new favorite. I'm not saying anything like that happened here, but did you see the bottle in the cabinet?"

Steadman had. It was more than half gone. If the discarded box in the wastebasket indicated it was a newly opened bottle, someone had taken a hefty dose of the antihistamine.

Steadman fished the empty box from the trash and held it up. "Which one of you is using the Benadryl?"

Will rolled to a standing position and joined Steadman and Frost in the kitchenette. "That was Lance's. He had a cold and he didn't like swallowing tablets."

"And the liquor in the cabinet? Whose is that?"

Will turned on the kitchen tap and splashed some water on his face, ripping a paper towel off the roll to dab against his wet skin.

"We all had a drink or two this afternoon, deputy. No reason not to. We're stuck here and none of us planned to get behind the wheel of a car or operate heavy machinery."

"Is there someplace we could talk privately?" asked Steadman.

Will crushed the damp paper towel into a ball and lobbed it into the wastebasket. "Sure. We can use my office."

Steadman followed the man to a room near the lab. A large desk, credenza, and file cabinets took up one end of the oblong room, with an arrangement of chairs around a coffee table filling space at the other end.

"Let's sit here," Steadman said, indicating the chairs. They chose seats perpendicular to each other, and Steadman let the silence grow, waiting a full two minutes before he spoke.

"Cathcart doesn't have an MBA program," he said, breaking the tension.

Will shifted in his chair. "Okay. So what?"

"I'm just trying to understand why you lied. Did Lance misrepresent himself to you? Or did you misrepresent him to the higher-ups in order for him to get the job?"

"What does it matter? He got the job, and he did it well."

"It might matter a lot. I'm sure there are very specific requirements for getting a drug approved by the FDA. I suspect having the documentation handled by qualified personnel is one of them."

"What are you implying? If you think I killed Lance to take him out of the equation, you're delusional. Lance was my best friend."

Will's voice, and the color in his face, had both risen. Steadman made a motion with his hand, easing him down.

"I'm not really implying anything here," he said. "I'm only trying to piece together a puzzle that isn't making any sense."

"The only puzzle I see is why Lance walked out that door to his death, and I can't think that has anything to do with me, or any of my associates."

"You're probably right, but it's my job to check. Could you send Janet in here to talk with me?"

Will stood. "Sure," he said tersely, and left the office.

Janet entered a moment later and Steadman motioned her into a chair. The pallor of her face was so pronounced he wondered if they should have sent her off with the paramedics. Bloodshot eyes, enormous in her white face, blinked at him and she hugged herself, rocking back and forth in the chair.

Steadman took a stab. "Janet, I think you're the one who used Mandy's old card to leave and come back. What did you do out there?"

She dropped her gaze and the pace of her rocking increased, but she didn't speak.

"Did Lance know about your drug habit?" Steadman asked.

She went still. "Okay, I took the swipe card so I could go out to my car without leaving a record. I had some stuff...some stuff I needed...in my car."

Steadman remembered the mounded heaps of snow covering the cars in the parking lot. Each had been covered with a pristine shell.

"And then you altered the video recording?"

She stared at him again, and Steadman could almost see the throb of her heartbeat in the red veins of her eyes. She looked haunted, tormented by ghosts of grief, regret, and what might have been. She dropped her head in a weary nod and spoke in a voice devoid of emotion. "Yes, I altered the recording."

"Can you describe to me how you did that?"

A long moment passed before she simply said, "No."

"All right," he said. "Go on back to the lounge and try to get some rest."

"That's it? That's all you're going to ask me?"

"For now," he agreed.

She left, and Steadman once again pulled the cell phone from his pocket, noting the symbol that told him he'd still be unable to reach his wife. But now, it was the camera function he was interested in. He pulled up the gallery of shots he'd taken at the snowy scene of Lance's death, and scrolled through them. He stopped on one that showed Lance's body loaded onto the stretcher. Using his fingers on the screen to zoom into a corner of the photo, he focused on a segment of orange canvas.

He'd noticed the tiny anomaly before, but hadn't given it any thought. He dropped his chin into his hand as he stared at the picture and thought about it now. A tiny shred of thin black plastic clung to a grommet in the stretcher, standing out against the orange of the fabric.

Steadman didn't believe Lance Medford had died by accident. He had a good idea now who'd killed him and how it had been done, and he thought he understood why. But he had no proof, and he was out of his jurisdiction, separated from his support system. Except for Frost.

Not for the first time, Steadman was grateful to have the man beside him. He needed a sharp pair of eyes and an eager brain.

They had some searching to do.

Steadman stood in the glassed-in vestibule, staring out the thick-paned doors at wind-tossed pellets of ice falling, still falling, from a black, malevolent sky. No stars were visible. Nothing was visible outside the globes of yellow light cast by streetlamps in the parking lot. They flickered once or twice as he watched, but the power held.

A vicious gust hit the doors and they rattled in their frames, sending a shiver down his spine. He didn't want to be here, but the thought of braving *that* to get somewhere else was not appealing. In any case, he and Frost had to finish the business at hand before they could leave. A weary sigh escaped him, and he switched on the radio, holding it away from him as it went through its initial hiss and squeal.

"Sheriff Calloway, Chief Steadman here. You really ought to come."

"What's going on, Steadman? I got word the ME has the body. If you've taken statements from everyone present, your job is done. Hike on back to the hotel and get some rest."

"Wish I could do that, Sheriff, but this is a murder case."

A short silence ensued and when the sheriff came back on, his words were clipped and chill as the wind outside. "I asked you not to overstep your bounds, Chief. This is my turf, and I'll be the one to make that determination. Sounded to me like you have precious little to back your suspicions."

"True enough," Steadman replied, "but now I have more—conclusive proof that will stand up in court."

"What are you talking about?"

"Come and see, Sheriff."

Steadman signed off and returned to the lounge where everyone was gathered in the seating area around the blank-screened television. An unpleasant odor, acrid and scorched, filled the room. Someone had made microwave popcorn and left the bag unattended. Steadman exchanged a look with Frost and handed him the radio.

"Hold on to this for me, would you please?"

"Sure thing, Chief."

"Okay, people, if I could have everyone's attention."

He felt a little foolish saying that as he realized everyone was already waiting to hear what he had to say. So he said it. "Lance Medford was murdered, and I know who did it."

Steadman looked around at their stunned expressions. Janet's face paled to the shade of whipped cream, a frightened frown creased Beth's forehead, Hector Arnez scowled, and Will moved to the edge of his chair, leaning forward.

"Who did it?" he challenged.

"You did, Will."

Will gave a disgusted grunt and threw his hands in the air, looking to his wife and associates for support. They avoided his gaze.

"And you did, Beth."

She gasped, but Steadman ignored her, turning to Janet. "And you, Ms. Ralston. And even you, Hector."

The investor's handsome face turned ugly. "You're crazy," he snarled. "Where are you getting this absurd idea?"

"When Will brought me and Deputy Frost to the body, I noticed a few things that didn't sit right. There was no sign of a cell phone, and in this day and age, who would venture out into such a storm without that lifeline of communication? When I opened his parka to search the inner pockets for a phone, I noticed snow on the inside of his coat, which got me thinking. And then, there was the absence of snowpack in the treads of his boots.

"Lance Medford did not walk to the site where his body was found. He was carried there, by two of you. I was puzzled by a fragment of black plastic that had caught on the stretcher. Then I realized you had cleverly covered the stretcher with garbage bags to keep it dry while dumping the body, knowing we'd soon be using it to collect the body. One of those bags snagged on a grommet, leaving that trace of plastic."

"This is all conjecture," Will said, his voice stone hard.

"That's true," Steadman admitted, "so let me continue with my conjecture. You all wanted Lance dead, and this blizzard presented you with the perfect opportunity. He wandered out into the extreme weather, became disoriented, and hypothermia claimed him. Such a sad story, but no one would have reason to suspect anything different.

"This is what I think happened: You all had a drink after work, except Lance's drink was laced with liberal amounts of Benadryl, enough to knock him out. Then you bundled him in Will's coat and carried him out into the snow on the stretcher, leaving him to die from exposure. In these conditions, it only took minutes, and his death would be attributed to hypothermia. Any Benadryl left in his system would be explained by the cold you claimed he had."

"He did have a cold," Janet insisted.

"It hardly matters at this point," said Frost.

"How are we supposed to have gotten the body out?" said Beth. "Surveillance video and the swipe system document everything."

"At least one of you knows how to alter the video, but you couldn't get around the swipe system. I believe you drugged Lance, and while he lay sleeping, Will put on Lance's coat, pulling up the hood, and used his card to swipe out. On the video, it looks like Lance leaving, and the swipe appears to corroborate that. Then Beth and Janet used Mandy's card to carry Lance out on the stretcher where Will switched coats and that's how the snow got inside Lance's parka. Then you all returned to the lab, using Mandy's card to get in, and one of you erased that part of the video."

"Why would we do such a thing?" asked Beth.

"And how do I figure into your accusations?" Hector demanded.

Steadman patted his pocket, assuring himself the solid object was still there. "I can answer those questions by telling you about a little hunt Deputy Frost and I conducted this evening on the premises. We found two items of interest. The first was a pair of crumpled, dirty black garbage bags. One of them has a small tear which I'm sure, under lab analysis, will match the scrap caught in the stretcher's grommet."

Janet Ralston let out a little moan and Steadman saw that she again had her knees pulled to her chest and was rocking with agitation. Part of him felt bad for her, but he pressed on.

"The other item was Lance Medford's cell phone."

"What?" Hector screeched, his voice shooting up an octave, spurred by fear and indignation.

"Yes. Deputy Frost found it stuffed under some hanging folders in Beth's filing cabinet. It contains some enlightening text messages regarding falsified test results for the Alzheimer's drug and Lance's intention to report the fraud to the FDA, losing millions of dollars for this lab," he pointed at Hector, "and its investors."

"I had nothing to do with any of this," shouted Hector. "I wasn't even here when it happened."

"You hypocritical snake!" Beth ground out the words through clenched teeth. "You're the one who told me to get rid of the phone."

"Then why didn't you?" he shot back, anger getting the best of his self-preservation.

"How?" she said. "Where? I couldn't toss it in a lake, all the bodies of water are solid ice. The ground is frozen so I couldn't dig a hole. Garbage men aren't running their routes—wherever I threw it, it would be vulnerable to discovery. I couldn't think of any good way to dispose of it and so much was happening so fast. I hid it to deal with later."

"And how's that working out for you?" Hector spat the words out, his face twisted in a furious sneer.

Out of the corner of his eye, Steadman detected motion and glanced sideways to see that the sheriff had at last arrived.

"Sheriff Calloway, I'm so glad you could make it. We've got a roomful of murderers here."

The sheriff drew his weapon and slowly raised it.

"You can put the gun away, Sheriff. I think they'll go with you peacefully, but we're going to need more handcuffs."

"They're not going anywhere with me, Steadman. You are. You and the deputy."

Steadman hesitated. The sheriff's revolver was leveled right at him, the black hole at the tip of the barrel staring like an unblinking eye. It was disconcerting. Steadman knew he had to keep the man talking.

"Where are you taking us, Sheriff?" he asked.

"For a walk outside. A couple of fools from the Northwest who don't know how to handle themselves in this kind of weather could die real fast. I wish you'd simply done as I asked, Steadman. This all would have turned out a whole lot nicer."

So, the sheriff had arranged a date with the snow angel. Steadman shivered, thinking about how this might go down, how he and Frost could end up popsicles like Lance Medford had. It could go that way, but Steadman didn't think it would.

He had other plans.

"Let me guess," he said to Calloway. "Hector's company and the lab are big campaign contributors. They've got you in their pocket."

"I'm in no one's pocket!" the sheriff snarled. "Let's get going." He motioned with the gun for Steadman and Frost to start walking.

"I don't think we will, Sheriff," said Steadman. He raised his voice and spoke toward Frost who held the radio in front of him. "You getting all this, Hal?"

Frost released the transmit button and a burst of static tore through the room, followed by Hal Cooper's wavery voice. "Got it loud and clear, Chief Steadman. I've got a buddy here from The Grand Rapids Press and he heard it, too. Took some real good notes, but just in case he missed something, we recorded it. Incidentally, Chief, we've put a call through to the state police and they ought to be there real soon."

Frost offered the radio and Steadman took it, pressing the transmit button. "I appreciate that, Hal. Thanks for your help."

"Thank *you* for the story."

Steadman heard the gurgle of delight in the old reporter's voice. "I suppose you want to stick around for the wrap up?" he said.

"You suppose right, Chief."

"Copy that."

Steadman nodded to Frost who took the radio and resumed pressing the transmit button. Just then, a loud buzzer announced the arrival of the state police. No one moved to let them in.

"I suggest things will go easier for you all if you give your full cooperation to the investigation," Steadman said. He looked around at the ring of sullen faces, staring at him with varying degrees of heat and resentment. He turned to Janet. "I know you didn't want to be a part of this. You didn't want to kill Lance. I think you really loved him."

An anguished moan broke through her lips and she choked down on it, her eyes welling over with silent tears.

"You can't bring Lance back, but you can do something for him going forward. Open the door, Janet."

She stared at him, her face the picture of a ruined life. But he thought he saw a spark of light in her eyes, a tiny glimmer of hope. It was more than just his imagination.

The buzzer rang again, and with a suddenness that startled him, Janet Ralston sprang from her chair and bolted for the door release button, sobs tearing from her throat in desperate abandon. The police entered and apprehended those responsible for the death of Lance Medford.

Outside, the snow finally stopped.

Amid the bustle of arrests and Miranda rights, Steadman excused himself and found a quiet corner where he lifted his phone and found, at last, a signal. It was after two o'clock in the morning. He'd missed Vivi's birthday and that didn't sit well with him. He'd made her a promise.

He punched the speed dial and she picked up on the second ring. "I knew you'd call, you lovely man," she exclaimed, the smile in her voice coming through across two thousand miles of winter-blasted country. "I've been worried about you. How's the conference? Are you keeping safe?"

"Conference got canceled," he told her. "I've been working a case."

"What? How does a Mason County sheriff's deputy end up with a case in central Michigan?"

"It's a bit of a long story. I'll tell you when I get home. The important thing is that Frost and I managed to wrap it up in the course of a few hours. Arrests are being made as we speak."

She gasped. "Randall Steadman, you are my hero! And you never cease to amaze me."

A small stab of regret knifed into his chest, a bit of guilt to go with the pleasure he got from her glowing praise. "But I failed you, darling. I promised to call on your birthday, and I just wasn't able to pull it off."

"But you did!" she said, surprise in her voice. "What do you think this is?"

"I'm glad as I can be that I was finally able to get a call through, but it's well after midnight. I missed it."

"It's after midnight where you are, but it's still my birthday here."

He'd forgotten about the time change, just hadn't given it a thought with everything else occupying his mind. A tiny weight lifted off his heart. "I love you, Vivi Steadman. Happy birthday!"

She laughed, a silvery tinkle that brought the image of her face sharp to his mind, the shine of her china-blue eyes and curving lips. Frost appeared, beckoning him, and he gritted his teeth, sorry to have to end the call.

"I've got to go, hon. I hope your birthday was awesome and I can't wait to celebrate it again with you when I get home."

"I look forward to it," she answered. "Remember, Rand, you'll always be my hero."

He smiled and tucked the phone back in his pocket. A lawman—any man—couldn't ask for a better wife.

AUTHOR'S NOTE

DEATH MAKES A DINNER DATE

We all have secrets. Every one of us hides something from someone.

And when characters have a secret, we want to know what it is. Our curiosity grows with each layer that's peeled back.

This is one of those kinds of stories. The seed for "Death Makes a Dinner Date" was planted when I was invited to submit a story for an anthology with the theme of "Secrets."

I thought it might be fun to explore what two characters in conflict are hiding from each other, from everyone else, and even from themselves, pulling back the curtain just a little bit more with each unfolding scene.

The editor I originally wrote the story for gave it a pass, which turned out to be a good thing because "Death Makes a Dinner

Date" got picked up by *Alfred Hitchcock's Mystery Magazine* and was published in their July/August 2021 issue.

Now that I've served the appetizer, I invite you to tuck in. I hope you'll find this dinner date suspensefully satisfying and delicious.

Death Makes a Dinner Date

The secret burned inside her like the flickering candle at the center of the cloth-covered dining table, warming her from within. She watched the tiny flame as it guttered and glowed inside the crimson glass which held it, a small, licking tongue so benign when contained and so utterly dangerous if let loose.

The smell of hot wax enveloped the intimate table for two, but Serena scowled across at an empty seat. Gavin was late. She had no doubt, however, that he would show. She'd caught him looking at her with that intrigued expression in his eyes just as often as he'd caught her stealing glances at him. No mistake—there was something between them.

There always had been.

Serena buttered a slice of dark brown bread and bit into the tang of caraway and rye, chewing slowly, letting the flavors play over her tongue. She blessed her love for good literature. It had been the Bay Ladies' Book Club that brought them together. Or at least it had brought her and Daphne together and the rest fell into place like destiny. Serena had been so pleased when Daphne volunteered to host the meetings. All the ladies had a good excuse for not doing it themselves—apartment too small, rowdy children at home, pets people are allergic to—but Serena wondered how many of the others, like she, harbored a hidden passion for Daphne's sexy husband.

The hostess returned, a touch of smirk behind her solicitous smile.

"Would you like to order a drink while you're waiting?"

"I would, thank you. Dubonnet, with a twist."

"Straight up?"

"Club soda please."

She watched the hostess retreat to the bar, her hips swaying a little to the Bossa Nova beat. A faint stab of envy over the girl's well-defined calf muscles troubled her briefly and she took another bite of bread. Glancing at her watch, she saw Gavin was now ten minutes late. Another five, without a call or explanation, would verge on rude and Serena could not envision Gavin being rude.

Daphne always loved having him around, showing off her house husband. Serena—and the whole book club with her—rejoiced that his job allowed him to work from home. How else could he have been there to help serve up the refreshments when their literary discussions were concluded?

Over the weeks and months, Serena had found an increasing number of excuses for dropping by between meetings. She and Daphne became friends, dragging yoga mats into the living room or scrapbooking at the kitchen table. And Gavin remained ever in the background, offering his opinions, exchanging those surreptitious looks, until they'd practically become a threesome.

In fact, the three of them had been together the day the police discovered the first body.

Gavin dreaded this dinner appointment. He parked his car as far back in the lot as he could manage, under a drooping pine that looked like something from Dr. Seuss, and glowered down at the steering wheel. The ticking of the cooling engine reminded him of the warning a rattlesnake gives, just before it lunges with fangs outstretched.

His secret was becoming harder to keep. Some days he felt as if it was etched on his forehead and anyone who looked hard enough might read it there. He wondered if Daphne's friend,

Serena, had done just that. Is that why she suggested they have dinner?

If he'd known, really understood, how dark and twisted this path would become, could he have refrained from starting down it? He remembered the story about the frog who was persuaded to carry a scorpion on its back across a wide river. Halfway into the crossing, the scorpion sunk its stinger into the frog, dooming them both. With his dying breath, the frog asked the scorpion why he'd done it.

Because it's my nature.

No, he could not have turned from this course, however challenging. It was his nature, and the truth was he relished it, every twist and turn.

Except for maybe this one.

He cracked open the car door and threw out a leg, letting it stretch a moment before heaving the rest of himself onto the pavement. He was thirteen minutes late already and it wouldn't pay to be rude. He crossed the rutted surface of the parking lot in loping strides, his boots setting up a rhythmic clatter on the asphalt. At the door to the restaurant, he took a deep breath and pushed inside, letting his eyes adjust after the burning glare of the streetlamps.

Careful to arrange his face into a suitably neutral expression, he located Serena and made his way to her table as the hostess arrived and took his order for a pint of Blue Ribbon.

"Sorry I'm late," he apologized. "Traffic."

"I figured you'd have a good reason."

She smiled at him, revealing an almost flawless set of teeth, marred only by one front incisor appearing longer than its neighbors. He met her gaze and they locked eyes briefly before she swept her lashes down and looked away, a blush of pink coming up on her cheeks.

He was aware the moment had been somehow significant, but was less certain about what it meant. Was the woman merely attracted to him, or was she trolling him for something deeper? Something darker?

"Have you ordered already?"

"No, I was waiting for you." She paused and when she spoke again, her voice had taken on a throaty undertone. "I wondered if we might try the platter for two."

Gavin froze, a mild shock running through him, rocking him a little in its wake. What was her game? He looked around at the other tables, wondering if anyone was watching, noting the woman's brazen behavior. He knew the police were still interested in him and they'd attach more importance to this meeting than Gavin could afford. He'd have been smarter to avoid this date.

But had that been a veiled threat he'd seen in her eyes when she extended the invitation? Did she intend to hold some kind of power over him? If she suspected something and was willing to use it to manipulate him, he needed to understand her terms.

Still, she was shaving awfully close to the carotid here, playing as if they were a couple.

After all, Daphne had been dead for less than two months.

The Bossa Nova faded out and a moody jazz piece dominated by a mournful saxophone took its place. Gavin had been right to decline the dinner platter for two. It was far wiser to be more circumspect. She could take it slow, building the anticipation, if he could. There might be a few good reasons for rushing it, but she'd put them aside for now and just enjoy this dinner.

Her mouth watered, triggered by the aromas of garlic and cooking meat. She ordered a grilled chicken salad and waited while Gavin explained how he wanted his steak cooked. Or rather, uncooked, as he demanded a mere ninety seconds on each side and a bloody, red middle.

The hostess brought another round of drinks and Serena saw Gavin's eyes follow her legs. Ah well, men couldn't help it. Like metal to a magnet. She watched him fidget, toying with his fork, and realized he was nervous. Because he wanted to make a good impression on her?

Or because he was afraid of being seen in public with another woman so soon after his wife's murder?

It would be a tender subject, but Serena thought it might help him to talk about it. They'd spoken of sensitive things before, delicate subjects lingering in the air after the book club discussions. She reached out a hand and placed it over his, giving a gentle squeeze, trying to ignore the sting when he pulled away.

"Did you hear there's been another victim?" she asked. "I caught it on the news in the car on the way over. A couple of early morning skateboarders found a woman's body dumped in a half-pipe. Nine knife wounds, like the others."

Like Daphne.

She shuddered. It must have been awful for those young kids, such a shocking way to start the day. Of course, Gavin had been the one to find Daphne. Her heart plunged a little at the thought. She wished he might have been spared such a horror.

"I heard." His voice was dry, just short of sarcastic. "The police are keeping me well informed. They still think I might be the guy."

Serena almost choked on her drink and swallowed quickly, clearing her throat. "I thought they crossed you off their list of suspects when they confirmed your alibi."

"They might have scratched me off, but if they did, they used a damn skinny pencil. Until they get someone else in their sights they'll never stop looking at me."

"Well, that's just silly. Even the dimmest of them must realize this is the work of a crazed maniac, not a scheming husband. Are they questioning the husbands of the other victims?"

"None of the others were married."

"Oh." That did cast a slightly different light on the matter, but she had no doubt he was innocent of his wife's murder.

The waiter brought Gavin's salad, doused in bleu cheese dressing. She could smell it from across the table and it had never been a favorite. She wrinkled her nose and faced the unpalatable fact that the police had focused their spotlight on Gavin the moment his wife turned up dead. There was no getting around it.

Gavin Wix, the man she loved, was the prime suspect in the murders of eight women.

Gavin chewed his steak with resignation. It was overcooked and tougher than it should have been. Despite his detailed instructions, few chefs ever got it right. He forked another bite into his mouth and gnashed his teeth into it, tasting blood on his tongue.

The woman had broached the subject and danced around it. When would she get to the point? What was it she wanted from him, and what kind of leverage might she wield in order to get it? This dinner was starting to feel like a waste of time.

A dangerous waste of time.

He swallowed the meat and lifted his beer glass, watching his dinner partner pick through her salad like a housewife at a bargain bin. The icy liquid went down smooth, refreshing his throat, one of the simple pleasures in life he'd miss if he went behind bars.

He was in hot water—no doubt about it—and he didn't know how much longer he could keep afloat. A dire certainty kept residence in one corner of his brain that Detective Foster saw through him already, and the irony of this did not escape him.

His feelings about his wife's killer were complicated. On the one hand, he cursed the fellow for invading his home and robbing him of his mate. But he couldn't help feeling a perverse sense of gratitude toward the perpetrator. For one thing, he'd committed the deed while he, Gavin, was indisputably a thousand miles away at a conference in Ohio. The police had tried—and patently failed—to break his alibi.

On the other hand, the killer had been sloppy in following his own *modus operandi*, neglecting certain details that made Daphne's murder stand out as a possible anomaly. The pet theory of the police was that Gavin had taken advantage of a serial murder spree to engineer the copycat killing of his wife.

Which was ridiculous—he would never in a million years have done such a thing.

And so his feelings in regard to the killer were a mass of confusion. His feelings about his wife's death, however, were uncomplicated in the extreme, and this is where he really ran into trouble. His efforts to keep the façade in place were waning and soon everyone would know his secret.

He was delighted she was dead.

The music now filtering into the dining room through hidden speakers had a Vince Guaraldi feel to it, an upbeat piano rhythm that brought a smile to Serena's lips. She finished mining the best bits from her salad and pushed the plate away, regretting the trace of onion that lingered on her breath. She caught movement in the periphery of her vision and saw the hostess heading over again to refresh their drinks. Serena shook her head and made a little brushing motion with her hand.

It was time to move this discussion to a more private venue.

Gavin's jaw still worked over the last bite of his steak. She watched the strong bones and muscles of his face flex and move, his Adam's apple bobbing slightly as he swallowed. She loved these types of little details about Gavin, had observed them through lowered eyelashes for months under Daphne's unsuspecting gaze.

Serena believed some of the other women in the book club had sussed out her secret, probably because it mirrored their own. Gavin was an exceptionally attractive man and Daphne had been foolishly cavalier, holding him so loosely in her naïve, innocent hand. At least she had died in a happily married state, a condition that couldn't last forever with a man like Gavin.

So, her secret was out and Serena would make certain Gavin knew all about it before this night was over. She was ready to come all the way clean with her feelings toward him, the passion that took her beyond the difficulties of death and a murder investigation.

But Serena had a darker secret—a secret she tucked and pushed and tunneled deep within her, as if beneath layers of mud and hard-crusted snow. So deep that in the blue-light spaces of day, she could almost forget it was there.

The secret lay buried within her. She didn't think about it. She didn't worry that it might sprout like a seed, sending fragile, uncurling tendrils above ground, ruffling the surface and breaking up the shell which surrounded it. Her heart did not pound or grow faint because of it. She was building it an airtight coffin.

Once or twice, she had caught Gavin looking at her with such a queer expression as if the question—that all-important question—trembled on his lips. Did he suspect? But he couldn't, not really. Neither one of them would be here if he did.

Or would they?

Love moves in mysterious ways. After tonight—after she and Gavin cleared the deck of all ambiguity and started planning for the future—she could close the lid on that coffin, sealing away the secret it contained. Forever.

And life could begin with the man of her dreams, a man she knew—beyond any shadow of a doubt—had not murdered his wife.

Because Serena had.

Relief flowed over Gavin, relaxing the tense fibers and bowstring-tight muscles in his back and neck. Serena had signaled she was ready to leave. She was not going to make a public scene. They'd find somewhere quiet to bring this to a head. He helped himself to a toothpick, removed the wrapper, and began a systematic cleaning of his teeth.

The hostess brought the check and he let Serena pay, ignoring the dirty look she gave him as he watched the sexy calves walk away. This was Serena's show, and she ought to foot the bill. The after-party would belong to him, and it was bound to be expensive.

In the parking lot, he gave her one last chance.

"Thank you for a lovely dinner, Selena. I should probably get going."

"It's *Serena*, as you well know. Why are you being so coy, Gavin? I think it's time both of us dropped the act, don't you?"

He did. Gavin felt his deeper self—his true nature—surface, his scorpion stinger rising to the ready. The law was closing in, forcing him to the river's edge with only one way forward.

"I thought you'd never ask," he said. "Why don't we drive down to Viewpoint Park and find a spot under the stars?"

Whatever she had in mind, she wouldn't get him to confess to the murder of his wife. Whatever evidence she thought she had, they'd never get him on that charge. He had not killed Daphne, and there couldn't be much for Serena to hold over his head.

But she could try.

He was willing to listen to what she had to say, as long as she took it with her when she went. Every detail of her death would match that of the other seven—clothing removed, nine stab wounds in the back, body posed face-down with the arms and legs drawn up, knees and elbows bent.

Like a frog.

Gavin had no illusions about how this night would end. He'd play it to the finish, true to his nature, and accept the consequences. After tonight, Detective Foster would have all the pieces he needed. Women across the city and even neighboring towns would breathe easier and walk on the streets after sundown with greater confidence.

Gavin would pick up his share of the bill for this dinner date with death and everyone would know that he had not murdered his wife.

He'd killed the other eight.

Author's Note

Beyond the Horizon

I've always been a little fascinated by black widows—both the spider variety and the kind that walks on just two legs.

So, when Leah Cutter, the editor of *Mystery, Crime, and Mayhem* chose Black Widows as the theme for an upcoming issue of the magazine, I was excited to get to work on a story.

Poisoning is the method of choice for most black widow killers and I wanted to come up with a completely different weapon, a chilling scenario, and flip the script on the "woman in jeopardy" storyline.

After a bit of brainstorming, the idea for "Beyond the Horizon" was born.

This story made its first appearance in *Mystery, Crime, and Mayhem: Black Widows*, May 2022.

Beyond the Horizon

Geneva Marks sat in the church pew and stared straight ahead as the strains of Wagner's Bridal Chorus swelled through the chapel, carried on a blare of organ. The bench beneath her felt cold and hard, unyielding against her spine, and she needed that right now. Something to keep her from sagging.

A current of air brushed the side of her face as the bride swept past with the scent of lilies, moving a little faster than Wagner had intended. Excited, no doubt, to become Mrs. Gabriel Bradley. Neva swallowed the bitter lump that rose in her throat and forced herself to look at the groom, standing tall in front of the altar.

On the pew beside her, Tasha Bradley cleared her throat and took Neva's cold hand in her own, squeezing it gently. The gesture nearly broke her. Neva clenched her teeth and drew a long, shuddering breath through quivering nostrils. The organ sent out one last vibrating chord and the church fell silent.

Straightening her spine against the wooden bench, Neva lifted her chin and watched Gabe greet his bride with a wide smile. He wore a beard now, neatly trimmed against his smooth, cocoa brown skin. But it didn't hide the dimple as he beamed across the altar at the white-gowned Celia.

Neva had to admit Celia looked gorgeous. She glowed in a simple, white satin gown, blond curls cascading around bare shoulders beneath the sheer veil. Her white, even teeth glistened between coral-pink lips, and the mole high on her left cheekbone only served to accent her beauty.

A sharp stab of pain rippled through Neva and her hand moved convulsively. Tasha strengthened her grip, sending comfort and support. They exchanged a look.

The day Neva had learned about Gabe's engagement to Celia, a weight had settled over her breastbone, making her feel as if she were slowly suffocating. A year on the good side of a bad divorce found her renewing ties with her best and oldest friend, Tasha Bradley, while the crush she'd always had on Tasha's brother firmed into something far more substantial.

Her hopes that Gabe might come to feel the same were dashed to bits when Celia breezed onto the scene. She entered Gabe's woodturner studio, fell in love with the beautiful pieces he crafted, and commissioned him to build her a coffee table. By the time he'd finished, they were engaged.

And now they were married.

Neva watched Gabe slip the ring onto Celia's finger and suddenly, she couldn't draw breath. Heart pounding, eyes blurring, she struggled to pull air into her lungs. This was wrong.

This was *so* wrong.

It wasn't just watching the man she loved pledge his life to another woman. Her deep misgivings went beyond that. Celia had raised prickles on the back of Neva's scalp from the moment they'd met. Her smile, her sweet southern accent, her congenial manner—all seemed as genuine to Neva as those emails that pop up in your inbox promising money from a dying cancer patient.

Unable to help herself, Neva had done some poking around. She'd gone to the ad agency where Celia worked and found a spiteful secretary willing to gossip over a double latte and Danish pastry.

"I don't like to stick my nose in," said the secretary, taking a big bite of Danish, "but she worked a lot of late nights with Mr. O'Donnell. I file the payroll records and I noticed she's had two pay hikes since she started here last June." One eyebrow rose on her lined forehead. "I've seen her work, and it's not that good."

Neva smiled encouragingly. "You mean you've seen her *ad copy* work."

The secretary nearly choked on her mouthful of pastry. She swallowed and patted herself on the chest. "Exactly. How she works behind closed doors is apparently on another level."

Neva had to take everything she said with a gargantuan grain of Himalayan pink—it was clear the woman was motivated by jealousy—but Neva's impression of Celia as conniving and manipulative was strengthened.

The secretary mentioned that Celia had come to them from another agency across town. When Neva called there, posing as a prospective employer checking references, no one had heard of Celia Alexander.

Neva had told Tasha about this, aware of how desperate she sounded, like someone grasping at straws from a haystack of spite. She had to acknowledge that's precisely what she was.

"Don't be petty, Neva," Tasha had warned. "It won't make you any more attractive in Gabe's eyes. If you're right and she's bad news, the marriage won't last and you can be there to help him pick up the pieces."

"Wonderful. Then he can pat me on the head and bid me lie down at his feet. I'll always just be his little sister's bestie."

Tasha had cocked her head, looking thoughtful. "Perhaps not," was all she said.

Now, in the church, Tasha let go of Neva's hand and placed an arm around her shoulder, bracing her for the moment when Gabe walked past with his beautiful new wife. The couple approached and Gabe twinkled at the two of them as he passed.

The organ started up again. The voluminous chords vibrated in Neva's stomach, stirring her to nausea, and she felt an urgent need to get out of the church and into the open air. Rising, she pushed past guests crowding the aisle and burst through the arched doors of the chapel.

Sudden sunlight dazed her vision and she nearly stumbled on the stairs when something hit her in the face. Reflexively, she grabbed it and a cheer went up from those gathered on the church steps. She blinked down at the bouquet of lilies and white roses in her hands.

As Gabe stepped into the waiting limousine, he paused to catch Neva's eye. Grinning, he gave her a thumbs up and the last thing she saw as the car pulled away from the curb was Gabe's face through the window, still watching her.

Neva worked hard to scrub those wedding images from her mind and not to think about the honeymoon in Tahiti at all. She focused on her job cataloguing specimens and relics at a natural history museum downtown. She found the work fulfilling and fascinating, though the chemical fumes emanating from the preservatives and fixatives sometimes gave her a headache.

One evening as she headed home, windows down to blow off the faint ache behind her eyes, Neva impulsively turned onto the street where Gabe lived. With Celia.

She drove slowly past the small craftsman cottage set well back from the street on a neat lawn. The porch swing hung empty, a thing of beauty Gabe had created in his workshop and polished to a golden shine. She and Tasha had spent many evenings gently swinging there while Gabe perched on a stool, strumming his guitar and singing softly into the night.

Neva's eyes blurred as she pulled to the curb. She blinked and swallowed hard. What was she doing here? Unbidden, the memory of Gabe's face watching her through the limousine window pushed into her mind. His expression had seemed wistful and a little sad.

Convinced that neither one of them wanted to lose the friendship they shared, Neva squared her shoulders and stepped out of the car. She passed Gabe's ancient blue BMW in the driveway and climbed the steps to the porch, careful not to look at the empty swing.

Two newly potted geraniums flanked the door and the smell of damp earth floated on the evening air. Pulling in a deep breath of it, Neva raised a trembling finger and pressed the bell. After a long pause, Celia opened the door and gave Neva a plastic smile.

"Hello, Geneva. Thanks for the waffle iron. I'm sure we'll get a lot of use out of it."

Celia's tone suggested Neva's wedding gift would be relegated to the dusty back of a cupboard.

"I'm glad. Is Gabe in?"

Celia puckered her forehead in apparent regret. "No, I'm sorry. He's not home right now." She lifted one shoulder in a half-shrug. "I'd invite you in, but I'm just heading out to meet him."

Neva let her gaze wander to Gabe's car in the driveway, but Celia let the unasked question go unanswered. "I'm in a bit of a rush, so if you don't mind…"

"Of course. I won't hold you up. Tell Gabe I dropped by."

"Will do, Geneva. Goodnight."

The door closed with a decisive snap and Neva walked slowly back to the street. Standing in the shadows next to her car, she stood looking at the tidy cottage. From this vantage point she could see through to the den at the back of the house.

Gabe sat in his favorite chair, laughing at something on TV.

The blinds blinked shut, blocking the sight. The impact of it hit Neva like a boom to the gut. With shaking hands, she started the engine and pulled onto the street, trying to convince herself the episode wasn't as menacing as it felt. Celia didn't like her. So what?

Problematic as that was, it didn't mean Gabe was in danger. So why did the roiling in her stomach send the hairs at the back of her neck standing to attention?

Over the days that followed, Neva tried to forget about it, to brush it off, to rationalize the incident and put it out of her head. She went to a movie with friends and even met Tasha for lunch without mentioning it.

Just as she started to believe she might get past the hurt and forget about her qualms, something happened to bring it all back and nail it home.

Neva drove by the dry cleaner after work, looking for a parking spot, but nothing opened up nearby. She had to leave her car two blocks down and around the corner, beneath the shady elms of a waterside park. As she walked back with two freshly cleaned dresses draped over her arm, Neva caught a glimpse of a couple walking hand-in-hand along the bay.

Gabe and Celia.

She stood transfixed, watching as they picked their way along the pebble-strewn beach. The lowering sun created a soft light around them and they appeared almost in silhouette, their features shadowed and indistinct. But there was no mistaking them.

Gabe wore his signature hat—a tweed flat cap he'd bought on a trip to Scotland and rarely left at home. The sunlight glinted off the gold of Celia's curls and played up her curvaceous figure.

And there was no mistaking they were in love.

They gazed at one another as they walked, stopping to kiss more than once. Neva looked away, letting her gaze travel to the far-off horizon, wishing she could float out to the edge of it with Gabe at her side. Wishing he'd been able to see beyond it to where she waited for him.

But he hadn't.

Neva heard a faint lilt of laughter carried on the evening breeze and watched Celia toss her head back, curls tumbling. She felt her stomach tighten. As the couple drew closer, she pulled back into the shadows but couldn't stop staring.

And that's when it happened. Gabe raised a can to his mouth, tipping his head back, and drank. He crumpled the can in one hand and tossed it over his shoulder into the bay.

Neva gasped. The action was so out of character. The Gabe she knew would never pollute the environment like that. He'd given her and Tasha sermons on the evils of littering. Celia was clearly having a detrimental effect on Gabe, destroying the kind and thoughtful man of Neva's dreams.

Dusk deepened on the scene and in Neva's soul. As Gabe and Celia disappeared in the distance, Neva moved with leaden limbs to her car and threw the dresses in a wad on the back seat, not caring one whit about wrinkles. Without something definitive with which to accuse Celia, she could do nothing but watch Gabe dissolve into the malicious maw of a stranger.

She let out the clutch with a jerk and steered into traffic, pointed toward home, more sure than ever that something was terribly wrong.

And more determined than ever to do something about it.

Neva pulled into the parking garage beneath her apartment and eased her car into the allotted space. As she left the garage and climbed the stairs, her cell phone pinged with a new message. Digging it out of her purse, she was surprised to see a text from Gabe on the screen.

Been a while since we talked. How ya been?

A little thrill of pleasure shimmered over Neva, melting some of the chill she'd felt since leaving the park. It was tempered by a touch of bewilderment. Just moments ago, Gabe had been walking on the beach with his wife. Kissing her, holding her hand, defiling the bay.

She tried to picture what he might be doing now. Sitting at a waterside café while Celia visited the ladies' room? Leaning against a coffee bar, waiting for the barrista to deliver their drinks? They wouldn't have had time to finish their stroll and return home. It made Neva feel a bit better to know that Gabe occasionally thought of her during his spare moments.

I'm well. Keeping busy. How's life treating you?

Splendidly. My work is getting some attention. House and Garden Magazine has approached me about a possible interview.

That's fantastic! I'm so happy for you. Did Celia tell you I dropped by?

She didn't mention it. When was that?

Neva thought about how to respond without sounding like a nine-year-old tattling on big sister. Before she figured out the right words, Gabe messaged back.

Gotta go. Take care, Neva.

A dozen things she wanted to say coursed through Neva's brain but in the end, she simply typed, *"Bye."*

Gabe had sounded like his old self, like the man she knew. Like the vibrant and spectacular individual she intended to preserve from Celia's numbing grasp.

In the apartment, Neva made herself a cup of lemon tea and settled in front of her laptop at the kitchen table. She typed every search term she could think of into a variety of search engines but failed to turn up anything interesting.

The tea had gone cold by the time she finished the last sip and she was ready to shut down and go to bed when one last thought occurred to her. She typed, "black widow husband killer," into the Google search bar and was rewarded with pages of material.

Skimming quickly through the pieces, Neva discarded several that clearly did not involve Celia but carefully studied a few that appeared promising. The ninth article she examined, titled *Suspected Black Widow Killer Out on Bail,* featured a photograph. The image was grainy and blurred but it sent a feather of ice down Neva's spine.

The woman in the photo bore a striking resemblance to Gabe's new wife.

The name was different—Francine Howard—and the hair was dark rather than blonde, but the face staring out of the screen looked remarkably like Celia. The article was short and provided little beyond what the headline revealed.

Neva entered the name Francine Howard into the search bar, then narrowed the results by adding "black widow." The search yielded a subsequent newspaper article with more details. Francine Howard had been charged with two counts of murder in the suspicious deaths of two husbands. The prosecution cited the unusually large insurance policies as motive, but failed to convict because the accused produced ironclad alibis, clearing her in the deaths of both husbands.

Neva read the accounts of the incidents. The first husband had drowned in an isolated inlet on the northern coast of California. The couple had been staying at a seaside hotel but the death had occurred later, after they'd moved down the coast. An artist selling his wares outside the hotel had been a witness during the trial and shared his account with the newspaper reporter.

"I noticed them particularly because the woman had great bone structure. If I painted portraits, I'd have asked her to sit for me, but I'm a landscape artist. They came out early that day, dressed in swimsuits, and I tried to sell them a painting. They said they weren't carrying any money and promised to look at my artwork later.

"I saw them meet up with another man as they walked off toward the beach. Later, the couple returned and bought two of my paintings. Then they packed up the car and left. That's the last I saw of them."

The reporter had followed the couple's progress down the coast where they'd checked into another hotel. She'd interviewed the waiter who supplied Mrs. Howard's alibi.

From the reporter's narrative, Neva learned the couple had lunched together at a table on the terrace. Then the husband went off for a swim. He was gone all afternoon while the wife sat at the table, reading a book and drinking iced fruit juice. She only left once, briefly, to use the restroom.

Dinnertime arrived and the waiter said Mrs. Howard had seemed annoyed that her husband hadn't returned. She ordered a steak and ate it while she continued to read. Finally, she paid the bill and went up to her room.

The article explained that Mrs. Howard had called the police when her husband hadn't returned by ten o'clock. The next day, his body was found washed up on the rocks south of the beach and the medical examiner confirmed he'd died sometime during the previous afternoon—while Mrs. Howard read her book on the terrace.

The timing of the second death had occurred in similar fashion. Mrs. Howard had a modus operandi.

In this instance, the husband plunged to his death, falling from a coastal cliffside. Mrs. Howard—who was now called

Mrs. Seymour—had been attending a play with two friends who vouched for her unhesitatingly. Their husbands joined them for dinner after the play, except Mr. Seymour never showed up.

Neva finished reading the article and printed a copy. Like the first piece, the accompanying photograph was too blurry to be definitive. Still, Neva felt like she had something, at last, that went beyond petty resentment. She shivered.

Her suspicions were now based on reported facts.

Friday morning, on her way to the museum, Neva stopped and bought a large black coffee and a raspberry jelly donut. When she entered her supervisor's office, he cottoned on right away.

"I know that's for me, so just cut to the chase—what are you after this time?"

Neva smiled as she placed her offering in front of him and perched on a corner of the desk. He scowled and poked at the donut.

"It's fresh," she assured him.

"And so are you. Get to the point."

"All right, Don. You know how your wife works in Homicide?"

"Yeah?" His scowl deepened, but Neva saw the underlying curiosity and knew she had his attention.

"Do you think she'd meet with me? I've stumbled across something suspicious and I think my friend is in danger."

He dropped the donut. "If someone's in danger, you should call 9-1-1."

Neva hesitated. "The situation is..."

"Complicated?"

Neva considered. "Delicate," she finally said.

Don sighed. "I'll call Paula."

Paula Quimby met with Neva over a salad lunch in the museum cafeteria. The space was light and airy, open to the ceiling three floors above and rimmed by a mezzanine. The clank of flatware and soft murmur of voices from nearby tables provided a backdrop for their conversation, assuring Neva that no one was paying them the slightest notice.

After thanking Paula for meeting with her, Neva explained the situation in what she hoped was a concise and sensible manner. She spread the printed copies of the articles on the table and pointed out places she'd underlined with a yellow highlighter.

"I'm not a hundred percent certain it's the same woman, but I'm certain enough to be worried about Gabe's safety," she told Paula.

The police detective listened politely and skimmed over the highlighted passages. "I understand your concern," she said, "but we see this kind of thing all the time. A son thinks the attendant at his mother's nursing home is a wanted criminal. A husband thinks he recognizes his wife's new friend from an episode of *Unsolved Mysteries.*

"It's natural to be concerned about our loved ones, and not unreasonable to be suspicious of anyone new coming into the picture. But I have to tell you, Neva—" Paula speared a forkful of lettuce and chewed a moment before continuing. "It's usually a false alarm and then all you've done is raise resentments."

"I know. I'm sure you're right—in most cases. But I really think this is the exception to that rule."

Paula finished her salad and gathered the printed pages, shoving them into her shoulder bag. "Tell you what, I'll take a look at this, do a little checking up, and let you know if I come across anything dodgy."

Neva stifled a sigh and met Paula's proffered hand for a parting shake. "Thanks for giving me your time," she said.

"No problem." Paula handed her a card. "Call me if anything comes up. I'm going to go blow Don a kiss."

"Okay."

Neva watched as Paula disappeared through a door marked, Staff Only. She fingered the card Paula had given her and programmed the number into her speed dial. Just in case.

She finished the workday in a sort of daze, giving her tasks less focus than they deserved. As she put away her work things, she made up her mind to talk to Gabe, tell him her concerns, show him what she'd found. He would be angry, and she cringed at the thought, but for now it was the only way she could think of to protect him.

She pulled up outside the cottage and sat for a moment, letting the song on the radio finish, gathering her courage. Gabe's car was not in the driveway, but he might have parked it in the garage. The old BMW could even be in the shop which Gabe referred to as its second home.

Three songs later, Neva switched off the engine and rang the doorbell. Celia answered with the same plastic smile as before.

"Oh hello, Geneva. Gabe's not home yet."

"Do you expect him soon?"

"I do."

A moment passed, neither of them spoke. With an audible sigh, Celia stepped back, opening the door further. "Why don't you come in and wait for him?"

Neva stepped over the threshold and dropped her handbag beside the door. The house felt cold and alien. This had been a bad idea. She should have arranged to meet Gabe elsewhere but hadn't wanted to create the appearance of a clandestine meeting.

"Come through to the kitchen," Celia called over her shoulder. "I'll make us some tea."

As Neva followed, she wondered if Celia intended to poison the tea or maybe just spit in it. Sinking into a chair at the kitchen table, she let her gaze wander over the familiar space. The large wooden cutting board where she and Tasha had chopped loads of vegetables every summer for their homemade salsa. The beautiful acacia salad bowl Gabe had fashioned in his woodturner shop, one of his first pieces and still among the best.

Celia filled a teapot from the tap and put it on the burner. "Keep an eye on the kettle for me. I need to grab some more teabags out of the storeroom."

While she was out of the kitchen, Neva snooped. She studied the corkboard beside the refrigerator and poked through a stack of mail, not sure what she was looking for but frantic to do something useful. No cryptic notes or smoking guns came to light.

She heard Celia returning and hurried back to her chair just as the kettle whistled.

"Perfect," Celia said as she poured steaming water over the teabags. "We'll let those steep for a bit." She joined Neva at the table, carrying the two cups. "Is there anything in particular you wanted to discuss with Gabe?"

Neva's tongue felt glued to the roof of her mouth. She swallowed to work it loose and tried to decide how to answer. Before her brain fully engaged, she heard herself say, "How many husbands have you had, Celia?"

As soon as she spoke, she wished she could call back the words, but they were out and running. Celia's eyes held a malicious glint as she replied. "I understand why you resent me, Geneva. I came out of nowhere and snatched away the man you thought you could have for yourself."

Neva flinched, but Celia kept talking in a light, casual tone as if chatting about the weather.

"It was never going to happen, Geneva, and you needn't blame me for that. To Gabe, you're his baby sister's best buddy and that makes you his. Buddy, I mean. That's all it could ever be."

Celia thrust her knife in with surgical precision. And then she twisted it, leaning in close to Neva's face. "And now, since you ask so nicely, I think I'll take that away from you, too."

Neva shot up so fast she knocked over the chair. She stood, heart pounding, blood coursing, shaking like an aspen in a hurricane.

"You're evil," she sputtered. "A murderer!"

Celia laughed. A palpable menace filled the room and Neva felt an urgent need to get out, away from Celia's mocking, toxic presence. As she ran for the front door, she shouted, "I won't let you hurt Gabe."

On the porch, Neva bent double, feeling like she was going to retch into the bushes. Behind her, the door slammed and Neva heard the deadbolt ram home. What a stupid thing she'd done. As she fell into the swing and worked to steady her breathing, she realized a new level to her stupidity.

She'd left her handbag inside.

With her keys, her wallet. Her cell phone. And a copy of the pages she'd printed out for Gabe.

She remembered dropping the bag right at the entrance so she'd be sure to pick it up on her way out. She pictured the scene, the living room and entry hall as she'd run through them on her way out the door.

The bag hadn't been there.

Was Celia in there right now, pawing through her personal possessions, reading about herself from the carefully highlighted pages? Maybe that would be best, the safest way for Gabe. If Celia knew her past had caught up with her, she wouldn't dare try it again.

Or would she?

And the thought of an unscrupulous person like Celia digging through her private, sensitive information like ID's, credit cards, photos of friends and family, made Neva desperate to get the handbag out of her clutches. Who knew what kind of hell a vindictive Celia could create from such tinder?

Neva rang the bell and tried to quell her rising panic. The sonorous chime went unanswered and Neva pushed the button again and again without result. She clanged the brass knocker vigorously.

"Celia! Open up."

Nothing.

Giving up on that tactic, Neva ran around to the back of the cottage. She peered in through the window at the top of the kitchen door but there was no sign of Celia, or her handbag. She tried the door, but it was locked. She banged on it with her fist.

"Celia, I need my bag."

After a silent moment, Neva tried a reasoned approach. "I know you'd like me gone, but I can't drive away without my keys. I need my bag, Celia."

No response.

Neva sank onto the back step, head in her hands, and wished Gabe were here, could witness his bride's irrational, maniacal behavior and question her motives. She fantasized a dozen ways out of this mess but had to acknowledge none of them would come to pass if she sat on the step, doing nothing.

She thought she heard movement inside the house. Rising, she went to the door and started pounding, yelling and screaming her frustration, demanding that Celia let her in. The door flew open under her upraised fist and Gabe's astonished face swam into view.

"What are you doing?" he asked. His brows were drawn together, furrowing his forehead, and the dimple Neva adored was nowhere in evidence.

She couldn't answer him, and saw now that her wish had backfired. The only irrational, maniacal behavior Gabe had witnessed was her own.

"I left my bag inside," she finally stuttered. "Celia wouldn't give it back."

Celia appeared beside Gabe, rolling her eyes. "I was in the bathroom. Give me half a sec and I'll get it for you," she told

Neva. As she turned and headed for the living room, she shot Neva a vicious glare.

"Are you okay?" Gabe asked.

"She took my handbag, Gabe, and wouldn't answer the door when I tried to get it back."

He frowned. "I nearly tripped over your bag when I came in. It was right where you always leave it."

"No, it wasn't," Neva insisted. "Look, Gabe, there's something I need to tell you. Could you come out—"

"Here's your purse," Celia said, holding out the bag.

Neva took it and looked imploringly at Gabe. He shook his head.

"We'll have to make it another time, Neva. We've got plans for tonight and I need to grab a shower. My hair's full of sawdust."

Celia wrinkled her nose. "And you smell," she added. "Go jump in the shower. Goodbye, Geneva."

The door shut, like a resounding slap in the face. Celia stood on the other side of the glass and watched with eyes like acid as Neva retreated down the steps and let the shadows claim her. As upsetting and humiliating as the episode had been, she hoped some good might come of it. Surely, Celia would have to back down now from any plans to harm Gabe.

But Celia's face, as Neva caught a last glimpse of it through the window, was a mask of grim determination.

The situation felt more dangerous than ever.

Instead of going home, Neva drove back to the museum and let herself in the staff entrance with her keycard. Her hands trembled so violently that it took three attempts for her to insert the card correctly and get the door open. Inside, the halls were dim, lit only by soft bulbs recessed into cinder block walls at twenty-foot intervals.

Neva's footsteps echoed in the deserted space and the after-hours emptiness did nothing to relieve her nerves. The lingering odor of toluene hung in the air as she passed through the laboratory and entered her tiny office, switching on the lights and waking her laptop computer.

The museum subscribed to more specialized and powerful reference databases than could be accessed by the average Joe on the internet. They were not intended for personal use and Neva was not a rule-breaker by nature, but she had no compunctions about digging into them now.

A database she often used for research carried millions of newspaper and magazine articles from thousands of sources. When she entered "Francine Howard husband murder" into the search box, twenty-three pages of results popped up on the screen.

Neva perused the articles, looking for new information or a more definitive photo of the black widow killer. After poring carefully through six pages, exhaustion kicked in, dragging her low after the adrenalin high of her run-in with Celia. Plundering the bottom of her handbag for loose change, she bought a Snickers and a bag of pretzels from the vending machine and ate her meager dinner while continuing to scan the articles.

By page ten, she was struggling to keep her eyelids aloft and when she realized she'd read the same paragraph at least four times without grasping a word of it, she pushed away from the desk. After a visit to the ladies' room, Neva curled up on the sofa in the break room and sank into oblivion.

Light flickered, pulling Neva up from the depths of dreamless sleep. Confused, she rose up on an elbow and shielded her bleary eyes with one arm.

"What did you do that's so bad you can't go home and sleep in your own bed?"

The nasal voice belonged to Victor, the night watchman. He chuckled a little at his own wit but didn't wait for Neva's reply.

"I saw your car in the parking lot when I came in," he said, "and I thought you might be at the midnight movie. But lo and behold, morning broke and you're still here. I came to see if you're okay."

Neva swung her legs into a sitting position and worked a crick out of her neck. "I'm fine, Victor. What time is it?"

"Seven o'clock. I'm just going off-shift."

"Oh my. I was working late and couldn't keep my eyes open. I really didn't mean to spend the whole night here."

"Tough nut, huh?"

"What?"

"You got a tough nut to crack and you can't give it up."

A shimmer of unease brought Neva to her full senses as she remembered the events of the previous evening. "You're exactly right, Victor. I can't give up."

"You want I should put on some coffee?"

With awareness, came a new pump of adrenalin and Neva was now wide awake. "I don't think I'll need it, Victor. Thanks for the wake-up call."

The guard waved a hand and shuffled off, whistling *The Girl from Ipanema*. In the restroom, Neva splashed water over her face and swished a mouthful around her gums before heading back to her laptop and the search results presented by the database.

Halfway down page twelve, she found an article titled: Black Widow Hatched from Web of Violence. The journalist had focused on Francine's past, citing instances of home-grown treachery and "daddy issues." There were nearly a dozen reports of domestic abuse during Francine's early years. When her mother died under suspicious circumstances, her father was convicted of manslaughter in connection with the death.

He served ten years in prison, was released, and remarried. Two days after their first anniversary, he beat his new wife into a coma and fled the country.

The article suggested Francine had murdered her husbands in a sort of proxy revenge for her mother's death. The sizeable insurance payouts were simply a fortuitous fringe benefit.

What Neva found even more interesting was the follow-up done by the journalist—Francine had disappeared. After being acquitted in the courtroom, she'd vanished to spin her web elsewhere, perhaps under another name.

Most interesting of all, was the photograph featured in the article. Sharper than the others Neva had seen, this one left no doubt as to Francine's identity. The shape of the eyebrows, the curve of the lips. And the mole, high on the left cheekbone.

It was Celia.

Neva turned on the printer and waited impatiently while it warmed up and registered her print request. Her chest felt tight, her stomach queasy, as the machine jerked and made inexplicable noises. She dug her cell phone from her bag and thumbed the call button for Gabe.

It went to voicemail.

At last, the printer cranked out the pages she needed. Neva grabbed them and ran for the door, trying Gabe's phone again. No answer.

In the parking lot, Neva hit the speed dial for Don's wife, Detective Quimby. "Hello," she blurted. "I've found it."

"Who is this?"

"Sorry, Detective Quimby. This is Neva Marks. We had lunch yesterday."

"Right. Look, I haven't had a chance to—"

"But I have, Detective. That's why I'm calling. I've found proof. The woman who calls herself Celia is definitely Francine Howard, the black widow killer."

"She was never convicted."

Neva ground her teeth. "I know, but I'm convinced Gabe is in danger. I'm headed over to his place now." She paused. "Please, Detective Quimby, look into it. Help me, here."

"I'll see what I can find out. Don't do anything rash in the meantime."

Neva ended the call without responding. She steered the car back to Gabe's cottage and hurried past his Bimmer in the driveway. Clattering up the porch steps, she rang the bell with one long push of a finger. When nothing happened, she rang again. Longer.

"No one's home."

The voice came from next door, and Neva looked over to see a woman in gardening gloves crouched over a flowerbed. "You missed them by ten minutes," she said, straightening up with a hand to the small of her back. "You supposed to be going with them to the beach?"

Neva smiled, coming down the steps and across the yard. "Yes, but I'm afraid I'm running late. Did they happen to mention which beach? I forgot."

The neighbor tossed a handful of weeds into a bucket. "You're lucky I'm a nosey old biddy. I heard them arguing about the best way to get to Salmon beach."

"Thanks a bunch," Neva said and started for her car. Pausing, she turned. "Did they take Celia's car? A red Camry?"

"I don't know one model from another, honey. But it was red, all right."

"Great. Thanks."

Neva drove fast, hoping she guessed correctly that they'd take the coast road. She watched ahead all the while for Celia's red Toyota, afraid to even blink. Reaching Detective Quimby once more, she spoke over the woman's exasperated greeting.

"They're headed to Salmon Beach in a red Toyota Camry. I'm on my way there."

"Why shouldn't they head to the beach on a Saturday?"

"Two reasons," Neva said. "One—it's started raining. And two—Celia's first husband drowned at the beach."

"You surely can't believe she'd attempt anything now, with you so keen on turning up the heat."

"She's brazen. She's obsessed. And she'll have an airtight alibi, like before. I don't know how she pulls it off, but I'm scared, Detective."

"You might as well call me Paula. I can tell we'll be spending more time together in future. Don will want to hear all about this over dinner and a good Chianti."

"Salmon Beach, Paula. Please hurry."

The highway wound along the coastline, slick with surface oil raised by the drizzling rain. Neva drove as swiftly as she dared, peering into the distance as she rounded each curve, never catching sight of Celia's car. She tried Gabe's phone again, but it went straight to voicemail.

Neva didn't trust herself to leave a coherent message, and it seemed clear that Celia was somehow keeping Gabe incommunicado. Instead, she pressed the accelerator closer to the floor mat and wished Tasha was in the seat beside her. She hadn't wanted to discuss this with her friend until she had something concrete to share.

Now that she had concrete, there was no time to share it.

At last, the beach parking lot loomed up on her left. It held only two cars, but one of them was a red Toyota Camry. A heavy weight plummeted inside Neva's stomach and she felt sick. Squealing to a halt beside the Camry, she leapt from the car and sprinted down the zigzag path to the beach.

It was deserted.

Squinting, Neva scanned the water for a bobbing head, searched the sand for a pair of abandoned sandals. Nothing. She ran along beside the sea, sand slipping and shifting beneath her feet, turning her head frantically left and right.

She saw no one.

Panic sliced through her like a knife. She narrowed her eyes, staring hard into the distant horizon, trying to see beyond it. Trying so hard to find Gabe.

Panting and near tears, Neva stopped to catch her breath and think. Think. How had Celia managed to drown a full-grown, healthy man? How had she succeeded in sending another over a cliff?

She couldn't have done it alone.

A violent shiver shot through Neva, leaving her cold. Two cars in the parking lot.

Celia had an accomplice.

Her next realization was even more bleak—the cliffs.

She raised her eyes to the line of craggy overhangs a hundred feet above the boulder-strewn beach and saw Gabe. With Celia.

He wore his flat cap and an argyle cardigan sweater, the one she'd given him last Christmas. They were walking arm in arm, close to the edge. Celia was keeping Gabe's attention on the ocean horizon, away from the third figure who now appeared behind them.

Neva screamed. "Gabe!"

The stiff sea breeze caught the sound, dissolving it like foam on the sand. She screamed again, jumping up and down and waving her arms. She must have drawn his attention for he turned in her direction, but in that moment Celia and her accomplice seized him from behind and pushed him toward the edge.

Gabe pivoted and almost slithered out of their grasp, but he was no match for the two of them together. They wrestled him toward the precipice while Neva watched—horrified, helpless, unable to breathe.

An unexpected sound grabbed her attention. The bark of a dog. Neva swiveled her head to see an elderly man with a Golden Retriever at his heels.

"Help!" She shouted, pointing to the cliffs.

The old man caught sight of the struggling trio, alarm registering on his face. Yet, he seemed uncertain about what he should do.

"Help me get their attention," Neva cried.

Together, they screamed and yelled, flailing their arms like crazed windmills. Celia might believe she could succeed in her plan with only one biased witness. But now Neva was not alone.

Hope surged, with the old man beside her and the dog barking its head off. Neva saw frenzied tension in the lines of Celia's body and knew she wouldn't give in. But when her coconspirator caught sight of them on the beach—two witnesses very aware of what was happening—he dropped Gabe's arm and moved away, disappearing over the bluff.

With a shriek of fury, Celia ran at Gabe, heaving him closer to the edge. Stones and divots of grass and earth rained down, hitting the rocks below with a thud that turned Neva's insides to water. Gabe scrambled back from the brink. The tide had turned in his favor, but he was fighting a woman obsessed.

No longer able to simply stand and watch, Neva grasped the old man by the shoulders and planted a kiss on his whiskery cheek. She turned and tore up the path to the clifftop. As she neared the summit, she saw flashing blue lights.

Paula had arrived.

Two strobing patrol cars were parked at angles, blocking off the parking lot. Neva saw Paula speaking with uniformed officers as they pulled a man from the car next to the Camry and placed him in cuffs. Neva stopped dead.

It was Gabe.

But when she got closer, she saw it wasn't. Gabe was still on the cliff.

Neva shouted to get Paula's attention and pointed toward the cliffs. Then she ran, cresting the bluff, and saw Celia and Gabe. They were on the ground now, rolling like wrestlers on the mat. The grass was wet and very red.

So was Gabe's shirt.

He was flagging, loss of blood stealing his strength, and they were so close to the edge. So very close.

As Neva reached them, Celia shoved at Gabe's shoulders and he started to slide over the precipice on the slippery grass. Neva threw herself down on the turf and grabbed both his ankles, digging in with her toes.

She squeezed her eyes shut and prayed.

It was enough. The pound of running feet reached her and helping hands grabbed her and Gabe. And Celia.

It was over.

The hospital waiting room smelled of rubbing alcohol, latex, and floor wax. Somewhere down the corridor, a baby wailed while two seats to Neva's left, a boy played a hand-held device which emitted electronic beeps and boops on a continual basis. The noise grated like a rasp on Neva's fragile nerves.

She flipped through a magazine while she waited for Tasha to arrive. Nothing on the glossy pages raised a blip on her interest radar. She was too worried about Gabe and too keyed up about Celia. She'd called Gabe's sister as she watched the paramedics load Gabe into the ambulance, and then she'd trailed behind the speeding vehicle on its way to the hospital.

She couldn't stop thinking how red the grass had been.

Through the vestibule windows, Neva saw Tasha arriving and went to meet her. They clung to each other, drawing strength from their long friendship, each standing a bit taller for the other.

As they pulled apart, Tasha said, "What happened, Neva?"

"Celia had a knife."

Neva pulled Tasha into a chair and explained the events of the last few days, watching her friend's face go from puzzlement to horror to rage. She gripped Tasha's hand.

"It's all right," she said. "Gabe's going to be all right."

And he was.

A week after the cliffside tussle, Gabe was released from the hospital. He, Neva, and Tasha got together with Don and Paula over dinner and a good Chianti. Just as the detective had predicted.

The police had both Celia and her accomplice, the Gabe look-alike, in custody and under the circumstances, Detective Quimby was willing to impart some of the details of their ongoing investigation. After three glasses of wine.

"Francine's not talking. Hasn't said a word—not even to her attorney, as far as I can tell. However," she raised her glass, "Ricky Taylor was only too happy to lay it all out. He told us how Celia seduced him into participating in a crazy scheme for a big insurance payout.

"To convince him it would work, she told him about the other times she'd pulled it off. He said, and I quote, 'I don't think she even cared about the money. She just wanted to hurt the guy.'"

Gabe grimaced, patting the bandage over the stitched wound in his chest. "It hurt," he confirmed.

Neva and Tasha, on either side of him, rubbed his shoulders in sympathy.

"I'm sure," Paula continued. "But you were a stand-in for her father. What she really wanted was to kill you, like she'd done with at least two previous husbands."

"And Neva stopped it happening," Tasha said, pride and gratitude shining in her eyes.

"Neva stopped it," Gabe echoed. Neva felt heat rise in her face as she met his gaze, aware he was looking at her with fresh eyes, seeing beyond the limits of their past.

"Celia always chose a male accomplice who bore a marked resemblance to her husband of the day. Ricky told us how she schooled him, made sure he dressed and walked and gestured like Gabe. Because in a very critical moment, he would *be* Gabe."

Neva remembered the time she'd watched the couple in the waterside park, thinking she was seeing Gabe with Celia. She shivered. What she'd really witnessed was a practice session, a dry run to see if Ricky could pass for Gabe. And he had. Except for that one slip.

Gabe would never litter the bay.

She should have known, should have realized. She might have been able to stop it sooner. If anyone had believed her.

"We found a duffle bag in Ricky's car," Paula said. "It contained an argyle sweater and a Scottish flat cap. Exact duplicates of what Gabe was wearing, or near enough. That's how Celia cemented her alibis.

"She lured her unsuspecting husbands to an isolated beach or cliff and with the help of her accomplice, killed them, and left the bodies to be found later. Then the accomplice assumed the identity of the husband and they paraded in public, making sure the time of death would be set a bit later in the day.

"After that, she made a show of sending the 'husband' off on his own while she established her alibi and the husband disappeared, only to be searched for and found dead as the result of a tragic accident."

"Wicked," Don said. His hand shook as he poured another glass of wine.

"Exceedingly wicked," Paula agreed. "It's fortunate that Neva persevered and got her locked up. For good, this time."

"I'll drink to that," Gabe said, lifting his glass. Everyone followed suit, clinking glasses and looking at Neva with approval.

It felt great.

And when Gabe squeezed her hand and took a long time letting go, it felt even better. Something had shifted. Neva sensed it and hope rose within her, shining like the dawn. Somehow, she knew they would move forward together, toward the horizon.

And beyond.

Author's Note

No Rest

My thriller novel, *Nocturne in Ashes*, introduces my series heroine, Riley Forte, a concert pianist and undercover agent. In *Nocturne,* the first book in the series, Riley gets recruited by an elite under-the-radar private security firm. The second book, *Staccato Passage*, has her training at an ultra-secret spy academy in the heart of Bavaria, where she acquires the skills and builds the team that will carry the series forward.

This story, "No Rest," takes place between those two books as Riley interrupts her concert tour to attend a spycraft training session in Georgia during an unexpected blizzard.

And the road she's on takes a wicked turn.

Riley got no rest and neither will you, until you finish the very last word!

NO REST

Concert pianist Riley Forte, renowned for her classical repertoire, tuned the rental car radio to a classic rock station and cranked it up hard. *Proud Mary* blasted through the confines of the little car as she beat out the rhythm on the steering wheel, enjoying the vibrations under her fingers, feeling the need for sound and movement after the long, trans-Atlantic flight.

By the time she'd sung the last rolling chorus, she'd passed the environs of the Savannah/Hilton Head airport and made it onto the freeway. Opening the vents, she turned the temperature dial to blue, letting icy air flow until the flesh of her arms rose in goosebumps and her nose dripped. She shivered, adjusting the knob to a more moderate setting, and watched the road signs for a convenience mart. Loud music and a brisk climate would only get her so far—she needed snacks and a refreshing beverage.

Riley activated the windshield wipers, clearing a layer of misty droplets from the glass. Her original plan had been to stay the night at the airport Marriott, saving the last leg of her trip, a hundred-and-fifty-mile drive to the countryside north of Valdosta, for the morning.

If only she'd stuck to the plan.

It seemed sensible to catch a good night's sleep after sitting upright for sixteen hours in planes and airports, but her attendance at this training was vital and her ability to get there—or not—would reflect on her resourcefulness. The training, an intensive course in spycraft, would prepare her for her first undercover assignment, coming soon.

After playing a crucial role in stopping a serial killer, Riley had been recruited by the head of a private security organization who saw her concert pianist persona as the perfect cover for travel among certain circles. She'd interrupted a concert tour to make this trip, and time was short for her to learn and train. Now that she'd arrived back in the states, the weather report was predicting a blizzard of the magnitude native Georgians saw once in a lifetime. She had to tackle the drive now or risk missing the training.

Traffic on the freeway was sparse as folks settled in to wait out the coming storm. Riley exited and found a 7-Eleven, pulling into the near-empty parking lot. She shrugged into her favorite knee-length coat and zipped up, snagging her finger on a raw piece of the metal zipper.

"Ouch!" Wrapping a tissue around her bleeding finger, she examined the zipper, concluding it must have caught in the conveyor belt at airport security. "I must find something to file that down," she muttered, grabbing her purse.

A blast of heat and the bitter smell of burnt coffee hit her as she entered the convenience store. She made a quick trip through the aisles, deciding on a bag of tortilla chips, some honey-roasted peanuts, and a box of Junior Mints. Not the healthiest fare, but interesting enough to stay awake for, she hoped. She also found a box of peppermint teabags and an insulated vacuum flask large enough to hold a quart of tea.

"Do you have anything smaller?" she asked the clerk, holding up the flask.

"That's the only thermos we got."

Happy to find a plentiful supply of near-boiling water near the coffee dispenser, Riley filled the flask and unwrapped four teabags, dipping them in to steep. After a moment's thought, she added two more. The stronger, the better. She fastened the lid and took her purchases to the counter.

The clerk, a gentle-eyed man with the slight facial droop of a former stroke patient, pushed aside a crossword puzzle and slid the pencil behind his ear. Riley noticed it was sharpened to a point keen enough to draw blood. It had been little used on the black-and-white grid.

"It's a toughie," said the clerk. "Cryptic, you know. Brit style."

His accent surprised her. Not a southern drawl, but the tones of New England. "I adore cryptic crosswords," she said. "Ordinarily, I'd love to help solve a clue, or two, but—"

"I know, dear. You'd best get home, and quick."

Riley shrugged, giving him an apologetic smile. "I'm a long way from home. I'm driving to Valdosta tonight."

He fixed her with a stern gaze. "You'll do no such thing. Snow's on the way, and locals don't know how to handle the stuff. Roads will be bad. Hole up for the night—that's my advice."

Riley thanked him and ran her credit card through the chip reader, taking the bag of snacks and the heavy thermos. She nodded a goodbye and headed for the door.

"I'll put you in my prayers tonight," the clerk called after her, retrieving the pencil from behind his ear. "You'll need it."

In the car, Riley placed the flask in the center console and popped the top, letting the aroma of peppermint fill the air, breathing it in. Firing the ignition, she re-entered the freeway and drove fast, traveling south to the junction turnoff. The sky beyond the windshield loomed with the dull gray of unpolished pewter, the last of the daylight draining away like dirty bathwater. Riley drank tea and tried to ignore her growing fatigue, switching the radio to a classical station and concentrating on composers, arrangements, and fingerings of pieces she'd studied in the past.

Forty minutes into her journey, she'd drunk half the quart of tea, and her bladder let her know it. Chafing at the waste of time, she steered the car into a rest stop and pulled on her coat, avoiding contact with the jagged zipper tag. She took care of business and flushed, hearing someone else enter the restroom as she finished up. Pulling open the stall door, she stepped out, startled by a figure huddled against the wall.

The woman wore a torn denim jacket, hanging crookedly on her slender form above a pair of baggy yellow sweatpants. Her dusty blonde hair stood out in snarled disarray, framing a face so pale it appeared there was more blood on the outside of it, than on the inside. The blood on the outside came from her nose and a cut above her right eyebrow. She trembled, like only the cinderblock wall held her upright.

Riley went to her instinctively, raising a hand to the ravaged face. "What happened?" she asked.

The woman drew a breath and let it trickle out in a shaky sigh. "My boyfriend and I had a fight." Her voice sounded scratchy and harsh, but it was pure Georgian drawl.

Riley went to the sink and wet a paper towel, using it to dab the wound on the woman's forehead. "I don't think this will need stitches, but you should at least get a butterfly bandage on it." She paused, handing over the paper towel so the woman could wipe her nose. "You may not like me saying it, but you need a new class of boyfriend. Is he waiting for you outside?"

The bruised eyes squeezed shut, the brow wrinkling in pain. "No. He left."

"He left you here, wearing *that*, with a blizzard closing in?" Riley clucked in disgust and snatched a clean paper towel from the dispenser, waving it savagely under the stream of water. She wrung it dry and exchanged it for the bloody wad in the woman's hands. "What's your name?" she asked.

The woman sniffed, leaning her head back and pinching her nose. "Dee," she said, the single syllable like a blast from a broken kazoo.

"Hello, Dee. I'm Riley." Stifling a twinge of irritation over the delay it would bring, Riley said, "Come on, I'm driving you to the next town where you should go straight to the police station and file assault charges."

The woman didn't speak, only glared at Riley from the corner of one red-rimmed eye.

Riley sighed. "That isn't going to happen, is it?"

Dee lobbed the sodden towel into the trash bin and yanked down another. "No."

Riley washed and dried her own hands. "Well, Dee, how about you mull it over in the car, with the heater on. Let's get out of here."

The incident at the rest stop worked even better than peppermint tea for keeping Riley awake. Fury and indignation stirred her blood and kept her heart tripping along above the normal rate. The sign for her junction loomed on the sullen gray horizon, and Riley turned west onto the highway, heading into the approaching storm, still determined to beat its arrival. She glanced at Dee, the white face tipped up, cheeks like chiseled stone, eyes closed.

"I have some hot herbal tea in the thermos, if you'd like."

Dee opened her eyes like a woman coming out of a trance. She gave her head a little shake and looked at the flask between the seats. "Not much of a tea drinker," she said, but lifted the thermos from its hollow and hefted it with both hands. "Honey, this thing is heavy enough to brain a horse."

"Now there's a product feature I hadn't considered." Riley turned her gaze back to the road and covered a tremendous yawn with the back of one hand.

"Are you all right to drive?" Dee asked, returning the flask to the console. "You look pretty beat, if you don't mind me saying."

"I'll be all right."

"My mama always said there's no rest for the wicked."

Riley didn't answer, not sure how to interpret that. Her mother had often said the same thing, except in her version there was no rest for the weary. Either way, Riley figured she'd be getting no rest any time soon.

A tiny prickle of unease crossed her scalp. Now that she was isolated in the car with this stranger, the woman seemed less vulnerable and faintly menacing. As a rule, Riley didn't pick up hitchhikers due to the potential hazards, and now she realized what she'd just done amounted to the same thing.

"Y'all don't talk like I do," Dee said. "Where y'all from?"

Riley resisted the urge to peek into the back seat to see if there was anyone else there. "I live in Washington state, west of Seattle."

"I didn't realize there *was* anything west of Seattle. Except the ocean."

"Quite a bit, actually," Riley said. "The Puget Sound, the Hood Canal, about a hundred lakes, and all the land that lies between, including my house."

"What brings you to Georgia?"

"Business conference."

"Oh? What kind of business brings you clear out here?"

Riley gripped the steering wheel a little harder. "Just one of those confidence-builder type of things."

"I see. So you'll be spending time with a bunch of strangers? Or are you meeting friends there?"

The prickle across Riley's scalp grew more pronounced. Was this woman just nosy, or did she probe with sinister intention, fishing to find out who'd miss Riley if she didn't show up?

"I'm meeting friends," Riley said.

"That's nice. I hope you—"

The piercing signal of an emergency broadcast burst from the radio, cutting into Dee's response. "Oh, that storm," she drawled in annoyance. But the announcement wasn't about the storm.

Authorities in Georgia are searching for an escaped convict from Arrendale State Pri—

"Look out!" Dee shouted, pointing ahead with frantic jabbing motions, the passing headlights from an oncoming car highlighting her face like an x-ray lamp, turning it skeletal.

Riley pumped the brake and stared out the windshield, alert for danger signs and seeing none. "What was it?"

"You didn't see the deer?" Dee asked, incredulous. "Running alongside the road. It almost sprang out in front of you."

"No, I missed it."

"And thank heaven for that. If you'd hit the damn thing it would have put a real kink in your plans."

"Mmmm," Riley agreed. "Did you hear that radio announcement?"

"About the prison break? Some of it. The usual—consider inmate armed and dangerous, exercise caution, don't pick up hitchhikers or stop in rest areas."

She paused, and Riley glanced over. Instead of meeting her gaze, Dee looked out the window and said, "Guess I'm lucky you stopped for a pee before hearing that. I might've been setting up camp for the night and freezing my buns off."

"Yes, it's your lucky night," Riley said, working to keep her voice calm. Inside, she was a zinging mass of nerves. She'd missed parts of the radio alert, but Dee hadn't mentioned the one thing that stood out in Riley's mind. Police believed the escaped convict to be heading south, toward the Florida Keys. That would bring him—or *her*—right through this corridor.

Prison breaks don't happen often, but in every instance Riley could remember, the fleeing inmates had been male. No reason a woman couldn't do it, though. It was an equal opportunity crime. Did Dee's jacket hang so crookedly on her frame because it was ripped?

Or because one of its pockets held a weapon?

Riley swallowed and realized she was gripping the steering wheel so hard her knuckles stood out like luminescent pearls in the dim glow of the car's interior. She forced herself to relax, to breathe in deep, honing in on the last hint of peppermint lingering in the air, drawing comfort from it.

Outside the windshield, fat white flakes began to fall.

Gusts of snow-flurried wind shook the car and moaned past the door panels, pushing the little rental around like a playground bully. Dee pulled her knees up and huddled in the passenger seat, face hidden in shadow, while air from the heating vents battled against the invading cold, and lost.

Given the chance to do it over again, Riley would have chosen the airport Marriott and been snuggled under a fluffy duvet in front of a good movie by now. Instead, she gritted her teeth and steered carefully along the highway, hoping the rental car had a reliable braking system for icy pavement. Road conditions and visibility had turned treacherous in record time, and living in the Seattle area, Riley didn't have a lot of experience driving in such a setting. But if there's one thing her late husband, Jim, had hammered into her on the subject, it was to keep the gas tank above the halfway mark.

There wasn't much to choose from along this rural stretch of road. Houses and business concerns lay scattered along its edge like beads on a very sparse necklace, but Riley pulled over when she saw a little two-pump gas station. As she rolled to a stop and cut the engine, Dee stretched, letting out an enormous yawn, and opened the door.

"I got to powder my nose."

Out of the corner of her eye, Riley watched the woman start toward the shop entrance while she swiped her credit card and triggered the pump. She thought about what to do. She could drive off now, leaving Dee behind, and that might be the smart thing. But she had no actual reason to believe the woman was a danger to her, and if her story about the abusive boyfriend was true, Dee needed kindness and a helping hand. Abandonment was already an issue for her, and Riley didn't want to pile on.

A bracing wind buffeted her, sending icy fingers down her back, and snow fell in a silent, steady onslaught as she finished filling the tank and screwed on the cap. The lighted sign above the shop door flickered out and darkness descended like a curtain, leaving only the dim illumination of residual lighting. A man in a red lumberjack parka exited and turned to lock up, his keys tinkling like sleigh bells across the snowy asphalt.

"I'm closing up and heading home before this gets worse," he shouted. "You should, too!"

Riley ran across to meet him. "What about the woman who went inside?"

His brow furrowed. "There's no one inside, Miss. Hasn't been a soul come in all evening."

He pulled the cord on his hood, tightening it around his face, and flapped a hand in farewell. The tires of his truck sent up a rooster tail of feathery flakes as he turned onto the highway and disappeared into the gloom.

Riley ran back to the car and ducked inside, starting up the engine.

...If anyone sees Jackson, do not approach or contact her. Instead call 911 to report her location. If anyone has information on her possible whereabouts, call the dispatch non-emergency number...

The rest of the radio announcement faded into oblivion for Riley as she focused on one salient fact. The escapee *was* a woman. Whether or not Dee was the armed and dangerous fugitive, it was time to contact the police. Riley scooped the cell phone from her purse and dialed 911. It rang for a long time, and Riley realized the system was likely overtaxed between the snowstorm and the prison break. At last, someone picked up her call.

"911. What is your emergency?"

"I'm at a gas station on Highway—"

"I'm sorry, please hold."

Riley bit her lip and looked out at the crust of snow forming on her windshield. As she activated the wipers to brush it away, a sharp double tap vibrated the window beside her, startling a scream from her throat and cranking her pulse into the heart attack range. She turned to see a figure holding a flashlight and wearing a badge. The police.

Shaking with relief, Riley lowered the window. A woman officer in uniform blues and a heavy coat, hair pulled back beneath a dark, knit cap, switched off the flashlight and tucked it into a pocket. Before the glass was even half down, the officer spoke, her tone commanding.

"We've got an emergency, ma'am, and I'm requesting a ride into the station. My patrol car went off the road, and I'm unable to reach dispatch."

Before Riley could utter a single word, the cop circled the car and stood at the passenger door. She stooped and looked in at Riley.

"Please unlock the door, ma'am," she shouted through the glass.

Riley did.

Snowflakes fluttered across the windshield, matching the flurry of butterflies in Riley's stomach and making the world outside look like a snow globe in the hands of a two-year old. Riley made no move to shift out of neutral.

"Not supposed to snow like this in Georgia," said the cop. "We're spitting distance from Florida. Go figure." She made an impatient gesture. "Let's roll."

The police woman's coat gaped open, and Riley saw the butt end of a gun. It gave her an uneasy feeling, making her feel trapped in the confined space with an instrument that could kill by the tiny motion of one finger.

Reading the name patch stitched above the uniform breast pocket—Pylican—Riley said, "When I pull out onto that road, Officer Pylican, I'll need all my concentration to navigate the mess out there, so I want to tell you this now. I think I may have seen the escaped prisoner."

"You spotted Kim Jackson?" Her voice rang sharp in the stillness of the car. "Did you call it in?"

"I tried, but 911 put me on hold."

The muscles in the cop's jaw bunched as she gave a curt nod. "Everyone's understaffed tonight. Where'd you see Jackson?"

"Right here. *If* the woman I saw was the prisoner. I can't say for sure, but some of her behavior struck me as suspicious. She told me she was going to the restroom and then she just vanished."

"All the more reason to get to the station and pass on that info." The cop slapped her palm against the dashboard. "Let's go."

Riley felt a mix of relief and regret. She'd passed on what she knew, and the ball was out of her court. But she was savvy enough to realize she wouldn't make it far past the police station tonight. When she delivered Officer Pylican, she'd be asked to fill out a report, make a statement, or whatever procedure applied. She watched her chances of reaching the training facility on time dwindle down to dregs.

Resigned, she shifted into drive and pulled carefully forward, testing the icy surface. As she turned the tires toward the road, her headlights swept across the snowy terrain, picking out a moving shape in the storm. The figure's head jerked up, staring right into the glare, holding up one arm to screen her face. It was Dee.

And she was dragging a body.

"What the hell?" Officer Pylican leaned forward, squinting through the windshield. Riley pressed the brakes, and the car skidded to a halt just short of a ditch. The cop leaped out, gun drawn, and leveled the barrel in Dee's direction. "Drop the body and keep your hands out to the side where I can see them," she shouted.

Riley didn't know if the body acted as a burden or a shield for Dee, but she dropped it as instructed, and that's where her compliance ended. She turned and ran, disappearing amid the swirling snow as Officer Pylican fired into the night.

Without thinking, Riley switched off the engine and left the headlights burning to illuminate the scene. She ran to the abandoned body and knelt to examine the man, her hands shaking. He'd been stripped to his underwear and stabbed in several places, but shallow, ragged breaths still came and went between his blue-tinged lips.

"The prisoner must have attacked him and taken his clothes," the cop said.

Before Riley could respond, the officer turned back toward the car. "Put pressure on those wounds," she called. "I'll try again to reach someone."

She ran to the car, leaving Riley to tend the wounded man. She unwound the scarf from her neck and fastened it tightly around the man's trunk, pressing against a gash in his side. Through it all, he was unresponsive.

"Still nothing," Pylican shouted. "Stay with him!"

Riley watched as the officer took off in Dee's direction, her figure quickly swallowed by snow and darkness. Something about the situation tugged at the edge of her consciousness, something that didn't fit, but she couldn't bring it to the surface. Very little had happened during the evening to fit any expected pattern, so picking out a single anomaly seemed unlikely to help.

She shrugged out of her long, quilted coat. The wind chilled her in an instant, sapping warmth and energy from her body. Spreading the coat on a blanket of snow, Riley rolled the man onto it, kneeling to tuck his arms into the sleeves. She noticed he had several tattoos—a small dragon, a multi-colored geometric design, and a goofy-looking bird with a big bill. At least the authorities would have something by which to identify the body.

If he didn't make it.

Determined to do what she could to avoid that outcome, Riley zipped the coat shut, pricking her finger once more on the raw barb of broken metal. She hardly noticed as she grabbed hold of the fabric and started sliding the bundle across the snow toward the car. She paused to access her suitcase in the trunk, pulling on a sweater and a hooded sweatshirt, feeling a small degree of relief from the bitter cold.

Getting the man to the car across the slippery snow hadn't been difficult, but wrestling him into the back seat took every ounce of Riley's strength. He was small and trim, but a muscular deadweight is hard to shift and she wished for some help. The cop did not return and Riley decided her best course of action was to get the man to a hospital. She could alert the police from there.

Placing the injured man in the most comfortable position she could manage, she secured the door and turned to survey the darkened horizon. Snow continued to fall, clustering in her hair, but the battering wind had lost some of its bite. Riley hoped it was an indication the storm was letting up. Running around to the driver's seat, she jumped in and reached to start the engine.

The key was gone.

The shock of it sucked the air from her lungs. She ran her hands over the floor mat and slid her fingers into the crevices around the console. Kneeling on the seat, she reached into the back and checked the pockets of her coat wrapped around the unconscious man. He didn't stir.

What could have happened to the key? She remembered shutting the car off and leaving the key in the ignition. Might the cop have taken it when she ran back to the car to try calling?

A chorus of alarm bells chimed off in Riley's head. Officer Pylican hadn't left a phone in the car. The key had been her sole purpose in going back. Riley conjured the image of the cop running off after Dee, the uniform pants too long, bagging up around the over-sized boots.

And the tattoo of the bird, its giant bill jutting out from the sturdy body, beady eyes fixed on a wriggling fish. A pelican. The man in the back seat was Officer Pylican.

And the woman with the gun was a dangerous fugitive.

The stark realization seemed to drop the temperature in the car another ten degrees. Riley slumped in the driver's seat, a juddering chill working its way down her spine, the brittle slap of icy snow pellets against the windows sounding like nails in her coffin. Twisting in the seat, she looked back at the wounded officer, hoping he might provide some kind of silent guidance. The man's eyes were open and glazed, staring up at the fabric-covered ceiling of the car but seeing far beyond, into another world.

She was alone.

Riley forced herself to reach over the seat, feeling for a pulse, knowing she wouldn't find one. Pushing her hand against the man's throat, she sought a beat in his carotid, willing it to thrum beneath her fingers, but nothing moved there. The flesh under her hand felt like rubber and she pulled away, stifling a whimper of desperation and fighting the urge to curl up on the seat and cry.

She had to move, had to get out of the vicinity and into contact with people. She grabbed her purse and spared one last look at the man in the back seat. She should take back her coat, but couldn't bring herself to deprive the dead. Pulling up the hood of her sweatshirt, she let herself out into the pelting snow. There was nowhere to go. The only building in sight was the tiny gas station, locked up tight.

Riley remembered there had been nothing else for a mile or more before she'd pulled in. What about in the other direction? Should she try walking west along the highway or retrace her route to the east? A surge of dread feathered through her as she realized she wouldn't last long at the mercy of the elements. She had to find shelter.

She examined the storefront and considered shattering a window, but shied from the idea. It went hard against the grain to break the glass and doing so would expose the interior to the harsh conditions. Further, it would give the escaped convict a clear sign where to find her if she came looking.

Riley went around to the back of the shop. With a burst of hope, she jiggled the door handle but it didn't yield to her optimism. She had only a rudimentary idea of how to pick a lock and wondered if she could somehow break the knob with a heavy rock. Opting for her first idea, she dug through her purse and found a hairpin.

"It works in the movies," she muttered as she pushed in the pin and wiggled the doorknob, trying different angles and positions. She worked at it for several minutes with no discernible progress. Here was a skill she'd make a point of learning in the future.

If she had a future.

The pin broke. She pulled it from the lock and hurled it into the woods behind the shop, yelping in frustration. As she leaned against the building, shivering and wondering where to go from here, the door beside her opened and a hand reached out to grab her, pulling her inside before she could even scream.

The sudden cessation of wind and snow sent a glorious warmth spreading through Riley. At that moment, she hardly cared if the fugitive killed her, the relief was so great. But it was Dee's face, not the pseudo-cop's that peered into Riley's in the dim recesses of the shop's back room.

"You scared the Mississippi mud out of me," Dee chided. "I thought you were *her*, until I heard your voice."

"How did you get in here?" Riley asked.

"Picked the lock, of course."

Riley swallowed a grumble. "What's going on?" she demanded. "Why did you tell me you were going to the bathroom and then just disappear?"

"You're not from here, so you wouldn't know, but this is how Kim Jackson ended up in prison in the first place. She took a hostage on the road and left a trail of bodies behind her. I remembered about how you picked me up at that rest stop and I thought you might be her."

Riley let out a pent-up breath. "I was thinking the same thing about you."

Dee hugged herself, shivering. "Maybe someday we can share a laugh over that, but right now, we got to get out of here. What happened to the naked guy? I tried to help him."

Riley swallowed the lump that rose in her throat. "I got him into the car, but...he died."

"Oh." Dee waited a moment before asking, "Why didn't you just drive away?"

"She took the key."

"Damn," Dee said, blowing into her hands and rubbing them together. "She didn't want you leaving without her."

"Guess not."

Now that she was becoming accustomed to the inside of the building, Riley realized it wasn't all that warm. She sank onto a crate, feeling it shift beneath her weight. An open bag of Doritos on a scarred wooden desk scented the air with nacho cheese, making Riley's stomach growl. She'd never eaten her snacks.

A whirr issued from the baseboard vent and a feeble breath of heat drifted out. A sudden crazy thought occurred to Riley, skating on a very thin blade of possibility. She remembered how her friend, Rick, had been recruited into the covert security organization.

"Is this my test?" she asked Dee. "Am I failing?"

Dee studied her. "What is that, some kind of a philosophical question or were you addressing God?"

"You're not with the...organization?"

Dee's brow wrinkled. "You're more sleep deprived than I imagined."

"You're right," Riley said. "I could use some rest."

A gloomy silence descended, broken only by a worrisome gurgle and swoosh from the struggling heating system.

"Heat pump can't handle these kinds of temperatures," Dee said. "I've never seen southern Georgia so cold."

Riley didn't comment. She was thinking about how to proceed, adding hotwiring to her mental list of skills to acquire.

"Maybe you didn't leave the key in the ignition," Dee suggested. "Maybe she doesn't have it. What if it simply fell out of your pocket?"

Riley considered, shaking her head. "I'm sure I left it in the car."

"Sure enough to bet your life on it? Let's go look."

It was better than sitting pat, helpless and waiting. Still, Riley was reluctant to leave the shop and step out into the storm—and possibly the sightline of a dangerous criminal. She steeled herself and ran from the building, Dee at her side, their shoes crunching into the ice-crusted drifts. Gone were the fluffy flakes of a snow globe world. The pellets raining down on Riley's head felt like assault fire.

The trough she'd formed by dragging the downed policeman through the snow was filling up, but still discernible. She searched the area, kicking aside clumps of snow, working her way back to the car.

And there it was. Not three feet from the side of the rental, the key lay, half-buried in frozen flecks.

"Yes!" Dee shouted, snatching the key and raising it to her lips. "Hallelujah. Let's get out of here."

Riley cleared a circle of snow from the rear window and peered into the back seat. The body lay humped there, wrapped in her bloodstained coat. A pang of regret shot through her—sorrow for the way events had played out, for the family that would be missing a member, and a spear of anger that she hadn't been able to do anything to stop it happening.

She took the key from Dee's outstretched hand and went around to the driver's door, not liking the amount of snow that had built up around the tires and hoping she'd be able to get the car down the road to safety. Sending up a silent prayer, she tried the ignition and felt a surge of relief as the engine fired.

She let the car warm up for as long as she dared, but the thought of the armed fugitive looming out of the snow to stand in their way, stopping them from going, was too much. Careful not to cause a tire spin, she applied the gas and turned the wheel, starting the car in a slow glide toward the highway entrance.

Dee fiddled with the heating controls as Riley guided the car down the icy pavement. "Can't tell you how happy I am to be away from there."

Riley nodded in agreement, but her unease increased even as she put distance between herself and the blighted gas station. She glanced at Dee and gripped the steering wheel tighter. "I was *positive* I left the key in the ignition."

A cold, hard object pressed against the back of her neck. "You did."

Kim Jackson rose from the back seat, wrapped in Riley's coat, a smirk on her face and a gun in her hand. "You left the key, and I took it. I have a special understanding of what it feels like to be trapped, and I knew you'd be back looking for it. Hope springs eternal when your back's up against the wall, doesn't it, ladies?"

Riley's heart pressed against her windpipe, squeezing the breath from her lungs. From the corner of her eye, she saw Dee's hands fly to her mouth, stifling a scream.

"This is just like old times," Jackson said, a raspy chuckle in her voice. "Got me an open road and some traveling companions." The convict tapped the nose of the gun against Riley's temple. "I learned this in lockup—keep looking for your ticket out, and one day you'll find it. Just keep driving, girl. And head south."

Despite the cold, Riley's palms were sweating, making the steering wheel harder to handle. Patches of ice caused the car to slide and shimmy, and she eased off the accelerator. A sharp, painful jerk tugged her head down as the fugitive grabbed a handful of her hair.

"No slowing down. We've got a lot of ground to cover."

Lock-picking, hotwiring, and hostage negotiation. Riley reflected on the irony that she might have learned one or all of these skills at the training she'd surely miss now. It rarely goes well when the practical exam comes before the instruction. Her brain raced, fumbling for a course of action to improve the situation. It was funny how she'd started this road trip exhausted and now she was so wired her blood sizzled. No more need for peppermint tea.

She glanced down at the thermos, remembering how heavy it was, remembering Dee's remark. Wondering if Dee remembered these same things. She tried to catch the other woman's eye without drawing attention to her efforts, but Jackson was having none of it.

"Keep your eyes on the road and forget any bright ideas you might be hatching."

"I'm not hatching anything. I'm just nervous about the roads. We almost hit a horse earlier."

"A horse?"

"Yes. Came out of nowhere."

Dee was staring at her, but Riley saw her head dip in the tiniest of acknowledgments. Riley met Jackson's eye in the rearview mirror. Wondering how to distract the woman long enough for Dee to take action, she noticed a trail of blood streaking down from the fugitive's thumb, dark against the bone-white hand.

Letting her face show a mix of revulsion and concern, Riley said, "You're bleeding. How bad are you hurt?"

The escapee looked down at her hand and saw the smear across her thumb. Riley could have told her it came from the jagged zipper pull on her coat, but that wasn't important. What mattered in that moment was her attention diverted just long enough for Dee to swing the thermos, smashing it hard into the fugitive's face.

The gun went off, a deafening roar in the confines of the car, and Riley felt—more than heard—the ping of a bullet passing through the roof of the car. The little rental skidded, sliding toward a drop-off at the side of the road. Riley struggled to turn into the skid, getting the tires back on track, narrowly avoiding the ditch.

Beside her, Dee was clambering into the back seat, her feet scrambling for purchase on the dashboard, one knee smashing hard against Riley's mouth. She tasted blood. In the rearview, Riley saw the thermos rise and fall, accompanied by grunts and moans.

A truck came in from behind, first vehicle they'd seen since getting on the road. It blew the air horn, warning Riley to get in her own lane. It was all she could do to hold the wheel steady with Dee wriggling beside her and the ice sliding past beneath the tires. The truck driver had either a death wish or a smoking hot date. He barreled past and gave no quarter, sending a wave of snow and gravel skittering across Riley's windshield.

Dee struck once more with the thermos, and Riley heard a sound like a melon dropped on pavement. Nausea rose in her throat, choking her, bringing tears to her eyes. She pumped the brakes, bringing the car to a shuddering halt at the side of the road. She swallowed hard, gasping for breath. Dee slumped back into place in the front seat and dropped her head into her hands.

For a while, there was only the sound of two women breathing.

Riley opened the door and leaned out, melting the snow with the contents of her stomach. Stretching her legs over the puddle she'd made, she pushed herself out of the car and leaned against it, trembling, letting the cold, cutting wind wash her clean. Dee exited from the other side and stood with her back to Riley, shoulders heaving under the thin fabric of her denim jacket.

The blip of a siren sounded, and a patrol car approached, pulling alongside. The window whirred as it lowered, allowing a friendly-faced officer to address them.

"This isn't a rest stop, ladies. You'll have to keep moving." He leaned out to emphasize his next words. "It's not safe to stop along this route—there's an escaped convict on the loose."

Riley glanced into the back seat of her little rental, and quickly away. Good thing she'd sprung for the extra insurance. *Budget* wasn't getting this one back any time soon. She cleared her throat.

"About that," she said. "I'd like to report a sighting."

Author's Note

Solitary

Solitary came about as the result of an assignment from acclaimed writer and editor, Kristine Kathryn Rusch, a mentor of mine.

In April 2020, she asked me to write a story using the Covid pandemic as a theme. We were all suffering through difficult challenges at the time, our world turned upside down and inside out. I still remember the eerie feeling it gave me to go grocery shopping or put gas in the car and see everyone, everywhere, wearing masks.

Surreal.

This story is short and packs a punch. I hope you enjoy it.

SOLITARY

T he day all this started and the world turned upside down, Gus Carver told me to get used to being alone. I remember his eyes, like smoking black holes above his paper mask. He stretched out his arm, straining forward like he wanted to touch me, but pulled back before we made contact. We were living in a different world. No touching here, no breathing on each other.

And very little pleasant talk of any kind.

These days, everyone sends their thoughts and ideas through electronic means, anyway. Like robots, transmitting signals and neural impulses through wires and silicon chips. Hygienic, and cold as hell.

That sort of thing is not for me.

When I got to my room, all by myself, the slam of the door echoed like the hammer of a nail in a coffin—loud, harsh, and final. No use in wishing I could go out again. I wouldn't.

Not for a long time.

Most everyone here kept to themselves. That was the rule passed down from on high, and infractions were stringently frowned upon. If living in a vacuum-packed bubble was the aim, the people pulling the strings were hitting the bullseye.

In my room, I stared at the bare, bleak walls and tried to block out the smell of rot and despair that radiated from them like heat waves on desert sand. I stretched out on my lonely single bed and thought about what I might do to spruce things up in here. Given the chance.

Maybe a framed panoramic print, like the one I saw once in a shop downtown. Or an island breeze air freshener so I could shut my eyes and imagine I was somewhere else.

I thought about Paul Gaugin. We learned about him in my high school Humanities class, his artist's life in Tahiti, and I remembered his paintings, full of life and color. Tropical parrots and women wearing nothing but pink and orange strips of cloth around their hips.

The girl who sat in front of me in class had hair the color of honey on toast and a lilting Southern accent that made me think of the wind chimes on my grandmother's porch. When Mr. Fontaine introduced the concept of the Golden Mean, he called the girl out as an example. She stood in front of the class, blushing, while he measured the length of her arms and legs and pronounced her close to classical perfection.

I couldn't recall her name.

That sent me into a panic. My ears rang, ripples of compressed sound inside my head, and I couldn't breathe. Pushing up onto my elbows, I gawped like a goldfish slopped from his bowl, working my mouth, straining my lungs to capture a wisp of breath.

What are we, but memory?

When we forget, we cease to exist.

Sagging back onto the bed, I breathed at last, but it brought no relief. Here, in this isolated world, I had already ceased to exist. One more breath didn't make a blade of difference.

I ordered dinner. The man who delivered the meal left it at the door, backing away to limit his contact with me. The smell of steak and fried onions joined me in the room, my sole dining companion—welcome, but hardly enough to make up for what I was missing.

I ate slowly, letting the mashed potatoes linger on my tongue, the tartness of the lemon meringue pie bringing tears to my eyes that I wiped away with a brown paper napkin. When I swallowed the last bite, I closed my eyes and leaned against the wall, imagining all the bits of nutrition being carried around to the various cells in my body, working to keep me alive.

Even *I* could appreciate the irony in that.

After dinner, I went for a walk. I didn't go far, just down to the end of the block where I got a shave and a haircut. When the barber had finished, I felt exhausted, too tired to walk anywhere else.

I sank down, arms at my sides, motionless except for the feeble rise and fall of my chest. A sudden frantic desire to see someone, to behold another human being and feel some sort of connection, seized me. The hot yearning speared through me like an electric jolt.

I turned my head to look out the window.

Where moments before had been nothing, something worth looking at now appeared. Through the open curtains, I saw people, separated from me only by a pane of glass and a world of harsh restraints. For so long, I had been buried in my own pain, my own isolation. It seemed incredible that people could be moving and interacting in a world that still bore some resemblance to the one I remembered.

I made out four individuals, spaced several feet apart, looking back at me. I recognized one of them as the mother of a girl I once knew. The woman's hair had been dark then, but now it was white, thin and frizzled, pulled back from her face in a sort of twist. Age spots stood out on her skin and the bands of sinew in her neck looked like the strings of a guitar I used to pluck on random summer nights.

Nights when I wasn't otherwise occupied.

On *those* nights, I was never alone. I had companions. Lovers, even. Girls to keep me company and keep me busy.

So busy, on those nights.

Looking at the woman through the glass, I thought about smooth summer darkness, the bite of excitement and shiver of almost unbearable pleasure. The sound of wind chimes and raptured, breathless euphoria. Warm skin beneath my fingertips.

Warm skin, turning cold.

The woman through the glass looked back at me, her eyes a pair of frozen marbles above the mask she wore. They all wore masks. Everyone did now. Everyone keeping *six feet* between them, buried in protective little bubbles.

Solitary.

I pressed my head back against the flat paper-covered pillow of the gurney and laughed. I'd been living in isolation for eleven years. It felt good to spread the pain, to share the burden. Their days now were like all the days I'd passed in confinement.

On Death Row.

The strident tang of rubbing alcohol bit into my thoughts and a sharp prick burned along the length of my arm as the needle slipped in. I closed my eyes, grasping to find and hold my fondest memories.

Those summer nights, the guitar, the chimes, the laughter.

The screams.

What are we, but memory?

AUTHOR'S NOTE

COLDER THAN GAZPACHO

Betrayal.

That was the starting point for "Colder Than Gazpacho," a theme chosen by the editor of *Mystery, Crime, and Mayhem*. For this issue, I wanted to write a Cathryn Harcourt short mystery and since I lived just off the beach in Spain for seven years, I decided to send Cathryn to my old stomping grounds to research her next novel.

There, in the warmth of the sun, Cathryn goes up against a clever and calculating adversary. Someone seeking to serve up a dish as chilled and blood-red as the famous soup of Spain.

If you enjoy the cozy atmosphere of Cathryn's company, I invite you to explore the other books in the Cathryn Harcourt Mysteries series.

And now, wrap up in a blanket if you need to, against the chill of betrayal, but come along for this intriguing mystery first published in *Mystery, Crime, and Mayhem: Betrayal*, February 2024.

Colder Than Gazpacho

Cathryn stood, hands on hips, feet splayed on the wet sand, waves lapping at her ankles, as she gazed out over the western horizon. In the first days of spring, the sun set early, even in southern Spain, and its golden rays melted across the copper ocean like butter on a golden pancake.

She dug her toes into the cool grains beneath her feet. Though the day had been fine, the breeze feathering across the bay from Cadiz raised a slight shiver along the hairs on her arms, and Cathryn hadn't gone past her knees into the aquamarine water.

She might have picked a warmer time of year to do the research for her next mystery novel, but she liked the relative quiet of the off-season, offering long moments of solitude, perfect for pondering and plotting. Licking the slight salt tang from her lips, she gathered her things and began trudging along the slithering sand back to her rented apartment, one block from the beach.

Climbing the steps to the promenade above, Cathryn skirted a few piles of dog detritus dotting the sidewalk. Everyone in Spain, it seemed, owned a dog and the messes were shrugged off and accepted by the locals as part and parcel. Cathryn tried to adopt an equally casual attitude, grateful the aromatic lumps hadn't been baking all day under a scorching sun.

Entering the foyer of the apartment building, she scraped the last of the sand from her sandals on a nubby mat before starting across the marble floor. Water from a fountain at the center of the space splashed gently into a ceramic bowl, and the soft strains of a Spanish guitar floated on the air. Cathryn liked the building, and her apartment offered a spectacular view of the bay.

From the corner of her eye, she caught movement at the manager's counter and heard the slight murmur of conversation as she headed to the elevators. She jabbed the button and as it lit, a resounding crash echoed in the airy space, making her jump.

Turning, she saw a woman staring down at the shattered mess of a potted plant, her palms pressed to her cheeks. Cathryn dropped her beach bag and hurried to help.

"I...I'm sorry," the woman stuttered as León, the property manager, came forward with a bag to collect the broken shards.

"Are you all right?" Cathryn asked her. The woman was shaking, her face extraordinarily pale. "Can I get you a glass of water?"

Cathryn nodded to León who handed her the bag and went to fetch the water. The woman pulled her hands from her face and began helping with the cleanup. As Cathryn worked, she studied the woman from beneath her lashes. There was something familiar about her, and as León arrived with the water and a broom, it came to her.

"Paige?" she ventured. "Paige Kincaid? Is that you?"

The woman's startled eyes flew to Cathryn's face and she stared hard, her mouth dropping open. "Cathryn?"

The two college roommates embraced over the pile of scattered soil. "It's been thirty years!" Paige said. "How can you possibly still look the same?"

Cathryn laughed. "I'm sure I don't."

"Nor do I. But you recognized me anyway."

She sat back on her haunches and was about to speak when León shooed them both away. *"Por favor, señoras.* Go now. I will handle this."

Cathryn helped Paige to her feet and they walked arm in arm to the elevator, Cathryn retrieving her bag on the way.

"I'm Paige Morrison now," her long ago roommate said.

"Is your husband here with you?" Cathryn asked.

Paige sighed, shaking her head. "My Walter has passed on. Been almost five years now."

Cathryn squeezed her hand. "Six and a half years since my Ryan died. I guess we're kind of in the same boat."

Paige gave a wan smile. "Paddling along with you was always a good thing."

The elevator arrived and they stepped inside. "Which floor?" Cathryn asked, her finger poised over the buttons.

"I'm on six."

"And I'm on seven," Cathryn smiled.

"Come in for a drink?"

Cathryn regarded her friend. "I think I should," she said. "Something really upset you back there, and if there's any way I can help, I'd like to do that."

The sparkle went out of Paige's eyes, but she nodded, leading the way as the carriage arrived on the sixth floor. Like Cathryn, she wore sandals that made little slapping noises on the polished marble floor of the corridor. Inside the apartment, she kicked off her sandals and padded into the kitchen, opening the refrigerator and gesturing Cathryn onto the sofa.

"Did you ever take up drinking, Cath, or are you still strictly no alcohol? I have a passable cabernet I could open."

"No wine for me. I still prefer water over everything else."

Paige shook her head. "I never could understand that, but...good for you."

She brought two bottles and settled next to Cathryn on the sofa—one water and an amber-colored cerveza which she drained past the halfway mark in one long draft before speaking.

"I've read some of your books, Cathryn." She thrust her beer bottle out, clinking it against Cathryn's water in a sort of salute. "They're good. You've come a long way from Professor Darnell's English class."

Cathryn smiled. "I'm glad you enjoyed reading my characters' exploits." She paused. "I don't claim to be an expert at solving mysteries, but I like to think I can help an old friend. So, what's up, Paige?" she asked gently. "What happened down there in the lobby?"

Instead of speaking, Paige dug a crumpled note from her pocket and handed it to Cathryn.

What can one admire more than the honest and pure?
What can lift the soul higher than noble truth?
What can hold us with fervent allure,
More than the sweetness of innocent youth?
Enjoy my gift,
Jane

Cathryn read the note twice, unsure what she should be taking from it. "This came with the plant?"

Paige bit her lip and nodded.

"It's a lovely poem," Cathryn said. "Why has it upset you so much?"

Paige clenched her fists in her lap and squared her chin. "The sender—Jane Lucas—couldn't have written that note." She raised her eyes to Cathryn's.

"Because I killed her, thirty-three years ago."

"Thirty-three years!" Cathryn exclaimed. Shock and disbelief washed over her in equal measure. "That was before we met. Why did you never tell me anything about this?"

"Would you, in my place? If you were trying to put the awful past behind you and start a new life?"

Paige's hand trembled as she raised the beer bottle and downed another long swallow. "I wanted to forget it, pretend like it never happened." She paused. "I wanted to be somebody else. And so, I was."

Cathryn remembered that bright college girl of long ago, the wistful hopeful air she'd carried. There had been a brittle edge that Cathryn had sensed but never come close to breaking through. And now, more than thirty years later, she was about to take that plunge.

"Tell me," she said.

Paige set the beer bottle on the glass-topped coffee table with a hard click. "I was a stupid teenager with a brand new driver's license. After a school dance, I took a carload of friends out for a ride."

Paige's nostrils flared and she swallowed hard, her face twisting under the bitter taste of it. "I thought I was so cool, so invincible. Driving fast, pedal to the floor, the road like silk under the tires. My friends were laughing, cheering me on, and everything was wonderful."

Creases rose on Paige's forehead as she fought to control her riling emotions.

"Until I saw the girl."

Cathryn could almost feel the words sticking in her former roommate's throat, knew it hurt her to spit them out. But also knew she had to.

"She was just there. Suddenly. Out of nowhere. And I couldn't stop in time. I just mowed her over."

Paige's face crumpled. "The awful, haunting sound of it." She shook her head, unable to say more for several minutes. When she spoke again, all she said was, "Her name was Jane."

Cathryn moved closer on the sofa, taking her friend's hand, lowering Paige's head to her shoulder while the woman sobbed into the silence of a Spanish evening.

After a while, Cathryn asked, "What happened to you after that?"

Paige sniffed, reaching for a tissue from a box on the end table. She mopped her face, pressing her lips together to quell further tears. "I served nine months in juvie for vehicular manslaughter. The judge ordered me to write a letter of apology to Jane's parents. They never replied."

Cathryn frowned. "And now, after thirty-three years, some-one pretending to be Jane sends you a potted plant?"

"It's not the only thing that's happened," Paige said. "I came here to get away from it."

Cathryn swallowed her surprise, realizing the tremendous amount of stress her friend must be operating under. "What else?" she prompted.

"About three months ago, I got an email from a woman claiming to be Jane's sister. She said she wanted to meet and talk about what happened, that it might bring us both closure."

"Did you agree?"

"Not at first. But after some thought, I decided to meet her. I went to the place we arranged, but she never showed up."

"What was the woman's name?"

"She just signed as Susan, and I remembered that Jane did have a sister named Susan."

"Did you ever hear from her again?"

Paige hesitated. "I'm not really sure. She never emailed again, but someone started calling me on my cellphone, whispering my name before hanging up. Sometimes, when I came home from church or running an errand, I'd find a poem tacked to my front door. Similar to the one that came with the plant. And then I got a friend request on Facebook from someone calling themselves Jane Lucas."

Cathryn felt herself squirming. This conversation was definitely making her uncomfortable. She couldn't imagine how awful it must feel for Paige to be going through it.

"Did you hold onto those poems?" she asked.

"The first time it happened, I tore up the blasted thing and threw it out. After that, I thought maybe I should keep them, in case...I don't know. In case the police needed them for evidence or something. I can dig them out for you."

"Sure" Cathryn said. "But later. Right now, I want to hear the rest of the story. How did you end up here?"

"I started to feel unsafe," Paige continued. "Like I was being watched or followed all the time. I just had to get away. Walter left me enough money to take a trip now and then, so I packed up and came to Spain. I thought I'd get a real break, and then..."

"Right. The plant. The poem."

"I'm scared, Cathryn. It seems like Jane's sister is set on making me pay for what I did."

Cathryn leaned forward, placing her water bottle on the table next to Paige's beer bottle. "But why now?" she asked. "After all these years?"

Paige slumped against the sofa, misery stamped on every feature. "You know what they say about revenge—it's a dish best served cold. Like gazpacho."

"That's one cold gazpacho."

Cathryn regarded her friend, noting the still-pale face, the trembling hands. "You need to eat," she said. "And so do I. Let's walk down to the Argentinian steakhouse."

After some persuading, Paige agreed and they exited the apartment building into the dusky evening, a long line of streetlamps sending spangles of light into the blue velvet sky. A couple of kids on skateboards sped past, their wheels setting up a rhythm on the squares of pavement.

The enticing tang of grilled meat drifted on the air and Cathryn felt her mouth water as she anticipated a tender steak, flanked by a medley of vegetables. The restaurant was just around the corner, but before they made the turn, a voice hailed them and a woman stepped from a tiny shop crammed with merchandise of every kind.

"Paige! I thought that was you. Are you headed to dinner?"

The woman cocked her head at Cathryn, smiling and holding out her hand. "Hi, I'm Anita. Paige's neighbor."

Cathryn shook the proffered hand. "Then you're my neighbor, as well. I'm Cathryn."

Paige gripped Anita's shoulder, a trace of excitement and pride in her voice. "Cathryn Harcourt," she told Anita. "The mystery writer."

Anita's hazel eyes widened and her gaze sharpened, appraising. "Really? How marvelous. I don't know how you do it. I can't string together a decent sentence unless it's steeped in code and executes a command."

"Anita is a software engineer," Paige explained. "Made a mint out of computer programming."

Anita nodded, grinning. "Maybe two mints," she agreed. "Which prompts my question—are you eating Argentinian tonight? That's where Gerald and I are planning to dine. Will you join us? My treat."

Without waiting for an answer, she swung her mane of long dark hair and hooked her arm through Paige's. They began walking. Cathryn fell in beside them, a little bemused by the woman's positive presence. She seemed genuine and friendly, and though her manner was a bit pushy, it came across as an odd sort of charm.

"Where is Gerald?" Paige asked.

"Oh, he ran down to that tobacco shop," Anita said. "He's discovered some kind of Turkish something-or-other to stuff in that pipe of his." She tossed a glance over her shoulder. "He'll be along any moment."

As she spoke, a man appeared out of the shadows of a side street, walking toward them.

"Speak of the devil," Anita said, giving her husband a fond glance and accepting his kiss on her cheek.

Gerald nodded a greeting at Paige and Cathryn as they rounded the corner to the steakhouse, the tantalizing aroma growing more alluring with each step. Cathryn's stomach growled, but as she moved forward, she bumped into Paige who'd frozen, standing stiff and staring.

Cathryn followed her gaze to something dangling from the arched entrance to the restaurant's patio, caught in a halo of light from a glowing streetlamp.

A pair of pink silk dancing shoes, almost like ballet slippers. Pretty things, with a delicate rhinestone-studded strap across the ankles. Quite lovely.

Except that they were slashed to ribbons. Gutted down to the leather soles.

Cathryn stood over the stove in Paige's tiny kitchen, heating a can of soup. She had to get some nourishment into her friend—she only wished she could've found something other than tomato soup on the pantry shelf.

It bore too close a resemblance to gazpacho, brought too blatant a reminder of the vengeance hovering over Paige's head.

It looked too much like blood.

She felt protective toward Paige, acknowledging a growing determination to find out who was terrorizing her old roommate and putting a stop to it. After finding the ruined shoes, she'd walked Paige back to the apartment, insisting that Anita and her husband stay at the restaurant and enjoy their dinner.

Cathryn finished heating the soup and poured it, steaming, into a mug, adding a splash of milk to mitigate the redness of it. Paige accepted the mug and sat warming her hands with it, staring blankly at the wall beyond.

"They were my favorite," she murmured.

Cathryn knew she meant the shoes and said nothing.

"I wanted to wear them a couple nights ago and couldn't find them. I decided I must have left them at home, and I wore a pair of black heels instead. I never imagined…"

Sitting beside Paige, Cathryn rested a hand on her friend's shoulder as she sipped the soup, finishing it like an obedient child. Cathryn rinsed the cup in the sink and suggested it was time for bed. Paige didn't object.

Leaving the apartment, Cathryn went down to the first floor and knocked on the door to the property manager's rooms. After several moments, León answered her knock, dressed in pajama pants and a silk robe open to the waist. His chest was covered in curly black hair going gray, like a dusting of talcum powder.

"Is everything okay?" he asked. "Mrs. Morrison was *muy afligida*—very upset this afternoon."

Cathryn regarded him, taking in the dark eyes full of concern. Genuine concern, she thought.

"May I come in?"

"What, now? Like this?" He gestured vaguely toward his state of undress.

She smiled. "My intentions are purely honorable, I assure you."

His olive complexion took on a rosy hue. "I never thought otherwise."

He stepped back and she walked past him down a marble-floored hallway, following the sound of a jazz piano to the salon at the back of the apartment. León followed, gesturing her into a chair and turning the speakers down to a faint tinkling.

"Your English is excellent," she told him, settling into butter-soft leather. "Where did you learn it?"

He shrugged. "Like most of us, I learned it from American movies and television."

Cathryn raised her eyebrows, inviting more, and he laughed.

"Okay, and I spent a couple of years on the beaches of southern California."

"Surfing?"

"What else, dude?"

Now they both laughed. A wooden cutting board with a glass dome sat on the coffee table between them, covering slices of Manchego cheese. He slid it toward her. "Have some," he suggested.

Cathryn waved a declining hand, and he leaned back in his own chair. "What can I do for you, Señora Harcourt?"

She decided to play it straight. "Someone is terrorizing Paige Morrison. I don't know who, or for what purpose, but I intend to find out."

León's brow furrowed, but he didn't seem to doubt her statement. Instead, he said, "You and she—you are old friends?"

"College days."

He nodded, understanding. "Then you must do all you can," he said simply. "What do you need from me?"

"I want to know how you came by that potted plant. Who delivered it?"

"*Vale,* that I can help you with. I know the florist personally, and she delivered it herself. I will ask her tomorrow."

Cathryn hesitated. "Can you ask her tonight?"

He rolled his eyes, pinning her with a wry gaze.

Leaning forward, Cathryn reminded him, "You said—very correctly, I might add—that I should do all I can."

Sighing, he pulled a mobile phone from the pocket of his robe and dialed a number. He spoke for a moment in rapid Spanish, then turned to Cathryn.

"She arrived at her shop this morning to find an envelope with a request for the plant to be delivered here to Mrs. Morrison, and the cash to pay for it."

Cathryn said, "What was the signature on the note?"

He relayed the question and shook his head. "No signature. Anything else?"

Cathryn lifted a shoulder. "Not right now. Please thank her for me."

"*Por supuesto.*"

Riding the elevator up to the seventh floor, Cathryn thought about the ragged bits of information she was gathering. It felt like the beginning of something, like when her first plot ideas came to mind, floating and formless until she shaped them into a cohesive story.

She hoped she could coax the true shape of things from what she was learning and find an end to this nightmare for her friend.

Back in her own apartment, she undressed and slid beneath the sheets, tired and still hungry. Regretting the loss of a fine steak dinner, she dreamed about it as she drifted off to sleep.

And woke an hour later to thunderous pounding at her door.

Cathryn pulled on a pair of sweatpants, wriggling into a T-shirt as she hurried to answer the frantic hammering. Paige stood in the corridor, her gray-blonde hair a tangled mess, dark shadows and creases beneath her eyes.

All of it punctuated by the reddening three-pronged scratch across her left cheek.

"She was there, Cathryn! Watching me while I slept."

Cathryn led her to the sofa, snagging the little first aid kit she kept in a drawer of the end table. Little beads of blood were oozing from the scratch and the skin around it was inflamed. Paige hugged herself, shivering, while Cathryn dabbed antiseptic over the wound.

"I heard someone whisper my name, right next to my ear. I felt her breath." Paige's voice cracked and trembled, like a warped and scratchy vinyl record. "I woke up and she was standing over me."

"Did you see her face?" Cathryn asked.

Paige closed her eyes. "No. It was hidden in shadows. Or maybe she was wearing a mask. I couldn't see. I was frozen in terror, and there was a peculiar smell in the air that somehow made everything more frightening."

Cathryn squeezed her friend's shoulder. "I'm so sorry, Paige. Can you describe the smell? Was it perfume?"

Paige shook her head. "I don't know what it was." She sniffed and her voice grew husky with unshed tears. "She leaned over me and I tried to scream, but I couldn't make a sound."

She broke off, shuddering, then gulped and choked out the rest of the story. "Her long black hair brushed my face, then she slashed me across the cheek and disappeared."

Paige caught at Cathryn's hand, held it tight. "Oh, it was awful! I can't take much more of this, Cathryn. What am I going to do?"

Cathryn kept her voice steady, her tone matter-of-fact. "I'm going to call the police."

Paige bit her lip. "Please don't," she said. "It's useless. I called them last week when I thought I saw someone on the balcony, trying to get in. They investigated and found nothing out of place."

"Well now—unfortunately—there's a little more for them to work with. This scratch across your face, for instance."

Paige still held her hand and Cathryn felt the trembling in her fingers. "Please don't call them. They think I'm loony. My Spanish isn't very good, but I know *poco loco* when I hear it. They won't take me seriously."

"*I'm* taking you seriously. Give me the key to your place. I'll investigate."

"No, Cathryn. Not tonight," Paige pleaded. "Let me stay here, and please don't leave me alone."

"I won't. I promise."

Cathryn tucked Paige into her own bed and curled up on the couch where she had line of sight to both the front door and the balcony slider. As she floated toward sleep, she reflected that she wasn't making much progress on her research project on crime in Andalusia.

Then again, maybe she was.

The click of the front door lock had Cathryn bolting from the couch as watery sunlight trickled in from the balcony. A woman with long dark hair was letting herself into the apartment. Cathryn's heart leapt into her throat until she registered the plastic bucket in the woman's arms, filled with spray bottles, sponges, and brushes of varying size and shape.

It was Wednesday. The maid's day for coming.

"*Buenos dias, Señora.*"

Cathryn released her breath and ran a hand through her hair, smoothing it down. "Good morning, Soledad."

"You sleep on couch? Something wrong with your bed? I fix?"

"*No hay problema,*" Cathryn told her. "I had a friend sleep over. Let's not wake her yet."

"*Vale, Señora.* I start in here."

While Soledad dusted and ran the vacuum cleaner, Cathryn scrambled eggs and made toast. By the time it was ready, Paige had joined her on a bar stool at the counter.

"I prescribe a day in the sun," Cathryn said. "Let's eat breakfast and go to the beach."

The day was fine, the salt air wafting on a gentle breeze as they descended the stairs to an expanse of shadowed sand. Gulls called overhead, their melancholy cries echoing against the rhythmic swell of the waves.

A woman in a blue bikini lay stretched out on an enormous rainbow-striped beach blanket, a shaggy golden retriever at her side. As they drew near, the dog rose, barking, and ran to greet them.

"Elmo!" Paige cried, sinking to a knee to give the dog a vigorous rub down. He wriggled with pleasure, tongue lolling as he followed them back to his mistress. The woman raised up on an elbow and removed her sunglasses, waving a welcoming hand.

"Come on in," she said. "The water's fine."

"How would you know?" Paige teased. "You never actually go in."

"Salt water makes me itchy." Shifting her long, well-tanned legs, the woman rolled into a sitting position and peered at Cathryn with curiosity.

"Kim," Paige said, "meet one of my oldest and dearest friends, Cathryn Harcourt."

Cathryn spread her beach towel out on the sand and Paige did the same. "Kim actually lives here," Paige told her. "Not just vacationing like you and me."

"Really? Cathryn asked. "What brought you to Spain?"

"US Navy," Kim said, waving a hand toward the nearby Naval base. "My husband's a Seabee, on the construction battalion. We're here for a three-year tour."

"Are you enjoying it? Doing any traveling?"

Kim replaced her sunglasses and stretched out on the blanket. "Charlie isn't able to get away much," she said. "But we've been to Morocco and Gibraltar, as well as Seville. They're close enough for day trips."

"Wonderful," Cathryn said. "I hope you'll get a chance to do more. In the meantime, you've got a lovely setup here."

"Mmm," Kim agreed, lifting her face to the sun. Cathryn watched the sweep of dark hair settle around the woman's shoulders. Shifting her gaze, she took in the well-manicured fingernails, long and red, entirely capable of inflicting a nasty scratch on vulnerable skin.

She didn't really think Kim could be Paige's night visitor, but she wasn't ready to rule it out, either. If Jane's sister truly was stalking Paige, intent on revenge, she might be hiding behind any innocent façade.

After a lunch of crusty rolls stuffed with crab salad, bought from a seaside bakery, Cathryn and Paige climbed the stairs, returning to the apartment building for a siesta. While Paige napped, Cathryn made a call back to the States.

Zach Dillinger, a PI she sometimes consulted, would just be starting his workday. After exchanging pleasantries, Cathryn said, "If an investigator, such as yourself, were to dig into a long-ago event, like a juvenile case of vehicular manslaughter, how would he go about it?"

"Is this research for a book, Cathryn?"

She hesitated. "Not initially, although it may spark an idea for a future plot. No, Zach, it's a bit more personal this time. An old friend is in trouble."

She heard him clear his throat. "As you are no doubt aware, juvenile records are sealed," he told her. "But sometimes there are ways around that."

"I'm not after the information in the file. I just want to find out who else might have accessed it."

She gave him Paige's maiden name, the approximate time frame, and any other information she thought might be useful. "I'll do some poking around and get back to you," he told her.

"Thanks, Zach. We'll talk later."

Ending the call, Cathryn peeked in on Paige and found her curled in a ball, gently snoring. Moving quietly, she let herself into the corridor and punched the elevator down button.

This time, when she found León in his daytime office, he was fully and properly dressed in slacks and polo, only a hint of his curly chest hair showing at the open collar. He greeted her with a grin.

"*Hola, Señora.* I am at your service. How can I help?"

Cathryn indicated the open door. "May I?" she asked, pulling it closed at his nod. "I'm sorry to tell you this," she said, sinking into a chair next to his mahogany desk, "but Paige Morrison's situation is getting worse."

"*Qué pasó?* What's happened now?"

She told him about the previous night's events.

"Did you call the police?" he asked.

"Paige preferred not to. She feels they wouldn't take her complaints seriously."

León pursed his lips. "As manager of this building, I could consider their point of view," he said, giving her an apologetic look. "I don't like to think crimes are occurring beneath this roof. Is this not perhaps the result of stress or an overactive imagination?"

Cathryn glowered at him. "Someone raked her across the cheek last night," she pointed out. "I've seen her face and it's no figment of the imagination."

He raised his hands in surrender. "*Vale,* I believe you. What do you suggest we do?"

We. Cathryn felt some comfort in having him come over to her side. She only hoped he would comply with her next request.

"These troubles followed her here from the States," she told him. "Which of your tenants booked their rooms in the days following Paige's arrival?"

He stared at her reproachfully. "I can't just dispense that information," he said. "My tenants have a right to privacy."

They locked eyes for a count of ten before Cathryn sighed. "Will you just verify, then, if any women with long dark hair fit that time frame? Anita Wilson, for example."

"I can at least set your mind at ease on that score. The Wilsons moved in before Paige Morrison's arrival."

"Really?" Cathryn said, surprised. "How long before?"

He shrugged. "A few days, a week." With a sly look, he said, "I will not consult the register on this. I am speaking only as an observant neighbor, you understand."

"I thank you, dear neighbor, for your quick and ready powers of observation." She paused. "And what about Soledad, the cleaning woman you recommended?"

"Soledad! She is the daughter of a close friend," he assured her. "Above reproach."

"That may be, but when did she start cleaning apartments in this building?" Cathryn asked pointedly.

León sighed. "Soledad has been working at another of my properties for more than two years. She transferred here just last week, about the time you arrived," he admitted. "But I am sure this means nothing."

"Did you initiate the transfer?"

He gave her a dark look. "No, it was at her request."

Cathryn rose. "Thank you, León. Can you tell me which apartment she is cleaning now? I need to speak with her."

Deciding to use the stairs, Cathryn climbed to the third floor. León had been reluctant to reveal the number of the apartment where Soledad could be found, but Cathryn had persuaded him with the argument that his friend's daughter must be innocent, as he believed. She might, however, possess information that could help lay this whole thing to rest.

Panting only slightly, Cathryn emerged from the stairwell and started along the corridor. Ahead she saw the sort of cart a bellboy uses to deliver luggage to the upper floors of a hotel. She knew the apartment building kept such a cart in the utility room next to the elevators for tenants to use.

The cart was loaded with bags of groceries and household items and stood next to an open apartment door. As Cathryn passed, she heard a murmur of voices from inside. She'd taken several steps beyond when the voices registered in her memory.

Anita and Gerald Wilson.

Cathryn halted and crept closer to the open door, staying close to the wall. Shamelessly, she strained to hear their conversation.

"...they can go on this bottom shelf," Anita was saying.

"Very well, my darling," Gerald replied, and something more that was lost amid a clattering of pots and pans. Then Cathryn heard, "Don't worry about the canned goods, my sweet Anita Sue—I'll take care of that."

"Way ahead of you." Anita's voice was suddenly loud in the corridor as she dipped forward to grip a bag of canned vegetables and saw Cathryn standing there.

Cathryn quickly assumed a pondering expression. "Sorry," she said. "I didn't mean to snoop, but the labels on those cans caught my eye. I'm not familiar with these Spanish brands. Have you tried that one? Is it any good?"

Anita broke into a smile. "Cathryn! Good to see you. How's Paige? We haven't seen her since...you know, last night at the restaurant. Is she okay?"

"Oh yes, she's quite recovered. Did you and Gerald have a good dinner?"

Anita snorted. "Have you ever had a bad dinner at an Argentinian steakhouse?"

"Come to think of it," Cathryn said, "I have not."

Gerald stepped out into the hallway. "Oh, hello," he said, lifting the bag from his wife's arms. "Did you come to visit?"

"No, I won't bother you. I was just passing by." Hoping to ferret out more information about Anita's movements the night before, she added, "Did you two do anything fun after dinner? Dancing? Moonlit walk on the beach?"

Gerald laughed. "Not a chance! We ate too much, drank too much, and came straight home to sleep it off."

Cathryn flapped a hand toward the cart. "Well, I'll let you get back to it," she said. "See you around."

As she continued down the hallway, she reflected that while Gerald was sleeping off a slew of margaritas, Anita could have crept out without his knowledge. She turned the corner, glad to be out of the Wilsons' sight as she knocked at Apartment 342.

After a moment, the door opened, and Soledad's hesitant face peeked out. "Oh, hello Señora Harcourt. I'm sorry, the Cuadrados are not at home right now."

"That's okay, Soledad. I came to see you."

The hesitation turned to wariness. "Me? *Por qué?*"

"There are some things I would like to ask you."

The maid shook her head, the dark hair tumbling around her shoulders and Cathryn saw the door closing—literally—on this opportunity to question the young woman. She put out a hand, speaking quickly.

"I'll only take a moment of your time. Please," she added. "It's important."

Soledad gave her a stoic glance, squaring her shoulders. "What do you want to know?"

Cathryn wasted no more time. Getting right to the meat of the matter, she asked, "Why did you come here, Soledad? To this building, at this time?"

The woman's chin rose a notch higher. With a touch of defiance, she said, "Why shouldn't I? America is not the only country whose people can do as they please."

Cathryn dipped her head in acknowledgement. "You are right, of course. But something brought you here and now. Will you please tell me?"

The woman's eyes narrowed suspiciously. "Did he send you?"

Cathryn blinked. "He? Who do you mean, Soledad?"

The maid studied her, and Cathryn sensed a shift in her attitude.

"No one sent me, I promise you," she hurried to say. "It was my own idea to seek you out. I have a friend in trouble and I'm trying to help her."

"You have nothing to do with José?" Soledad pressed.

"Nothing," Cathryn assured her. "I know nothing about this José."

The maid's shoulders relaxed, and her face softened. She regarded Cathryn solemnly, her dark eyes huge and strangely haunted. "I came here to get away from José," she admitted. "He does not respect my right to say no. He always wanting and wanting, and never leaving me alone. I had to escape him."

Cathryn nodded sympathetically. "I see. So, you asked for a transfer to this building. To get away from José."

The maid lifted a palm, her expression rueful. "*Cada maestrillo tiene su librillo.* Each of us must do what we think best."

"*La verdad,*" Cathryn agreed. "I wish you success. Thank you for telling me, Soledad. *Adios.*"

Back in the stairwell, Cathryn finished her climb to the seventh floor just as the phone in her pocket jingled. Pausing to catch her breath, she tapped to accept the call and greeted her PI contact.

"Zach, how's it going?"

"Good, Cathryn. I managed to unearth some information for you."

"Wonderful. Let's have it."

"I called the local courthouse, but the cagey clerk wouldn't give me anything. So I contacted an associate who lives in the area and he agreed to go in person and see what he could dig up. Turns out a woman calling herself Susan Fleming attempted several times to access the juvie file, claiming she was the sister of the deceased and had a right to know what happened."

"Susan Fleming? Paige did mention a sister named Susan. Was she granted access?"

"Officially, no. But my associate questioned the clerk in charge during this Susan woman's last visit. He suspects money might have changed hands for a peek at the file."

"I see," Cathryn said. "Thank you, Zach. Send me a bill for your time and give my thanks to your associate."

Cathryn entered her apartment and went to the glass slider overlooking the beach. She gazed out at the distant horizon where the setting sun spread a copper mantle over the shifting water, turning it into a molten sea, matching the ideas in her brain.

She thought about the women she'd met over the last two days who fit the age range of the dead girl's sister and the physical description of Paige's attacker.

Despite Soledad's long dark hair and access to the building's apartments, Cathryn crossed her off the list as being too young.

And she had no discernible motive for terrorizing a middle-aged American tourist.

That left Kim, Paige's friend from the beach. She had the requisite hairstyle and a set of claws capable of inflicting the sort of wound marring Paige's cheek. She could conceivably be the sister in question, befriending Paige on the beach for reasons of her own.

Anita Wilson fit the bill, as well. And probably a dozen more women in the vicinity.

Who, if any of them, was tormenting her old college roommate?

And why?

Cathryn slept late the next morning. She'd looked in on Paige the night before and found her friend white-faced and distraught. Paige had gratefully accepted Cathryn's offer to sleep on the couch, to be on hand if anything else occurred.

The couch was long enough, and the pillow and blanket Paige provided were comfortable. But Cathryn woke with the sort of crick in her neck that would be with her all day. As she sat massaging the muscles in her shoulders, she heard the flush of a toilet and seconds later, Paige padded into the living room.

"Good morning," Cathryn said. "Did you sleep okay?"

"Yes, fine."

The dark shadows beneath Paige's eyes said otherwise, but Cathryn didn't challenge her on it. Instead, she asked, "What are your plans for the day?"

Paige walked to the balcony slider and pressed the button to raise the heavy persiana shades, letting the weak morning sun dribble into the room. The day was overcast, gray-tinted clouds roiling in the distance, seagulls winging in the foreground, their plaintive cries faintly audible through the glass.

"I wanted to go to the gypsy market and look for those little—"

She broke off with a strangled gasp, standing frozen at the window, her face twisting in anguish. Cathryn jumped from the sofa and dashed to her friend's side. The balcony afforded a spectacular view of the beach, a wide swath of pale brown sand stretching out beneath, waves creaming up along the edge.

And written in large block letters on the slate of sand, it said:

I AM JANE.

"That's it," Cathryn said. "Enough of this nonsense. We are getting to the bottom of this. Today."

She put an arm around Paige and led her to the sofa, wrapping the blanket, still warm from her own body, around her friend.

"Let's get some breakfast," she continued. "And then I am going to talk to all the women on my suspect list, starting with…"

A sudden memory flashed across her mind, raising a flag that suggested here was something she needed to pay attention to. Focusing, she tried to hone in on the thought that fluttered at the edge of consciousness. She recalled the snippet of inconsequential conversation she'd heard yesterday while passing the Wilson's apartment.

Anita Sue. Gerald had called his wife sweet Anita Sue. Could Anita be the Susan she was looking for?

"My first stop will be the Wilsons," she announced.

Paige's stricken eyes grew wider. "Anita? No, Cathryn. She was already here when I arrived. They didn't follow me."

"Someone keeping close tabs on you, as it seems Susan is doing, would know your plans and act accordingly, staying a step ahead."

Paige shuddered. "I can't endure much more of this."

"And you won't have to," Cathryn assured her.

After a hasty omelet, Cathryn and Paige took the elevator down to the third floor and knocked at the Wilsons' apartment. After several moments, Cathryn tried again, but no one came to answer her knock.

"Let's try the beach," Paige suggested.

"Good idea. We might find Kim there as well."

"Kim? You suspect her, too?"

"Right now, I suspect everyone."

As they hurried along the sidewalk, Cathryn spotted Gerald Wilson strolling the promenade, puffing on his pipe. They rushed to meet him.

"Good morning, Gerald," Cathryn said. "Where's Anita?"

"Back at the apartment. She's not feeling well today."

"We stopped by the apartment," Paige said. "No one answered."

"She was probably sleeping. She pulled the persianas in the bedroom before I left. Is there something I can help you with?"

"Maybe," Cathryn replied. "Did Anita have a sister named Jane?"

Gerald stopped walking, his eyes wide and startled. "No, you're not going to talk to Anita about Jane," he said decisively. "That would be far too upsetting for her. Jane died years ago, and Anita doesn't like to remember it. She never even told me about her sister's death until after we were married."

"How long have you been married?" Cathryn asked.

"We just celebrated our first anniversary last month."

Cathryn heard a faint whimper from Paige and noticed her old roommate was hugging herself, her face a mask of misery. She looked like a piece of china about to break.

Making her voice firm, Cathryn said, "Gerald, we need to speak with Anita right away. I don't want to distress her, but it can't be helped."

"I don't like this," he grumbled, putting out his pipe. "But I'll see if she's willing to speak with you."

As they walked, Cathryn put her arm around Paige. "Are you all right?" she asked, feeling the tremors in her friend's fragile bones.

"No," Paige said. "I have a dreadful feeling. A sense of doom. I feel it in the air."

Gerald let them into the apartment and motioned them onto the sofa before disappearing down the hall. A moment later, Cathryn heard an anguished cry.

"No! Oh, no. Please, no."

She rushed to the bedroom, stopping behind Gerald's petrified form. Over his shoulder, she saw Anita Wilson sprawled on the bed, an empty pill bottle by her side. Pushing Gerald gently aside, she felt for a pulse but knew by the frozen rictus on Anita's face that the woman had passed beyond any help she could offer.

In the dim light seeping in through the chinks in the shades, Cathryn saw something clutched in the dead woman's hand. Without touching anything, she bent to peer closer. It was a photograph of two young girls together, laughing in the sunshine.

And on the back of the photo, she could make out a single word.

The name Jane.

Cathryn watched the last rays of sun streak across the ocean and melt into darkness as she stood at the window in Paige's apartment. Paige sat curled in a chair, her feet drawn up, arms locked around her knees, silent and shell-shocked. Gerald slumped on the sofa, hands splayed on either side, palms up, his face blank, eyes staring.

All three of them jumped when a sudden loud knock sounded at the door. Cathryn went to answer it, admitting a pair of blue-uniformed members of the Policía Local. Both held their hats in hand as they entered, solemn-faced, and expressed their condolences.

Cathryn, Paige, and Gerald had already given their statements at the scene before retiring to Paige's apartment to commiserate and wait for what came next. The older officer, a slim gray-haired man with an impressive Roman nose, approached Gerald and spoke in a soft, melodious voice.

"I apologize for intruding at such a time like this," he said. "But I must clear off a few matters before we can proceed any further. Is okay?"

Cathryn saw the Adam's apple bob in Gerald's throat as he swallowed. "My wife," he said, his voice coming out in a croak. "I didn't know, I didn't think she would…"

His words trailed off and he swallowed hard again. The officer held out the photograph, bent and crumpled, that had been clutched in Anita's hand. It was encased in a sheet of plastic, but the handwriting on the back was clearly visible now.

Summerhill, Susan and Jane.

"The girls in the photo?" prompted the officer. "Your wife, and...?"

"Her sister, Jane. She was killed decades ago by an out-of-control teenage driver. Anita never got over it and recently she's been...brooding on it. But I never imagined she would harm herself. I didn't realize how badly it was affecting her. It happened so long ago."

"These things catch up when someone is already depressed," the officer said. "Everything stacks up together. *Entiende?*"

Gerald sank his head into his hands. "Yes, I understand," he murmured. "I just wish I'd done something to help."

"Do not blame yourself. We found a box of old pictures similar to this one." He turned to Paige. "As well as several recent photos of you." He paused. "With red X's marked across them. Do you know why this may be?"

Paige's answer was so muted that Cathryn barely heard her say, "Because I killed her."

The officer frowned. "Are you confessing to murdering Mrs. Wilson?"

"No!" Paige burst out, her pale face going red. "I was the out-of-control teenage driver. I think Anita wanted to kill *me*." She choked back a sob. "And I don't blame her!"

Gerald stared, speechless. Cathryn went to her friend huddled in the chair and bent to put an arm around her. She'd caught a glimpse of that box of photos. An open shoebox on the bed beside Anita's body. She'd seen those red crosses.

And she'd seen something else she'd like to get a closer look at.

A sheet of pink paper printed with wedding bells at the top and a scrawl of writing down the page. She'd be willing to bet Gerald and Anita had written their own wedding vows and that the pink paper contained Anita's composition.

And that the blue paper behind it held Gerald's own vows.

An awkward silence fell in the room, broken only by a periodic sniffle from Paige. The officer in charge made a slight bow from the waist.

"It should not take long to wrap this up," he said. "Again, I apologize for the intrusion and I'm so sorry for your loss."

The officers departed and Gerald let out a long, mournful sigh. He looked at Paige. "I don't hold you responsible for Anita's death. She clearly had mental issues I didn't know about."

Paige gulped, looking small and miserable. "I'm so sorry."

Gerald made a brushing motion with his hands, as if to push the whole thing from his sight. "I'm glad to hear they'll soon close the case," he said. "I'm ready to go home."

"Yes," Cathryn said. "Once they find the private detective and confirm the details, I'm sure they'll complete the file and let you leave the country."

"Private detective? You've lost me, Cathryn. What are you talking about?"

"Anita would have needed help to discover the identity and current whereabouts of the woman she held responsible for her sister's death." She paused, watching Gerald closely. "You arrived here a week or so before Paige—how did that come about?"

Gerald seemed at a loss for words. Finally, he said, "I don't even remember. We were in the south of France and suddenly Anita said she didn't want to be there anymore. She suggested Spain, she made the arrangements, and...we came."

Cathryn nodded. "She must have received word from her PI, letting her know where to find Paige."

"No," Gerald said, anger tinging his voice. "We got here first. Paige came after."

"Yes, but...Paige, how much time passed between when you booked this apartment and when you actually arrived here?"

Paige had unspooled from her curled up position. She stared at Cathryn, puzzlement in her eyes. "I had to wait almost two weeks for all the arrangements to come together," she explained.

"Plenty of time for Anita's investigator to discover your plans and pass on that information. And then," Cathryn added, "someone must have helped her write those poems."

"What poems?" Gerald asked. His face had grown florid, his brow creased.

"Paige, do you still have those poems Anita left for you? Your wife," she said to Gerald, "has been terrorizing Paige for some time now." She raised her eyebrows. "You knew nothing about it?"

"Nothing."

Paige left the room and came back moments later, holding a plastic bag containing several cards computer-printed with the poetic verses. Gerald glanced at them and gave an aggrieved shrug.

"If, as you say, Anita wrote those poems, I'm sure she composed them herself. She was quite an eloquent writer, you know. And now, if you'll excuse me, León has prepared a room for me to stay in until this miserable business is over."

He left the apartment, shutting the door a little more firmly than necessary. Cathryn watched his exit, her gaze fixed on the door long after he was gone.

"I'm sorry for bringing you into this Cathryn, and ruining your vacation," Paige said.

"I'm not on vacation," Cathryn replied. "I'm doing research, and you've helped me immensely. You have nothing to apologize for."

Paige gave her a bitter smile. "I have a mountain of a mess to apologize for. A woman just committed suicide over something I did. It's just so...sad."

"I disagree," Cathryn said. "Sad is not the word. It's wicked. Anita Wilson did not kill herself. She was murdered."

"What! Oh, Cathryn—what are you saying?"

"I'm saying Gerald Wilson murdered his wife. I just need to find a way to prove it."

Later that evening, Cathryn let herself out of Paige's apartment and made her way down to the fifth floor. She'd been busy in the interim—talking, determining, arranging. Once more, she'd prevailed upon León for information, and after a few half-hearted sputters of protest, he'd told her where to find Gerald.

Reaching the apartment, she raised her fist and gave an authoritative knock. Gerald opened the door, his questioning face turning hostile when he saw who'd come calling.

"What do you want?" he growled.

Cathryn eyed him levelly. "I want to let you know that I'm going to the police first thing in the morning. I plan to tell them everything I know."

Gerald gave a derisive snort. "What could you know? We met you only two days ago. My Anita was alive, and now she's dead. I don't think I want to hear anything you have to say."

"You may want to listen to this," Cathryn warned. "I'm a writer, Mr. Wilson. I know that a person's style of writing is distinctive. Not as definitive as a fingerprint, perhaps, but a style analyst will easily determine that the woman who wrote those wedding vows in the box taken by the police is not the same person who wrote the notes and poems to Paige."

Gerald's eyes narrowed, but he said nothing.

"Anita told me herself that she couldn't string a decent sentence together unless it was written in code and executed a command," Cathryn continued. "I'm willing to bet an analyst, comparing those poems to the wedding vows you wrote—also in the box held by the police—would conclude it was you who wrote those poems."

Gerald's lips curled in a nasty grin. "That's thin, Cathryn. Really. I doubt it would hold up in a court of law."

"Maybe you're right," Cathryn agreed. "But when the police speak with the PI you hired to find the driver responsible for Jane's death, I believe the pieces will start adding up to something more substantial."

Eyes smoldering, Gerald moved to slam the door, but Cathryn planted her foot in the way.

"You are an evil man, Gerald Wilson. You married Anita for her money, planning all along to find a way to get rid of her. When she told you about her sister's tragic death, she handed you the key to her own demise. You made it look like Anita was deranged and out for revenge. And when she couldn't stand the pain any longer, she killed herself."

"Apparently that's what happened," Gerald said, his eyes taunting her. "And you can't prove otherwise."

"I won't have to. You're not as clever as you think you are. I'm sure you left plenty of indicators behind."

"Such as?"

Cathryn shrugged. "Perhaps strands of hair from that wig you wore when you attacked Paige in her bedroom. Or traces of your Turkish tobacco in the wound you left on her face. It's just a matter of time before the pieces fall into place and you're arrested for the murder of your wife."

"You're crazy!" Gerald snarled.

Cathryn removed her foot from the doorframe. "Goodnight, Mr. Wilson."

Turning, she walked down the corridor, keeping her pace even and unhurried, showing she wasn't afraid.

But she was.

Her heart pounded painfully inside her chest and her palms, clammy with sweat, shook like leaves in a windstorm. When she turned the knob on the stairwell door, her hand slipped, and she had to tighten her grip.

Glancing back, she saw no one. The hour was late, and the hallway was deserted. Her footsteps echoed eerily in the barren chamber of the stairwell as she walked to the top of the marble staircase and stood looking down, breathing deeply to calm herself.

She stood motionless, staring down the long flight of hard stone and listening hard. After a moment, she heard it—the metallic click of the door opening behind her, the padding of soft-soled shoes. The hairs on the back of her neck rose like tiny sensors as she felt the presence of another person at her back.

"You shouldn't have meddled, Cathryn. Without you sticking your nose in, this all would have worked like a charm."

Cathryn braced herself, felt the rough hands grip her shoulders. But she was ready for it. Crouching down, she clutched the banister rail and held on tight. She heard a scuffle and shout behind her as the two police officers grabbed Gerald and pulled him off her.

León helped her to her feet and wrapped his arms around her, steadying her.

"*Ay, caramba!*" He spoke the words against her hair. "Are you okay?"

"I'm perfectly fine, León. You needn't hold on to me so tightly."

He grinned. "My intentions are purely honorable, I assure you."

Cathryn felt her face go red. She laughed.

"I never thought otherwise."

The next morning, Cathryn walked once again with Paige on the cool sand of the beach. The sun shone lemony yellow up on the promenade, its rays yet to reach and warm the stretch of shingle rimming the murmuring waves.

A freshening breeze carried the smell of salt and seaweed, reminding Cathryn of something that had danced at the edge of her awareness ever since they'd accosted Gerald on the promenade above.

"Do you remember how you felt that sense of doom yesterday?" she asked Paige. "Right before we went up and found Anita?"

Paige shivered. "I'll never forget it."

"I think I know why you felt that way."

Paige gave her a sidelong glance. "Are you trying to tell me I'm clairvoyant?"

Cathryn smiled. "No, something much simpler than that." She paused. "You smelled trouble."

Paige wrinkled her brow. "So, I'm a bloodhound?"

"No. Gerald was smoking his Turkish tobacco when we encountered him. I believe you smelled that same odor on him while he was leaning over you in a wig and nightgown."

Paige gasped. "You're right! Now that you say that, I can smell it again and it brings back that sense of terror." She let out a long breath and patted herself on the chest. "You have no idea how much better I feel now, Cathryn. Thank you so much for rooting out my demons."

Cathryn heard a shout and looked up to see León loping toward them, kicking up sand in his wake.

"I wanted you to know," he said when he reached them. "When the police hinted that you had a recording of your conversation with him last night, Gerald made a full confession. He'll be extradited and tried in the U.S. for first degree murder. And thanks to you, Cathryn, the prosecutor ought to be able to make the charges stick."

Paige nodded her head vigorously. "Fantastic!"

Cathryn gazed out over the blue-green horizon, hazy with mist, and pondered the fate of Gerald Wilson and others like him. She shivered.

"So callous," she said. "So calculated. He'd planned it for months, knowing Anita had to die in a way that would make him appear blameless. He hired and bribed and cajoled his plan into action, all the while playing the adoring husband. That's cold!"

Paige hooked an arm in hers. "Colder than gazpacho," she agreed.

León turned, peering up at the apartment building looming above them. "Sadly, I've got to get back to my desk, ladies. I'll see you later."

Cathryn watched him retreat across the sand, the backs of his calves brown and well-muscled, covered in curly dark hairs. To match the rest of him.

"Ugh," Paige grimaced. "Let's talk about something cheerier. I'm glad my Walter left me with a lot of good memories. I can think of him with sincere fondness. Right to the end."

"Same goes for my Ryan," Cathryn added. "Here's to good husbands. Not perfect men, but good men who tried hard and lived well." She paused. "I still miss mine so much."

"Me too," Paige said. "Terribly sometimes."

Cathryn let her gaze wander once more to the far horizon, the farthest point before the sea dipped out of view and the unknown began.

"Times like these," she agreed.

Author's Note

A Study in Cashmere

I wrote "A Study in Cashmere" for a literary competition during the summer of 2020. The world, at that time, was deep in the midst of the Covid crisis. It touched all our lives in many ways and set the scene for this twisted little story.

"Cashmere" won second prize in the Short Fiction Break Summer Writing Contest and was first published in their online venue, July 2020.

It's short, and that's good because it's a long way from sweet.

A Study in Cashmere

I've wanted to do this for so long.

Gordon stood in front of the open hall closet, running his hand across the row of hanging coats, feeling their different textures beneath his fingertips. Scratchy wool, smooth poplin, the slippery impervious surface of a rain slicker. So many coats. Why did one woman need so many?

He removed his own charcoal-gray dress coat—his only dress coat—and shrugged into it, replacing the sturdy wooden hanger. From upstairs, he heard the click of the bathroom door, the ventilation fan firing up like a helicopter engine.

She was awake.

Gordon stared at the pile of scarves on the upper shelf of the closet. The faint smell of mothballs floated out at him, reminiscent of those sickly-smelling tablets he sometimes saw in the bottom of urinals. He wrinkled his nose.

The time was right, he recognized that. Before, there had always been something going on, getting in the way—deliveries, neighborhood commotion, Mabel's friends popping in unannounced. Now, thanks to Covid-19 and social distancing, he had a blessed respite from all that.

It was time to act.

He selected the scarlet cashmere, pleased with the aptness of his choice. Red was a power color. He'd be using the scarf to reassert power in a situation where he'd lost control. Red was the color of blood, of passion, desire. All appropriate to his situation. And red was her favorite.

He savored the irony in that.

Upstairs, the fan switched off. Gordon stuffed the cashmere scarf into his coat pocket, picked up his messenger bag, and let himself out the front door, pulling it quietly closed behind him. He didn't want to see Mabel's disheveled hair, her smeary bedroom eyes or the pillow creases in her sallow cheeks. He didn't want to speak to her before he left for work.

Plenty of time for that when he got home.

Gordon was one of the lucky ones. Only a handful of the agency's employees were allowed to come in to the office. Most worked from home now, deprived of the daily escape from their cloying family lives. Gordon didn't believe any man was truly happy in the shackled, society-mandated condition of marriage.

He hung his coat on the rack beside his desk. Once upon a time, he'd subscribed to the idea of wedded bliss, but life with Mabel had pulled back the curtain on that myth. Before they'd even reached their first anniversary, she'd scoured most of the rose-colored tint from Gordon's expectations.

Reaching into his pocket, he stroked the velvety cashmere of the scarf. It had a calming effect on him. He was still getting used to the hush of the office. No clients, no Muzak, no background murmuring of a business in swing. Movement caught his eye and he looked across the top of the cubicles, seeing the back of the vice president of marketing as he disappeared into his inner sanctum.

No one else was in sight.

Gordon pulled the scarf from his coat pocket and sat with it in his lap while he did his work, feeling its warmth and gentle weight, occasionally running a finger along the fine weave of the fabric. It thrilled him to think about what he'd be doing with the scarf later that night.

Opportunity had presented itself, and Gordon was not going to let it pass unheeded. Even the dreaded weekly visits from his sister, Della, had ceased and there would never be a better time.

The enforced isolation brought by the Corona virus would give him the privacy he needed to carry out the act, and an uninterrupted interval in which to dispose of the body. With the luxury of time and social seclusion, he could free himself from Mabel with the reasonable assurance of continuing that freedom, unhindered by force of law.

It was practically a license to kill.

Gordon finished a report, printed a hard copy, and filed it in the proper folder, letting the credenza drawer slide shut. The metallic click echoed in the empty space like a gunshot, but no one complained. Gordon liked the decisive, defiant sound of it. He reopened the drawer and gave it a shove.

Bam!

He'd considered using a gun, but the cashmere scarf was a far more elegant solution. As the day passed, Gordon thought constantly about his plan. He'd glimpsed the credit card bill from Veronica's Secret and knew Mabel would have "a surprise" for him when he got home. She was nothing if not predictable in her futile attempts to put the bloom back on the rose.

She'd be cooking what she deemed a romantic dinner, wine chilling on the sideboard. She'd have something to chat on about, a topic she'd read up on or google-searched, designed to catch his interest and impress him with her cleverness. She'd be utterly thrilled when he stepped close and put his hands on her.

Gordon wondered at what point she'd stop being thrilled.

The days were getting longer now, blue-gray light stretching into the hour it took for Gordon's drive home, and beyond. He parked the car in the driveway, made sure the locks chirped when he clicked the button, and walked up the stone path to the front door, kicking at a few stray lumps of bark mulch. Mabel's daffodils were fading, their golden days over, petals drooping on spent stems.

Gordon stopped on the porch. Once more, he put a hand in his pocket, touching the scarlet cashmere like a talisman, smiling to himself to tamp down a small wave of uncertainty. There would be no better time.

The rich aroma of beef stroganoff, Mabel's specialty, greeted him as he opened the door. He came straight into the kitchen.

"How was your day?" Mabel asked, offering her cheek.

He ignored the offer and grunted, unwilling to tip her off with any uncharacteristic behavior. Putting his bag down on a chair, he looked around the kitchen. The slender neck of his favorite Cabernet protruded from the ice bucket next to a crystal plate displaying a frosted cake adorned with curls of chocolate.

"I have a surprise for you," Mabel said, the girlish lilt in her voice irritating him.

"I can see that."

"Oh, but there's more, sweetheart." She turned from the stove and raised her eyebrow in a provocative leer. "Just wait and see."

He was done waiting. Gordon stepped behind her, noting the glossy flow of her honey-blonde hair, remembering how it had once seemed that all his problems would melt away if only he could stroke that hair and call it his.

A cruel illusion that would end now, once and for all.

Pulling the scarf from his pocket, he wrapped it quickly around her neck, pulling the ends tight. Mabel's startled cry choked off, bubbling like the pot of creamy stroganoff on the stove. She dropped the spoon, spattering hot droplets of sour cream sauce across Gordon's hands and the scarlet cashmere scarf.

Her fingers clawed at his, nails gouging his flesh, leaving red half-moon marks on his skin. The strawberry scent of her shampoo clogged Gordon's nostrils, turning his stomach as the gagging sounds she made faded and rasped away into silence.

Gordon held tight to the scarf, knotted in both fists, cashmere biting into the raw flesh of his hands. His breath came in rapid gulps and as he relaxed his grip, his wife's body slumped down and away, sagging to the floor with a resounding thump.

Gordon knelt to unwind the scarf from her neck, his hands shaking.

He'd done it.

He was free.

Before he had even a moment to savor the solitude, he heard a sound from the back room that sent his heart racing.

Footsteps.

"I know you told me to wait, Mabel."

The voice grew louder as it approached the kitchen. "But are you sure you wouldn't like some help?"

Della.

Gordon watched the shock register in his sister's face as she entered the room and took in the sight of him crouched over Mabel's body, the red scarf in his hands trailing away like a river of blood.

Mabel's treacherous surprise.

AUTHOR'S NOTE

THE WOLF & LAMB

"The Wolf & Lamb" represents the silver lining in a black cloud for me. I was invited to write the story for a particular team of editors and I was crushed when they said they didn't want to include it in their anthology after all.

So, I submitted it to my all-time favorite mystery magazine, *Alfred Hitchcock's,* and editor Linda Landrigan not only bought "The Wolf & Lamb," but made it the cover story for the May/June 2020 issue.

This was my first time being published in *AHMM* and it fulfilled a life-long dream. I'm delighted to say that I have since had a number of stories published in the magazine, a trend I hope will continue for many years.

Fair warning: "The Wolf & Lamb" is a Jack the Ripper story. It does not, however, go into graphic detail, focusing instead on how the events during that time impacted a naive young orphan newly arrived in Whitechapel to work at her uncle's pub.

The truth about what became of The Ripper remains a mystery to this day. No one really knows why he suddenly dropped off the map, though all can agree it wasn't a moment too soon.

If you enjoy suspenseful mysteries set against a historical backdrop, why not check out my Historic Suspense series?

For now, settle in and take a step back in time to the streets of London and the days of a courageous young girl's life in The Wolf & Lamb.

THE WOLF & LAMB

LONDON, SEPTEMBER 1888

J ennet stirred as fingers of watery sunlight poked through the grimed glass of the bedroom window to tease at her eyelids. Consciousness arrived and, with it, a sense of dread. She sat up, clutching the blanket to her chest, and listened to the flurried footsteps and raised voices. A yearning enveloped her, so sharp and strong that it knocked the breath from her lungs, and she wrestled it down. It was no use wishing none of this had happened, that her father had not died, that she'd not been transported to the filthiest part of London, that a madman wasn't killing women in the streets.

She rose, shivering in the morning air, and splashed her face with chill water, ignoring the greasy sliver of soap that smelled of rancid fat. She slipped into her green-sprigged morning frock, grateful that she could still dress as befitted a parson's daughter. For a while, anyway. When these clothes were worn to rags, she was afraid there would be no money to replace them. The advertisements she'd answered to serve as a ladies' maid or governess had so far come to nothing, and it seemed she must work as a barmaid at her uncle's Whitechapel inn far longer than she had hoped.

She tugged a brush through her dark hair, remembering how her father had laughed over her unruly curls.

"You are a fine, obedient daughter. It's no fault of yours that your head hosts a nest of rebellious curls. That was your mother's doing, though she was a good Christian woman, God rest her soul."

Jennet pushed the memory from her mind and swallowed the lump of self-pity. Life had dealt her a new hand, and she must play it to the best of her ability. Her father had not raised a milquetoast daughter. As she bent to lace her boots, a pounding came at the door and her Uncle Smither's voice bellowed through the thin walls.

"The bar's half full already, though it be morning still, so get a move on. There's a crowd of constables and committee men needing a stiff belt after the night's events."

Jennet ran to catch him as he started down the stairs. "What's happened now? Another woman dead?"

"Aye, and worse. Two this time, a double event, they're calling it."

Jennet followed his broad back down to the barroom of *The Wolf & Lamb*. Her stomach shimmied and swam inside her, and it was just as well there was no time for breakfast, for she couldn't have swallowed even the crust of bread that had become her usual morning's fare. In the bar, a beer haze was already rising, and the fresh-strewn sawdust was swirled through with footprints. Half the room's tables were occupied—constables to the left, committee men to the right, with a gaggle of working girls huddled between, their faces haggard, eyes wide with trepidation.

"I thinks you boys should pay for our drinks," said one of the women, raising her mug into the air and thrusting out her chin. "A girl can't do business in the streets these days, and you lot have been bloody useless."

"Here, Wendy, that's not fair," protested a burly, ginger-haired constable. "We've tripled our patrols. We're doing all we can. The Ripper is an audacious blighter!"

"He's got guts, I'll give him that," piped up a man from the Vigilance Committee. Groans and growls of protest buffeted him into silence.

"Your joke is in poor taste, Bill, but your point is well-made," a grizzled veteran of the constable force spoke into the strained hush. "This killer is bold, determined to have his fun and take his prize. He was interrupted before he could properly carve into poor Long Liz, and less than an hour later, he takes down Kate so's he can finish the job."

"Louis, here, is the one who interrupted him and saved Lizzie's skin," said a committee member, motioning to the steward from the Worker's Club.

"I saved her skin, but not her neck. He heard me coming, and slashed her ear to ear so she couldn't scream out."

"How'd it happen, Lou?"

"I drove my cart and pony into Dutfield's yard, and ole Bobtail shies up with a whinny. He doesn't want to go in. The gaslight was out and I had to light a match to see my way round. Rather wish I hadn't done. The blood was still flowing from the gash in her neck and I could feel him there in the dark, watching me."

"Did you see him?"

"Nay, and I didn't want to. If I'd lifted the flame his way, I'd a seen the devil staring back at me. Fair raised the hair on the back of my neck, and make no mistake. I know what it feels like to stand in the presence of evil."

Murder was no newcomer to the streets of Whitechapel. In the few months since Jennet's arrival, she'd grown almost used to hearing of the atrocities that were daily reported in the poverty-stricken east end of London. She was only glad that her gentle father had not lived to see her in such circumstances. Yet, if he was still living, she wouldn't be here at all, but back in their Yorkshire village where her father served as parson and she, as his assistant.

The illness which had taken him had been swift, and she was thankful for the mercy in that. But she was unprepared for the equal swiftness with which her father's replacement had turned her out, and she'd been forced to seek out her only living relative, her mother's brother, Uncle Smither. He'd taken her in gladly enough, seeing her as an able-bodied serving girl, fit to shift trays of beer and spirits and clean the rooms for let on the upper floor, as she was doing now. Though to give him his due, he'd been kind to her, and as generous as his circumstances allowed.

There was little soap or time for laundry. Unless the sheets were noticeably filthy, she'd been told to shake them out and make up the beds. The folk who stayed in these rooms were a slovenly lot, and the floors were scattered with debris and scummed with all manner of muck—spilled beer, spattered tobacco spittle, and worse. It was an unlovely job and Jennet deplored doing it, but she'd a thousand times rather be a scrubbing and serving girl, working on her feet, than a strumpet, working on her back, as so many of the women in Whitechapel seemed to be.

The frankness with which these women hawked their wares continued to shock and distress the parson's daughter. No older than her, some of them, and yet their lives and experience were so vastly dissimilar that Jennet classed them as different creatures, distinct from her own kind. She watched them with revulsion, appalled at their dress and behavior, unutterably mortified to see them leaving, arm in arm, with a paying customer.

Many a night, after her prayers were said, she squirmed in bed, trying to shut her ears to the noises on the other side of the thin walls, her face hot with shame for the degeneracy that surrounded her. She adopted the habit of drifting to sleep by remembering her father's sermons, strengthening her embrace of the principles he'd taught, renewing her determination to remain untainted.

That last day of September 1888, the day Jack The Ripper killed two prostitutes less than a mile from her home, Jennet hoisted drinks and wiped tables for many hours. At the end of the day, she lay exhausted in bed, a pillow pressed over her head to blunt the sounds of the night, and thought about her father's last sermon. The text had been based on Proverbs 31:10. "Who can find a virtuous woman? For her price is far above rubies."

Another night in the barroom, and business was booming. Hearty talk and shouts of laughter floated above the yeasty atmosphere, and a hurdy gurdy sounded from the drafty corner near the door, cranked by a shabbily dressed widow with a cup set out for coins. The woman's smile was faint and sad, her eyes distant and almost gone. Jennet felt a kinship with her. They were both bereft and struggling to maintain some sense of gentility amidst the squalor of their situation.

After the Ripper's double event, the night streets of Whitechapel had been near deserted. Women were careful to get indoors before sundown and men avoided walking in the streets after dark as that made them a target for police questioning. Custom at the pubs and in the streets was slow, and her uncle's face was grim as he counted out the takings at day's end.

Three weeks had passed, and then four, without another murder, and the year tipped into November. The story was kept alive in the press by delivery of sensational letters alleged-ly penned by Jack The Ripper, himself. One of the epistles came with a small box containing a section of kidney believed to be that of Catherine Eddowes, the killer's fourth victim. It suddenly became the fashion for the west-end crowd to tour the streets and frequent the pubs of Whitechapel, slaking their curiosity along with their thirst. They traveled in groups, bois-terous and determinedly gay, as if their levity could protect them like a shield.

The pub and street trade picked up again, and as Jennet served drinks and mopped up spills, she gathered bits and pieces of gossip, speculations from police and press over the character-istics and behavior of the Ripper. Some said he must be one of the constables patrolling the streets or how else could he keep getting away with it whilst they were so thick on the ground. That idea was hotly contested by the lawmen in the room, and roundly denounced by the majority. Some authorities in the press said he had a medical background, while others denied it, saying even a butcher's boy displayed more finesse. There were rumors that he was left-handed, fair-haired, a west-end toff, that he wore a peaked cap and owned a red scarf. A brazen few even suggested the Ripper might be a woman.

In the midst of all these suppositions, Jennet realized, for the first time, that the killer may have been in *The Wolf & Lamb*. She may have served him, wiped the glass his lips had touched. A wave of revulsion shuddered over her, tinged with terror. He might even have taken one of the rooms upstairs and slept close to her, with only a thin wall separating them. The thought was unnerving, and Jennet reminded herself that he only targeted prostitutes, that her kind was safe from his killing knife.

She kept a closer eye on the clientele, noting that the number of fashionable gentlemen who frequented the establishment was increasing. The working girls fussed and flirted, deals were arranged and presumably consummated somewhere out of sight. Jennet watched their seductions with a faint sense of horror.

Her uncle appeared at her side. "What's wrong, my dear? You look as if you've seen the Ripper."

She pulled her gaze away. "No, uncle."

He regarded her, his face twisted with exasperation, yet softened by something like concern.

"You're still bothered by the sluts, I'm guessing."

Her face burned. To discuss such a subject seemed the height of impropriety, yet so much of her life was now, by all former standards, improper. She took courage and forced herself to look her uncle in the eye.

"I find their behavior disgusting! Don't you?"

He turned to watch the women in question, with their bunched breasts and painted lips, their braying laughter and coquettish performance. When he turned back, a dark and pensive grief shone in his eyes.

"I don't suppose a one of them took up the profession out of choice. They're playing a game called survival, Jennet."

She flushed. "There are other ways—"

"What would you have done if you didn't have me to come to?"

Jennet pressed her lips together, refusing to go down that road. "I'd have found something."

He regarded her, his face kind. "Yes, perhaps you would have."

"They're like ravening wolves!" she burst out. "Look at them!"

Her uncle didn't turn his head, holding her gaze instead. "Aye, they're hungry, just like everyone else on the east end. You see them as wolves, but if you look more closely, you'll see they're merely lambs in wolf's clothing. It's the proper gentle-men, who come here sporting their fine lamb's apparel, that are the true wolves."

Jennet's eyes widened in astonishment, and she opened her mouth to protest, then shut it with a snap. She considered her uncle's perspective. Why else would the men come from across town, if not to hunt?

"I'm not a completely Godless man, Jennet. I don't set foot in church but once a year or so, but I was raised up the same as your mother, and I remember a few of my Sunday School lessons. I try not to judge, but to have charity. At any rate, it's a mutually advantageous relationship when the lambs and wolves all get along. Note the name bar hanging outside the door."

Jennet hadn't given a thought to the name of her uncle's establishment until that moment. "You named your inn *The Wolf & Lamb*," she said, comprehension dawning.

"And now you know why."

He sent her off with a tray of drinks. Jennet felt a bit dazed, so radical was her uncle's philosophy to anything she'd considered before. The scriptures were full of admonitions against forni-cation and whoredoms. Yet, as her uncle had pointed out, they abounded also with mandates for charity and mercy. Her head spun, trying to reconcile what seemed like two clashing ideas.

She set mugs of beer and glasses of gin on the crowded tables and delivered a whiskey to a lone gentleman at a back booth. He wasn't known among the regulars, but Jennet had seen him here before, and remembered that he occasionally took a room for the night. As she thought about it, a little shock went through her. She was almost certain the last time he'd come was the night of the double event. The first woman to die that night had been Elizabeth Stride, known as Long Liz, and she'd drunk a glass of beer in *The Wolf & Lamb* just hours before her death. It was likely a coincidence, but Jennet found her gaze darting back to the stranger as he nursed his drink, his attention on the action at the other tables.

He lifted the glass with his left hand, and that might be significant, but the experts had argued over the left-handed conclusion and no one could say for sure. The man was fair-haired, and a peaked cap rested on the table, next to the glass of whiskey. Jennet shook herself—surely she was attaching too much meaning to these small, speculative details. His interest seemed to be in Dark Mary, an Irish doxy a decade or two younger than the Ripper's preferred victim, so Jennet put her fears down to imagination and wiped the scarred surface of the bar, pocketing a meager tip left by one of the regulars.

Dark Mary was drinking too much and Jennet knew that would lead to a round of maudlin Irish crooning, followed by a rash of bad temper. True to form, the woman started in with *Rosemary Faire* before moving on to *Believe Me, If All Those Endearing Young Charms*. Three lines into *Danny Boy*, she lashed out with a fist and fetched young Jeremy a bloody nose.

"Ow, Mary! What was that for?"

"You was lookin' down my dress."

"Bloody hell, woman. Last week you clouted me for *not* looking down your dress. What do you want from me?"

"Leave me alone. I want you all to just leave me alone."

The drunk girl stumbled from her chair, weaving a zig-zagged line for the door. She stopped to adjust her bonnet and pull a shawl around her shoulders before stepping out into the night.

"Jeremy, you should go after her," said one of the other girls.

"You heard her. She wants to be left alone. With a left hook like that, no one will mess with our Mary," he said, pressing a bloody handkerchief to his nose.

"She lost the key to her room. How will she get in?"

"Oh, she took care of that by breaking the window pane so she can reach in and turn the knob."

There was a titter of laughter. "That's Dark Mary for you."

Jennet turned away to put a row of glasses on the shelf behind. A current of air stirred the hairs at the back of her neck and she was startled to see the stranger pass out the door, the peaked cap pulled low over his brow. A rush of fear washed over her, a primal tug at the core of her instinct. He was going after Dark Mary, she knew it.

She moved her gaze about the room, looking for her uncle, but he was nowhere in sight, having stepped out on some errand. Without stopping to think, she rushed out the door after the strange man, ready to raise a hue and cry if she should find him accosting the drunk prostitute. Pockets of fog wafted in the night air, obscuring great swaths of the street scene. Jennet saw no one about as she ran a ways down Duke Street, staying to the center of the lane to avoid the open mouths of dark alleys. She peered into the night, calling out Mary's name. For answer, she heard only the barking of a distant dog.

Her foot caught on an uneven cobble and she fell to the frost-rimed stones, the breath knocked from her body. As she struggled to fill her lungs, her gaze was drawn by a movement in the shadows. She looked on in horror as a dark figure materialized in the fog. The face was in shadow, but the silhouette included the shape of a peaked hat atop the head. Unable to draw breath to scream, Jennet worked to get her feet under her. The fog parted, and in that moment, she saw a glint of steel.

A clatter of hoof beats sounded from the top of the road, and Jennet felt their vibrations beneath her palms. The carriage moved at a fast clip, and if she didn't move soon, she'd be trampled. She rolled to the right, away from the dark figure, and the carriage came into view, cutting between them. At last, she was able to pull breathe into her lungs and she used it, not to scream, but to propel her legs in a desperate run for safety.

At the threshold of *The Wolf & Lamb*, she paused to look back, her heart racing with fear and the exhilaration of escape. The street was once again empty.

By morning, all of London knew about the most vicious murder yet. Dark Mary was dead, not killed in the street as the other victims, but in her own room with the broken window pane. And on this instance, the Ripper had taken his time, slicing and mutilating until the corpse was well-nigh unrecognizable.

Jennet told her uncle about her suspicions, and what had happened in the street. He went to the police and Jennet's suspect was identified and taken in for questioning, like dozens of other men had been on the tales and suspicions of witnesses. Jennet was dismayed to hear the man was released within a day. He had connections among the influential, and the police had no more reason to hold him than they had for any other citizen in good standing.

Both the Metropolitan Police and Scotland Yard were stymied, and Jennet was at least as baffled by her own behavior. She had run out into the night, unprotected and unarmed, for the sake of a harlot. The messy reality of life was not as clear-cut as it had seemed from the comfort and security of the parsonage. She felt real grief over the death of Dark Mary, and a sense of failure at being unable to stop it. Almost dizzied by the harrowing events and her shifting perceptions, she began to understand that she'd rushed out that night in an instinctive defense of a fellow human being against an unspeakable evil.

By late morning, the *Wolf & Lamb* usually held a sprinkling of working girls, in for their morning tea and milk. Jennet included a cup for herself and joined a table with three other women.

"Bless us all, the queen's dropped in for tea." The girl named Clara cocked her pinkie finger and took a delicate sip with lips still bearing traces of last night's lipstick. Jennet felt her face flush as Bess and Margaret, eyebrows raised and chins thrust forward, regarded her over the scratched surface of the table.

"My name's Jennet. Would you mind if I sat with you?"

"Take care, Jennet," Bess said, leaning so far forward that Jennet could see the pores in her unwashed skin. "Not too close, or you might catch our stain."

An ember of irritation flared within her, then winked out, like the ash of a dying fire. These girls had to test the waters and throw up defenses in order to survive.

"I wanted to say I'm sorry about what happened to Mary."

A moment of silence, tinged by regret and horror, passed between them. The three women clanked their tea mugs together and after a slight pause, Jennet joined hers to theirs. They drank without speaking. Jennet finished her cup and wrapped her hands around its residual warmth.

"I also wanted to say that I hope you'll take extra care on the streets, and do all you can to watch out for each other."

Clara gave a cackle and tossed back a wave of midnight-colored hair. "It almost sounds as if she cares what happens to the likes of us."

There was a round of hostile laughter and Jennet, solemn-faced, waited for it to fade before rising.

"Tea's my treat this morning. I really do hope you'll be careful."

Another lull descended over the east end, and business at *The Wolf & Lamb* was slow. The height of action came from a wrangle between Jennet's uncle and Thomas Winger, one of the regulars. The day was chill, and a gray pall hung in the air that couldn't be dispelled by a fire in the hearth or a drink in the belly. Uncle Smither and Thomas sat at the bar, nursing their beers and sharing a dish of sausages while Jennet wiped glasses and neatened the counter.

"It seems the Ripper is cleaning up the streets of London, one whore at a time," said Thomas.

"That's a crass way of looking at it, Thomas. That's not how you really feel, is it?"

"Do you read the Bible, Smithers?"

"I've been known to skim a passage or two."

"Let me quote you one. Jeremiah, chapter five, verse six: 'Wherefore, a lion out of the forest shall slay them, and a wolf of the evenings shall spoil them, a leopard shall watch over their cities: every one that goeth out thence shall be torn in pieces: because their transgressions are many, and their backslidings are increased.' If that don't describe our situation, I don't know what does."

"I recall a different chapter and verse. The one about a God who loved the world so much that He sent His Son, that whoso believeth in him should not perish, but have everlasting life."

"If it's the New Testament you prefer, there's one in Acts about abstaining from pollutions, fornications, things strangled, and blood."

"And how would you have responded to Jesus when he invited the one who was without sin to cast the first stone?"

"Enough with the clash of the Bibles! Those sluts bring the indignation of God down upon all of us, and you know it."

"Get out of my bar, Thomas."

"Eh? What are you saying, Smithers?"

"I said, get out of my bar."

Her uncle's voice was low and measured, but Jennet sensed the banked fire beneath.

"Come on, Thomas," she said, leading him to the door. "Here's your coat and hat. Take care on the way home, the stones have gone icy."

She came back to the bar and laid a hand on her uncle's shoulder.

"I grew up on scripture," she said, "but I'm finding I still have so much to learn."

"We, none of us, get out of this world alive, Jennet, but the good Lord gives us to the very end to figure it out. The worst thing about a murderer is he takes away that chance for his victim."

Jennet studied her uncle's reflection in the bit of mirror above the bar.

"Do you think anyone ever goes past the point of no return?" she asked.

"I don't know, Jennet." He paused, rubbing a hand against his temple. "It's hard to believe the Ripper could ever be human again."

Jennet tossed in her narrow bed, shivering a little, though her uncle had given her the best duvet in the house. The moon, nearly full, peeped in through the frosted panes of her tiny window, painting the floor with stripes of silver, intensifying the shadows of the far corner. Her mind writhed under a myriad of conflicting thoughts and memories, an attack upon the foundational blocks of her upbringing, and yet that foundation was firm. She had no doubt of the core principles; it was a question of application.

A command as basic as "thou shalt not kill" was offset by the command for the children of Israel to destroy every living thing within the fallen walls of Jericho, sparing only the harlot Rahab and her family. God blessed David with the power to slay Goliath. And what of Jael, the wife of Heber the Kenite? In the book of Judges, she was called blessed above women because she drove a nail through Sisera's head while he slept, killing the dreaded enemy.

These heroes had not killed out of revenge, but to preserve their people. Each had been in a unique position and given the opportunity to strike against evil and oppression. And each had lived ever after with the consequences of their actions. Had they slept easy, or did they wrestle, as she did now?

The moon lowered in the sky. As it dropped beneath the windowsill, Jennet's eyelids ceased their restless flutter, and exhaustion sent her finally to sleep.

In the morning, she rose from the bed and knelt beside it, drawing a small trunk from beneath. These were her father's belongings, the last she had of him. His Bible, with its beautiful hand-tooled leather cover, was on top. She lifted it, running her finger over the textured lettering before putting it aside. Next was her mother's diary, every word committed to memory.

That, and a few photographs, were all she'd ever known of her mother, apart from what her father had told her.

At the bottom of the box, Jennet found the small capped vial. She washed and dressed, and just before going down to the bar, she slipped the vial into her apron pocket.

The days grew colder as November neared its end, and London held its breath; if Jack followed a pattern, it seemed to dictate an attack on the last day of the month. As the sun set on the 30th, a thick fog rolled in, like an accomplice to the Ripper. The constables put every man available on patrol, and the Whitechapel Vigilance Committee was out in force, while the working girls huddled in bars and taverns, moving outside only in groups. The killer would be hard put to find a victim or a place to do his deed, but few doubted that he'd be brazen and resourceful enough to find a way.

The atmosphere in *The Wolf & Lamb* was strained and too quiet. Without the shabby widow and her hurdy gurdy, or Dark Mary singing her folk tunes, the air was somber and empty. Men spoke in subdued voices, and women flirted without conviction or enthusiasm. Jennet stared into the hearth fire, mesmerized by the dancing flames and the soothing crackle they emitted. She watched the fire gutter and then strengthen as the front door opened and closed on the arrival of a new patron. Tugging her gaze away from the flame, she turned to take the newcomer's order, and bit back a gasp.

It was him.

He sat at the same table as before, but his attention this time was not on the assortment of available women. He asked for a whiskey, and Jennet felt his eyes bore into her back as she walked to the bar. She bit her lip, trying to control the shaking in her hands as she poured out the spirits. From beneath her lashes, she saw he was watching her carefully. Dare she do it? With a deep breath, she steadied herself and took the vial from her apron pocket, laudanum left over from her father's illness.

Her motions were hidden by the rise of the bar, yet she felt so exposed as she tapped measured drops into the glass of whiskey. Too much at once would leave a bitter and detectable taste. She hoped the stranger would order more than one drink so she could string out the dosage.

The tray trembled, and she had to hold it with two hands as she walked slowly back to the table and placed the drink before him. He gave a sardonic smile, raised the glass and tipped it to her before taking a sip. Jennet turned away, but he caught her hand, pulling her back.

"The coppers brought me in for questioning, and I'm thinking you had something to do with that."

Jennet wrenched her fingers out of his grasp. She thought of the laudanum, and raised her chin.

"I might have done."

"And all because I tried to help you up after you took a spill? What kind of thanks is that? Sit with me, Jennet, and ask my forgiveness."

Jennet dropped her gaze, hugging the tray against her chest. "I'm sorry, sir. I was mistaken."

He caught hold of her skirt and pulled her toward him. "Sit, let's have a drink together. I have friends in high places who will tell you what a nice fellow I am."

Jennet yanked the fabric from his fingers and he laughed. Aware that he was enjoying her unease, she straightened her shoulders and drew a breath, stepping sharply out of his reach.

"I'll bring you another whiskey."

As he drank, he continued to follow her with his eyes. When she served him his third drink of the night, now laced with enough laudanum to put him under, she could see that he was waning. His movements were slow, his speech beginning to slur.

"Ah, Jennet," he managed, "I'm finished with the appetizers. You'll make me a fine main course."

He tried lifting his drink in a toast, but his arm was too heavy. It was time to enlist help, but she could not afford to call on the police again. He had influence, and if they turned him loose, as they had the last time, she'd have lost a prime opportunity to stop his butchery. Maybe her only opportunity.

She found her uncle in the kitchen, washing dishes. "Uncle Smither, one of the customers is drowsy drunk. He asked for a room earlier. Perhaps we should take him up?"

Together they succeeded in getting him up the stairs, though he protested and struggled against them. By the time they dumped him in bed, he was snoring.

Jennet and her uncle returned to the barroom.

Custom grew sparser than ever into the wee hours of the morning, and Uncle Smither sent Jennet to bed. Boards creaked beneath her feet as she mounted the stairs, breathing heavy not from exertion, but from the turmoil in her breast. She listened at the stranger's door, and hearing no sound from the room, let herself in and stood trembling at the threshold.

The mounded shape under the blanket did not stir beneath the square of moonlight cast through the window. With cautious steps, Jennet approached the bed, alert for a break in the even breathing patterns, watching the sleeping face for fear the eyes might pop open and he spring upon her. His coat hung from a hook on the wall where her uncle had placed it, and she took it down to go through the pockets.

She drew out a long knife, thin and sharp, as the newspapers had described the weapon used by the Ripper. Though it looked as if an effort had been made to clean it, the surface was dulled by stains that would not wash out, and the seams between blade and handle were lined with a crusty, brown substance.

Jennet shuddered and her stomach rebelled. Biting her lip, she took hold of herself. She had started down this road, and she would finish it. Another shape was manifest in the coat pockets, something flat and metallic. She removed a tin of the sort that might hold gentlemen's snuff.

This one did not.

An odor, both sweet and fetid, assailed her as she opened the box. A slice of some internal organ rested there, drying in its own slime. A keepsake, but far more putrid and sinister than a loved one's lock of hair.

Jennet closed the tin and replaced it, along with the knife, all doubt gone, determination renewed. She hoped the dose she'd given him was sufficient for her needs as she eased the pillow from beneath his head and pressed it against his face, interrupting the soft snoring. His hand flew up, clenching her forearm, and she struggled, kneeling astride him to press all her weight against the pillow. It seemed an age as he flailed beneath her, but at last his grip grew feeble, loosening by degrees until his hand fell away to lay atop the blanket, a gnarled claw in the moonlight.

She felt no overwhelming sense of emotion. No elation, and no grief. For her, this was not an act of vengeance, for that belonged to the Lord, alone. This was an opposition to evil, like David's stone or the nail of Jael. An act in defense of humanity.

She waited a long moment in the moonlight before removing the pillow and looking down into the face of the Ripper. No horns or forked tongue marked him out, yet malice seemed carved into his features, something he'd invited in and allowed to transform him. He made himself a servant of the devil, and she had vanquished him.

A final scripture came to her mind, and she whispered it into the night air.

"The wolf and the lamb shall feed together, and the lion shall eat straw like the bullock."

She placed the pillow back under the dead man's head and left the room as she had come. Closing the door, she leaned against it until the quickened beat of her heart returned to normal. She missed her father with a physical ache, and the life they'd led together. That girl would never have snuffed out a man's life. She wouldn't have needed to.

But the field had changed. Jennet remembered her uncle's words. *They're playing a game called survival.*

So was she, and tonight she'd scored a major strike against evil.

She crossed to her own room and climbed into bed. There, under the gilded moonlight, she lay until her eyelids dropped shut, and she slept.

Author's Note

Chamber of Vengeance

"Chamber of Vengeance" started out as a Halloween story and although it does feature a few ghosts, most of them are the kind we all deal with—shades of the past coming back to haunt us.

The story is set in Seattle during the 1980s and readers old enough to remember the era will recognize bits of pop culture making an appearance.

"Chamber of Vengeance" was originally published in *Mystery Magazine*, October 2021.

CHAMBER OF VENGEANCE

Dozens of body parts lay scattered across the room like the aftermath of a bomb.

Tamsin sneezed, then sneezed again as dust motes danced in the beams of yellow light glowing from recessed bulbs in the dim hall.

Mood lighting.

Decisively spooky.

Probably more so than when the wax display had been open to customers.

Trying to hide her dismay, Tamsin surveyed the long, narrow chamber. Limbs from discarded mannequins jumbled alongside moth-eaten costumes, their musty odor sending her into another sneezing fit, loud in the stuffy space.

"You said you wanted the display ready by Halloween?"

Vanessa Bradley, of the family-operated Costumes & Curiosities, gave a brisk nod. "Yes, we'd like to host the grand re-opening of our Chamber of Horrors on Halloween."

"That gives us less than three weeks."

An acid voice cut in. "I told her it couldn't be done." Ingrid Bradley, matriarch of the business and holder of the reins.

Tamsin glanced at Kurt, her employer, but he didn't meet her eye. "We can make this happen," he said, "but we must begin immediately."

"Of course," Vanessa said. "Today, if you wish."

Kurt pursed his lips. "Is the original designer still alive?"

A short hesitation, then Vanessa said, "No. The sculptures were created twenty years ago by Irina Rostova. She was very good, and claimed to be descended from Rasputin, which gave her a certain cachet. As you see," she swept an arm toward a corner of the hall, "his is one of the figures you'll be restoring."

Tamsin walked closer to the tall, hulking form. Shadows obscured most of the face, but the acrylic-painted eyes peered out with startling intensity. She shivered. Half dread, half delight. This job would be creepy, but fascinating.

"Why was the display shut down?" she asked.

Another pause, longer this time, spread through the dusty air. Vanessa drew an audible breath to begin her answer, but before she could speak, a browsing couple stepped into the far end of the hall, the woman's harsh, nasal exclamations blotting out all else.

"Look at this, Frank! Isn't it marvelous?"

Vanessa rushed forward. "This area is off-limits to customers," she said, trying to herd them back out, but the woman was not to be stopped.

"A wax museum," she squealed. "How wonderful!"

She ran her hands over a delicate, aging brocade ball gown and Tamsin gasped at the woman's lack of consideration.

Ingrid sputtered, her cheeks turning an angry red. "Get that stupid cow out of here," she shouted. The man turned, eyes wide and incredulous. He made a rude gesture, taking offense for his partner's sake.

"Really," Vanessa said, her voice firm yet polite. "It's not safe here. This area is for staff only—"

But it was too late. The woman dislodged some anchoring item from a towering stack, starting an avalanche. A mannequin leaning against the wall turned, knocking down a pair of crossed swords. One fell harmlessly, slithering to a halt at Tamsin's feet.

The other sliced through the woman's sleeve, drawing blood as it passed, its point skewering her designer bag to the wooden floor like a stuck pig, its guts spilling out as the blade quivered in place.

The woman screamed.

Paramedics stitched and bandaged the wound. Amid a fluster of apologies and threatened lawsuits, Vanessa escorted the wayward customers off the premises. Tamsin tagged along behind Kurt. Despite the distraction, she sensed her boss champing at the bit, wanting to get the paperwork squared away on their new project so they could dive in and try to meet that impossible deadline.

They stood inside the glass storefront, waiting, and Tamsin stared out the rain-streaked windows at the movie theater across the street, a lump the size of a plum forming in her throat. Last July, Jason had taken her there to see the new Michael J. Fox film, *Back To The Future*, exactly one week before their scheduled wedding.

And exactly one day before he'd broken off their engagement.

She turned away, avoiding Kurt's sympathetic eye, and pressed her lips together, humming along with Huey Lewis and The News as she perused a shelf stocked with gag items and magic tricks. She looked up when Vanessa approached, a man and woman in her wake.

"May I introduce my brother, Darren," she said, "and his wife Gina. Darren runs the creative side of the business while I mostly look after the books."

Darren Bradley had his sister's straw-colored hair, and wore it almost as long, tousled wavy locks held back by a white tennis visor. A cream-colored sweater hung around his neck, tied at the sleeves. His wife was a paragon of golden-tanned glamor with frosty eyes. An attractive couple, but tense, like magnets whose like-sides repel.

Vanessa turned to go. "In light of what happened just now, I'm going to call our attorney. Darren will set you up with a work order. Okay?"

We agreed and followed Darren down a passage behind the front desk. Bradley's Costumes & Curiosities covered a quarter of a city block and had been a fixture in Seattle since the 1940s. It featured a full-service costume shop, a museum of magic, a dungeon with an impressive collection of torture devices, and sideshow alley, with a fortune-teller, bearded lady, and sword-swallower.

And three weeks hence, a Chamber of Horrors, if Kurt had anything to say about it.

"Coffee?" Darren offered as we took seats around his desk. Tamsin accepted the cup and used it to warm her hands.

"Vanessa was just going to explain about the display," she said, "why it closed all those years ago. Can you tell us about it?"

Darren leaned back, hands stuffed into the pockets of his khaki slacks. "Mother insisted we close it down. After what happened."

Kurt set down his cup. "What *did* happen?"

"You don't know?" He blew out a long breath and pushed a straying lock of hair into place. "Irina Rostova committed suicide in the chamber. It caused a sensation and brought in customers by the droves, but mother was right to shut it down. Very crass to profit off a young woman's tragedy."

He rocked forward in the chair and came to his feet. "Last week Vanessa and I were cleaning out a storage room when we came across this."

He handed Kurt a spiral-bound notebook with the name Weldon Bradley printed on the faded cover.

"Father's notes and ideas. We read the pages about the wax display and realized it was time to open it up again."

Kurt spoke. "Is your father deceased?"

"He died eleven years ago."

Tamsin took the notebook from Kurt and flipped through its pages. "May we keep this? I mean, while we're working on the project. To help with the details."

"Of course. Just make sure I get it back."

Darren plucked a form from a tray on his desk and started filling blanks, then paused.

"We're all getting together for dinner tonight in mother's upstairs apartment. Care to come? You can meet the whole crew and ask any questions that spring to mind."

"That would be excellent," Kurt said.

"Great. Come at seven." A girl rapped twice on the open door, catching Darren's attention. "I'll be back in a moment. Just finish filling those in, will you?"

Kurt worked on the form while Tamsin snooped. She stopped in front of a desk in the corner with four CCTV monitors running. Not much was going on in three of the monitors, but the fourth was very interesting.

"Kurt, come see this."

The grainy screen showed Darren's wife, Gina, behind a rack of costumes in a hot embrace with another man. And in the foreground, hidden from the oblivious couple, was Darren and Vanessa's mother, Ingrid, taking it all in.

Tamsin watched Kurt scrutinize the floor of the chamber, his eyebrows drawn together, one hand stroking his clean-shaven chin, Florsheim loafers clacking softly on the hardwood. A blotchy shape, stained a shade darker than the rest of the floor, was visible beneath a light layer of dust.

Marking the spot where Irina Rostova spent her last moments.

"Horrible to think about, isn't it?" she said.

"Disturbing," he agreed. "Working this project won't give you nightmares, will it, Tamsin?"

"No more than usual, though I can almost feel a presence here." She shook her head. "Imagination, of course."

Kurt looked thoughtful. "Perhaps. It's almost time for our dinner appointment. Let's wash the dust off our hands and go up."

They arrived a little early and Darren, wearing a blue-striped apron, let them in. A woman, soft and delicate as a water lily, stood in the hall behind him.

"Kurt, Tamsin, let me introduce you to Mei Ling. If you need any art supplies for the project, she runs a shop just around the corner. And she delivers. Thanks, Mei Ling, for bringing those over."

"No problem, Mr. Bradley. I'll see you later."

Tamsin caught a hint of frangipani as Mei Ling exited. She followed Darren and Kurt into the kitchen where dinner preparations were underway. "I'm running a bit behind," Darren apologized, "but we'll be eating soon."

"Can I help?" Tamsin asked.

As she sliced peppers for a salad, the front door opened again. Murmuring voices and footsteps grew louder as three more people entered the kitchen. Gina, Vanessa, and a dark-haired young man wearing tortoiseshell eyeglasses.

"This is my friend, Richard," Darren said. "You'll be seeing a lot of him. He does the alterations for our costumes."

Kurt shook Richard's hand and Tamsin smiled a hello. The others sat in bar stools around the counter, at home in the room and with each other. They chatted about the events of the day while Tamsin finished slicing and rinsed the knife under the faucet.

"I have a question," she said. "The plans for the wax display in the notebook include ten figures, but there are only nine in the chamber now. Did Irina...leave before she finished the tenth?"

"Yes, but not in the way you're thinking," Vanessa replied. "Mother sacked her."

"She'd started falling behind in her work," Darren added, "taking far longer than her contract called for. She did nothing, sometimes, for days on end, saying she was ill."

Vanessa swiped a carrot coin from Darren's chopping board. "She was upset about something but wouldn't say what. Leave it to mother to suss it out. She was pregnant."

Darren swept the remaining carrots into the salad bowl, out of Vanessa's reach. "We were just children at the time, and father was in Germany, bidding on some vintage costumes, or he might have had something to say about it. Mother told Irina to clear out, she wasn't running a home for unwed mothers."

"But I thought..."

"Yes, well, Irina came back about a year later, after having the baby and giving it up for adoption. She still had her key. She let herself in after hours and broke a case in the dungeon, taking one of the daggers. She used it to slit her wrists in the chamber."

Tamsin felt her mouth go dry. "How awful."

"Mother found her the next morning, lying between Rasputin and Vlad The Impaler. That's the day her hair went white."

"Now you're just milking the story," Vanessa protested.

"And it's said her malevolent ghost haunts the chamber to this day," he added.

"Enough! When's dinner ready?" asked Vanessa.

The story was clearly one they'd told many times. Maybe they'd been too young when it happened for it to hold any real memories or emotional impact, but Tamsin felt sick, not sure she was up to eating, and both Kurt and Richard looked pale. They hadn't said a word during the exchange.

The timer beeped and Darren pulled a casserole from the oven.

"I'll go fetch mother," Vanessa said, heading into the rear of the apartment.

"Let's get the table set," Darren suggested, passing out plates and flatware.

Tamsin placed napkins and salt and pepper, feeling detached and robotic. She hadn't realized the chamber of horrors she and Kurt would be working on had such a stamp of authenticity. But Kurt had signed the contract that morning and she knew he wouldn't back out of the project.

It was Halloween or bust for him, and she wouldn't desert him in his hour of need.

Tamsin looked up from the table to see Vanessa return to the kitchen, moving slowly, her face ashen.

"Don't go in there," she warned, her voice flat and drained of all vigor as she pointed toward the bedroom. "Mother's dead. She's been murdered."

She fell into a chair, eyes wide. "Call the police."

After a restless night, Tamsin was back in the dusty chamber with Kurt, making her first order of business a general sorting and cleanup. Ingrid's murder heaped another layer of grim tragedy on Bradley's Costumes and Curiosities, but a phone call from Vanessa made it clear their restoration project was still a go.

Ordinarily, Kurt liked to hum the jazz standards while they worked, but today the atmosphere in the chamber was subdued, with Kurt speaking only in grunts or eloquent gestures. Tamsin wanted to break up the oppressive silence.

"Are we in danger here, Kurt?"

He shook his head without looking up from the piece he was painting.

"Who killed Ingrid? And why?"

After Vanessa's warning not to go into her mother's bedroom, they all had rushed directly there, as if drawn by an invisible string, needing to see to believe. Ingrid was stretched out on the bed, staked through the heart with a chisel, a mallet lying next to the body.

Tamsin shuddered, and turned to the portable toolbox that went with them on every project. Three chisels, just like the murder weapon, occupied their regular spots.

She thought about the paper she'd seen on Ingrid's nightstand, hand-printed with a series of symbols. Before she'd gotten a proper look at it, Vanessa had gasped, pointing to a series of empty doilies on the tall-boy dresser.

"Mother's crystal—it's gone!" A collection of Swarovski crystal worth ten thousand dollars, apparently.

And then the police had arrived.

Tamsin stepped closer to Kurt, catching his eye. "I couldn't sleep last night," she admitted. "I sat up, looking through Weldon Bradley's notebook. And I found this."

She opened the notebook to a page near the back, blank except for a series of symbols with a box drawn around them. She showed Kurt.

"I think these are the same symbols I saw in Ingrid's bedroom last night. Do you have any idea what they mean?"

Kurt examined the page and shrugged. "Cyrillic."

"Yes, but I don't speak Russian. I'm going to ask if anyone knows about this."

"No!"

"So, you *do* think we could be in danger."

Kurt glared at her. He sighed. "I'll go with you."

The establishment was closed in observance of Ingrid's death. The only sound as they passed through the eerie, deserted showroom was the faint tap of rain on the metal roof high above. Strident voices and the smell of coffee greeted them as they opened the door into the rear corridor.

"...killed her to get your hands on the money and control." Tamsin recognized Gina's snide tone.

"I didn't. It's more likely you did it to prevent her spilling the beans to Darren about your extra-marital activities."

Gina snorted. "As if he didn't know."

Kurt raised an eyebrow and Tamsin motioned they should leave. "Now's not a good time," she whispered.

They retraced their steps and Tamsin said, "I'm guessing Darren and Vanessa inherit the business and assets. That gives them motive."

"Don't forget Mei Ling."

"Mei Ling! Why would she kill Ingrid?"

"I have no idea, but she was there, remember? And she probably stocks chisels identical to the murder weapon in her shop."

"Which is precisely why she wouldn't use one," Tamsin said. "Following your line of logic, we're both suspects, as well."

A woman in uniform stepped into the chamber. "You're probably right about that," she said. "Tamsin Gooding, Detective Lewis would like to speak with you."

"I've never been a murder suspect before," Tamsin told Kurt when she returned. "And now, they want to talk to you."

"The police think one of *us* might have murdered Ingrid?" he said. "For what reason?"

"Ten thousand reasons, encased in crystal."

Kurt threw down his paint-stained rag. "Ridiculous!"

He stalked off and Tamsin turned her attention to the wax figures, half wishing they'd never signed on for the job, though she had to admit it was the most stimulating project they'd ever taken. The odors of fresh paint and old wax mingled, forming a fitting backdrop for the weaving of past tragedy and present calamity. Tamsin sensed they were intertwined.

She began undressing Jack the Ripper. Her job was to strip and clean the wax hands and faces, getting them ready for Kurt's paintbrush. As she pulled the right forearm from the sleeve, she felt an indentation beneath her fingertips. Turning the arm to expose the inner wrist, she saw the letter H carved into the wax. On a hunch, she pulled up the sleeves on the other sculptures and found a symbol engraved on each, even the werewolf, amid tufts of fur.

Some of the symbols resembled letters from the English alphabet, but a few did not. Tamsin opened the notebook and compared them to the boxed cipher. The symbols were all there, but in jumbled order, and by matching the symbols with the original order of the wax figures, as contained in the notebook, she was able to confirm they spelled out the same message.

Whatever it was.

Tamsin rose from her crouch over the notebook and bumped her head against a framed portrait of Nicholas and Alexandra, knocking it to the floor. The sturdy glass remained intact. She sighed in relief as a blotch of red on the wall caught her attention and she stepped closer, squinting in the yellow mood lighting.

The wax formed a heart shape containing carved initials:

WB

+

IB

How sweet—Weldon and Ingrid Bradley. They must have made the heart, but why cover it with a painting? More curious than ever about the mysteries behind the Bradley's, Tamsin decided to try again to find someone who could decipher the cryptic symbols.

She stepped from the chamber, expecting a wall of spooky silence from the deserted building, and was surprised to hear faint murmurs from the costume showroom. Beneath the red velvet changing room curtain, Tamsin saw two sets of feet standing very close together. Darren, with someone other than Gina. A whiff of floral fragrance suggested it was Mei Ling.

Sauce for the goose, and none of her business.

Tamsin crept into the office area but found no one. Unable to resist a little light snooping, she scanned the area but came up empty. She used the bathroom and washed her hands, then splashed some water on her face to rinse off the dust.

As she stepped from the bathroom, she saw Darren leave his office down the hall and head toward the rear exit. She called out a greeting, but he didn't even look back—only lifted a hand, flapping it at her in a dismissive gesture, and hurried out the back door.

Giving up on finding someone to help her, Tamsin retreated to the book nook, a tucked away corner containing brocaded chairs and obscure reading material. She seized the Russian-English dictionary like it was the Holy Grail and sank into one of the stiff, padded chairs.

The symbols were indeed Cyrillic, but as far as Tamsin could tell, they didn't add up to anything in Russian. Taking the dictionary with her, she went back to the chamber where Kurt had arrived, bearing sandwiches.

They ate ham and mustard on rye, the tang of Dijon and caraway hitting the spot for Tamsin. When they finished, she showed him the wax heart.

"Weldon Bradley and his wife Ingrid," Kurt mused. "Those old-fashioned values don't seem to apply to the new generation. Married love's not quite the thing in the house of Bradley."

"I noticed."

Kurt continued to stare at the heart. "Wait a minute," he said. "The bottom of this B was made by the frame pressing against the wax for untold years."

He ran a finger over the carved initials. "Yes, it's definitely fainter. I think we're looking at

WB

+

IR."

"Irina Rostova! I'll bet Weldon was the father of her baby."

"Come on, Tamsin, that's some heavy speculation."

"Granted, but it makes sense, doesn't it?"

The air smelled crisp and fresh, like a good autumn apple, and for once, there was a break in the rain as Tamsin parked and ran uphill a block and a half to report on time. Her shoes pinched, and she knew by mid-afternoon she'd be working in her stocking feet.

She entered Bradley's by the front door and wished the girl behind the desk a good morning.

"Miss Gooding," the girl called, "a man stopped in to see you this morning—you just missed him. He left a note."

Tamsin opened the note. Her heart gave a painful twist and a flood of heat washed over her cheeks. With shaking hands, she crinkled the paper into a ball and shoved it into her pocket.

Before she could recover her composure, she was blindsided by another shock as police led Darren, clapped in handcuffs, past her and out the front. Vanessa followed as far as the door, then turned back, biting her lip.

"What's happened?" Tamsin asked.

"Darren's been arrested for the theft of the crystal. A murder charge is sure to follow."

"What evidence do they have?"

"They didn't share that with me, but I intend to find out." She zipped up her jacket and disappeared into the weak morning sunshine.

"One more thing, Miss Gooding," said the front desk girl. "Mr. Tomlinson wanted you to pick up some supplies from Mei Ling's. Here's the list."

Tamsin walked around the corner to the art shop, the clack of her heels keeping time with her heart. She filled a basket, according to Kurt's list, and was on her way to the register when the bell jingled and Darren's friend, Richard, entered. He went directly to the counter and they chatted while Mei Ling finished a phone call.

"How long have you worked for the Bradley's?" Tamsin asked.

"About a year. It's definitely an interesting place to work."

"I'm finding that out. Kurt and I are intrigued by some markings we've found on the wax figures. We're having fun trying to decipher their meaning. You don't happen to speak Russian, do you?"

"No. Are the markings in Russian?"

"I'm not entirely sure. They look like this." Tamsin showed him the page from Weldon Bradley's notebook.

He shook his head. "No, I'm sorry I can't help."

Mei Ling handed Richard a box of supplies and he paid for his order. "See you around," he said as the bell tinkled behind him.

Mei Ling's lips curved in a tiny smile as she rang up Tamsin's purchases. She was unaware of Darren's arrest, and Tamsin didn't want to be the one to tell her. Like a coward, she clutched the bag of supplies and slinked out the door before Mei Ling could ply her with questions.

Things were shaping up in the chamber. The dust had been cleared and the spare mannequin parts relegated to a corner. Kurt bent over his palette, mixing paint, and he was back to humming. Tamsin recognized *The Way You Look Tonight*.

"Any exciting new developments while I was gone?" Tamsin asked, picking up her own palette and getting to work on a backdrop. "Other than Darren's arrest, I mean. I was here for that."

"I happened to overhear Vanessa tell Gina the arrest was made on the basis of a tape from the security camera, showing clear footage of Darren stashing the figurines in the back of a storage closet. The police searched the closet and recovered them."

"I don't get it," Tamsin said. "Why would he steal the crystal?"

"Only reason I come up with is that he killed his mother and wanted to make it look like a burglary, but it just doesn't sit right with me. Despite the evidence. Things are not always what they look like."

Tamsin froze. "Say that again."

"All of it?"

"Just that last part—things are not always what they look like."

"Do you still need me to say it again?"

Tamsin ignored him. She put down her paints and picked up the notebook. "This looks like a Russian word. But what if it isn't? What if it's an English word, spelled out with Cyrillic symbols?"

She snatched up the dictionary and turned to a page showing the transliteration from Cyrillic to English. Using it as a reference, she transformed

ВЭНГЭАНСЭ

into

VENGEANCE

"Someone left an intentional message in those wax figures," she said. "And the intention was revenge."

"Yes, but who carved those symbols? Irina, before she took her life? Or Weldon, when he weighed the cost of his infidelity?"

"And what form did they expect vengeance to take?"

Tamsin stared at Kurt, wondering if her eyes were as wide as his were. A shiver passed through her.

"We may never know," she admitted. "On a different subject, guess who's coming to see me tomorrow?"

A scowl crossed Kurt's features. "Tell me you're joking."

"You know what's happened, don't you?" Tamsin said. "His high school sweetheart has dumped him. Again. And now he wants to come crawling back."

"Tamsin, don't let him. There's no healthy relationship for you with Jason. Breaking off the engagement was the best thing he's ever done for you."

"Don't I know it," she agreed.

But it was a lie. She *wanted* to know she was better off without Jason, longed for that assurance, but part of her still held on to a slender hope she couldn't quite smother.

"What are you going to do if he wants to make up?"

Tamsin allowed a few ideas to flit through her mind, settling on one that felt good in the moment.

"I can spell it out in nine letters. V-E-N-G-E-A-N-C-E."

The next morning, as Tamsin arrived, the girl at the desk motioned her to the phone.

"Call for you," she said. "Mr. Tomlinson."

"I'll be out for the morning," Kurt told her. "I have to meet with our auditor, but here's something you'll be interested to know—Darren's been released on bail."

"They didn't have enough to charge him with murder, then?"

"It appears not. Be careful, Tamsin. Lots of hazards for you today."

Tamsin spent the morning painting scenery for the display. A Flock of Seagulls reached her faintly in the chamber, but she'd have felt more comfortable with Kurt and his Big Band favorites.

Between the paint fumes and her nerves as the noon hour approached, Tamsin's stomach bubbled like a primordial swamp. She tried to keep her attention focused strictly on her work, but one moment she'd be practicing her scathing remarks for when Jason asked her to reconcile, and the next she'd be dreaming of the two of them back together.

At 11:30, she cleaned her brushes, fluffed her hair, and reapplied lipstick. It was time.

She walked to the cafe, her killer high heels living up to the name, but looking good. Jason was already there, in a booth, and she slid in across from him. He'd ordered her a coke and she busied herself unwrapping the straw and taking a sip, hoping he'd break the ice.

"So, you're doing a job for Bradley's." he said. "How're you liking it?"

"It's been interesting."

"Were you there when the old lady got skewered?"

She gave him a look that made her feel like a disapproving schoolmarm. "I was."

"What was that like?"

"Look, Jason, I don't want to talk about it. Why'd you want to see me?"

The primordial swamp evolved into a volcano. This was it.

"I hoped we might have some lunch first."

"I don't have time for lunch, just say what you came to say."

Jason blushed and looked away. He was working up the courage and finally the words came.

"Can I get the ring back?"

A punch to the gut.

Tamsin couldn't breathe, couldn't believe she'd heard right. "What?"

"I need the ring back, Tams. I'm going to ask Sammy to marry me. I'm sorry."

"You want to give her *my* ring?"

"No! Of course not. But I can't afford another ring. I got a guy'll give me fifteen hundred for it."

Tamsin stood up. She lifted the glass of coke and poured it in his lap. "I'll send it to you by post," she said and got out before the dam broke.

Back at Bradley's she walked past the front desk and across the showroom, holding it together, stiff upper lip. She entered the chamber and left the lights off, retreating to the far corner and sinking to the floor where she finally gave way.

Time to let go of her hopes and dreams. This is what Irina must have felt like, as she bled on this very floor.

Only, Tamsin didn't want to die.

A shadow, deeper than the dark of the room, moved across her. Tamsin peered into the gloom, transfixed by an image so ethereal it could only be her imagination, but it looked like a woman.

Or the ghost of a woman.

The mouth opened in a silent scream and Tamsin drew back. In that moment, a *whoosh* of air brushed her face as a sword sliced down, hitting the spot where she'd just been. She gasped and rolled to her feet.

In the dimness, she saw Darren raise the sword for another swing. He was between her and the exit. She dodged the sword as it came down, its point penetrating the hardwood.

He meant business.

He wrestled the blade from the floor's grip and Tamsin tried to run past him, but he kicked out, knocking her to the floor. She shouted and he stood over her, bringing the sword up for the killing blow, a spill of light from the doorway illuminating his face.

It wasn't Darren.

Richard, in a wig and visor, the cream sweater coming loose from his shoulders, loomed over her, wielding the long blade.

Tamsin shoved with both feet at the base of Rasputin's towering figure, toppling it and fouling Richard's aim enough for her to roll out of his reach, but he was on her again in a matter of seconds.

He raised the sword and there was nowhere left for her to go.

Once more, a dark shadow flitted across the room, catching Richard's attention, pulling his intent gaze away from her. The blow never fell.

Light flooded the chamber. Richard dropped the sword and tried to run, but Kurt stood in the doorway, with Vanessa behind him.

"What is going on?" she demanded.

Tamsin got to her feet. "He tried to kill me."

"Darren?"

"No," Kurt said, staring at Richard. "Your other brother."

Vanessa's mouth gaped. "What are you talking about?"

Tamsin turned to Richard. "When did you find out about Irina and Weldon?"

He glared at her, panting, his eyes defiant. "When I turned eighteen, my adoptive parents told me about my mother. They didn't know who my father was, but it wasn't hard to piece together. I've been biding my time and perfecting my plan until the moment was right. Vengeance—that's what my mother demanded. It's what she deserves."

Tamsin lifted her hands, mystified. "But why attack me?" she asked.

"You were getting too close to the truth," Kurt guessed.

"You saw me," Richard told her, "dressed as Darren. After I stashed the crystal. I fooled you then, but it was only a matter of time until you put the pieces together and figured it out."

He straightened the sweater, tying it neatly. "Ingrid drove my mother to kill herself. She was cruel and merciless. She deserved to die."

The police arrived and took the situation in hand, cuffing Richard and leading him to the door as Darren entered. The two men stared at each other.

"We were friends," Darren said. "Why did you frame me for murder?"

"I hate you." Richard's voice was cold, flat as paper.

"I hate all of you."

Halloween arrived and, with it, the Grand Re-opening of Bradley's Chamber of Horrors.

Vanessa had granted Tamsin and Kurt free costumes for the evening, a bonus for completing the project on time. The black wig smelled funny and made her itch, but Tamsin liked the way she looked as Cleopatra and Kurt cut a fine figure as a circus ringmaster.

Except for a brief shower around four o'clock, the sky remained clear, and trick-or-treaters were out in record numbers. It seemed as if nearly all of them showed up at Bradley's.

The spooky awesome wax display was a success and Tamsin watched hundreds of guests file past the real-to-life sculptures fashioned by Irina Rostova and restored by her and Kurt.

Munching a handful of candy corn, Tamsin said, "I think Richard saw his mother in that moment he was about to kill me. That split-second distraction saved my life."

Kurt looked affronted. "My arrival had nothing to do with it?"

Tamsin laughed. "Of course it did. I'll never forget your dashing contribution."

"At least, not as long as I'm signing your paychecks," he said, giving her a wry look.

"That long," she agreed, "and beyond."

Kurt twirled his circus master mustache. "I didn't want to pry," he said, "but I'm really dying to know. How did your meeting with Jason go? Did he want you back?"

"Oh, he wanted *something* back, but I put a damper on his party."

"Good. You deserve a love story with a happy ending."

Tamsin swallowed the candy, tasting the sweetness on her tongue. "I do," she said. "I really do."

AUTHOR'S NOTE

MOSES MEETS THE KARAOKE KILLER

"Moses Meets the Karaoke Killer" came about in a funny way. It's the origin story of the Tal Bannerman Thrillers, a series spinning off from my Riley Forte Suspense Thrillers.

The Riley Forte books are exciting and fast-paced but a bit gritty and more serious in tone.

The Tal Bannerman stories, on the other hand, are madcap, rollicking fun. They are lightning-paced stories with a *Mission Impossible* meets *Get Smart* vibe.

"Moses Meets the Karaoke Killer" was the result of an assignment from editor Kristine Kathryn Rusch. She asked for a short story based on a minor character from one of my novels.

If you've read *Nocturne in Ashes*, the first Riley Forte novel, you may remember the chapter that takes place at the base of the smoking volcano, just hours before it erupts. The scene was one of riotous revelry, a crowd of partiers defying the volcano and the government officials trying to keep them away. Here's the snippet that inspired the spin-off story:

"This reminds me of that scene from The Ten Commandments, when Moses brings down the word of God from the mountaintop and everyone's dancing around the golden calf."

"I'm no Moses," Topper replied, "but I guess I know what he felt like."

After writing the story, I submitted it to one publisher who bought it for inclusion in a thriller anthology. Before it went to print, that publishing company was bought by another publishing company who also wanted the story.

Before it got eaten by yet another publisher.

I gave up and pulled the story, so it has never been published until now, but what the heck—I already got paid for it. Twice.

If you enjoy this type of humorous, offbeat, fast-paced thriller, I invite you to check out the other books in the Tal Bannerman series.

For now, I hope you have as much fun reading this one as I did in writing it. Enjoy!

MOSES MEETS THE KARAOKE KILLER

I f Tal Bannerman had to die, he didn't want to wear a dress to the event.

He stared in horror at the flowing scarlet fabric spilling across the conference room table like a size 38 river of blood, taking in the accompanying headdress and other accessories. He raised his eyes and let them travel from man to man around the span of polished oak, each face more solemn than the last. As incredible as their news had been, it was no joke.

The ticking of the clock above his head fell into the room like a pile driver on an endless line of waiting poles, upping his anxiety with each stroke. Tal felt as if someone had steamrolled his heart and drop-kicked the flattened mass left behind. Every ounce of blood in his body seemed to rush through his eardrums, burning and thrumming, drowning out the doom-filled briefing delivered by the man from Homeland Security.

Not that it mattered. None of it made any sense.

He blinked his eyes and held up a hand, working to draw enough breath to make himself heard. "Hold on," he said, "I'm not the guy for this. I'm a doctor, not a field agent."

"Precisely," said Hawkins, the DHS man. "If we had time to train an agent to do your job, that's what we'd do. But it's not an option. Mt. Rainier could blow at any moment and Intikam is on the move."

"Buck up, Bannerman," said Ziegfeld, his Chief at the Epidemic Intelligence Service. "It's all in a day's work for us. You knew that when you signed on."

He certainly had not.

Tal had signed on because his girlfriend, Bridget, wanted to get married. Every time he looked into her gold-flecked green eyes, he saw the two of them with three kids, a mortgage, and a honey-do list long enough to paper the spare bedroom they'd have for the mother-in-law.

He panicked.

He remembered how the day after he'd graduated from med school, his study partner, Victor Hobart, had hopped a plane for Atlanta to join the elite medical detective branch of the CDC, known as the Epidemic Intelligence Service. Tal subsequently received a string of postcards from Malaysia, Tahiti, and pristine Alaska.

One evening he came home from work and saw by the beach-studded postcard in his mailbox that Victor was in Spain.

Hey, Talmadge baby! It's all sun, sangria, and senoritas for me. How's your day going?

Meanwhile, Victor's girlfriend had dumped him and got herself engaged to a dentist.

Tal knew Victor was taunting him—the use of his full name told him that—and it crawled under his skin like a flesh-eating bacterium. Feeling that both his dignity and freedom were under attack, he'd filled out the online application and hit "SUBMIT."

Ziegfeld's fist slammed down on the table in front of Tal, sending a ballpoint pen skittering to the floor. "Pay attention, Bannerman," growled his boss. "Your career in the CDC starts or ends here."

Tal strained to focus, but his brain bogged down under the effort of trying to trace a path from where he'd started to this moment. He'd entered his name into the official roster and completed his initial training. Within three months, he'd received a Dear John from Bridget and visited five exotic locales. It took him only half that time to realize he'd made a mistake.

A big mistake.

Most of the frequent flyers he encountered on the team's travels were disease-carrying insects and there was no way he was getting a tan covered head to toe in trendy Haz-Mat gear. Worse than that, the misery and deprivation he faced, both domestic and distant, appalled and depressed him beyond measure. He wanted out, but he was obligated for a two-year stint.

And now the Chief was ordering him to put on a robe and go undercover as a personage from the Old Testament. No one signing on the dotted line could have seen that coming.

"Any questions?" asked Hawkins, his voice brisk.

"How do you know all this?"

"One of Intikam's engineers, Larissa Goreham, got cold feet when she learned about their plans. She defected to our side. Thanks to her information, we were able to capture one of the terrorist cell's top operators, a man code-named Everglade. We're extracting information from him now, but there's no time to wait for the full picture. Ms. Goreham supplied evidence to support her story and we're forced to accept what she says as good information. We can't afford not to act on it. Thousands—potentially millions—of American lives are at stake."

"What bio-agent are we talking about?"

"Agent Bannerman," said Hawkins, anger vibrating through his voice, "did you pay any attention at all during the briefing?"

Tal felt lightheaded. "I tried, sir, but—"

"Cut him a break, Hawk. It's a lot to swallow," said the man on Tal's right, an agent with thinning blond hair and a rosy complexion that shone through it like a beacon. His name was Wrigley.

"We don't have time—"

"And you're wasting what little we have."

Hawkins pulled in a deep breath and turned to Tal with a curt smile. "It's a bio-engineered version of the Hantavirus. Goreham says they reversed the gene that causes it to die in direct sunlight. This mutated strain grows and thrives in heat and light. In fact, the higher the temperature, the more virulent the virus and the more exponential its proliferation."

Tal's stomach dropped as if he'd swallowed a brick and the sour tang of nervous sweat filled his nostrils. This was bad. This was beyond bad. Hanta had a forty percent fatality rate—the ordinary, unaltered version of it. This engineered megavirus would be far more potent and he didn't know how they could combat it. There was no cure.

"And you said they're planning to disperse it using Mt. Rainier's eruption?"

"As an atomizer, yes. When the volcano explodes, gas, ash, and hot rock will spew for miles, at very high temperatures. If they're successful in introducing even a small amount of the bio-agent into the blast zone, it will mushroom and rain down over half the state. Prevailing winds are to the east, which will carry it even further."

"And when people start getting sick," said Tal's boss, Ziegfeld, "the epidemic will be unstoppable."

It was more than Tal could deal with all at once, so he pushed most of it to the back of his brain. "What's with the Moses getup?"

"The man we have in custody, Everglade, said one or more suicide bio-bombers will carry packets of powder infected with the virus up the mountain and wait for it to blow. He says the powder is being smuggled into the country and will be passed off to the bombers some time this afternoon at the roadblock on Highway 165."

"Okay. I'm still not seeing how the Prince of Egypt comes into it."

"That roadblock is party town. Crazies from across the country are gathering there in defiance of the mountain, dancing and reveling like the Israelites around the golden calf in the shadow of Mt. Sinai. Moses will fit right in and the flowing robe will allow you to hide an essential piece of paraphernalia."

"Such as?"

"Such as this containment unit," said Ziegfeld, tapping on a metal capsule about the size of a football. "It has an inner chamber for extra protection." He demonstrated how to open the capsule and remove the canister inside.

"I'm supposed to wear this under my Moses robe?" Tal asked, shaking his head. "I'll look pregnant."

Ziegfeld waved a fist under Tal's nose. "I'm going to pop you one, Bannerman, if you don't get with the program. Millions could die, and you're worried about how you'll look in a dress."

Wrigley spoke up again. "It's shock, sir. It often shifts people's focus in funny directions. Let's go over the plan."

"All right," said Hawkins. "We'll have a command post set up in a van at the roadblock. Wrigley, Crowther, and Franklin will comb the crowd. Bannerman, you'll hang out on the fringes and wait for the cue."

"What cue?"

"Goreham told us Intikam is set up for karaoke. After the powder is handed off, one of their guys will sing a particular song, a signal for the bombers to head up the mountain."

Tal couldn't help it. The tension inside him was wound so tight there was no way to hold it back. He busted up, laughter billowing out of him until he was gasping for breath. Wrigley pounded him on the back.

"Easy now," he said. "Inhale nice and slow."

"This is some kind of elaborate joke, right? You guys are testing me, determining my psychological fitness maybe." Tal held on to that shred of hope until Ziegfeld shot it all to hell.

"Wake up, Bannerman! This is happening. Hanta is your wheelhouse and you're dealing with it."

Tal swallowed hard. He deserved this. He was a bad person, getting what he deserved. If he'd married Bridget, he'd be mowing the lawn right now.

"What song?" he asked.

Hawkins looked uncomfortable. "We're working on it, but Everglade hasn't told us yet."

"Okay, so I wait to hear the secret song no one knows the name of and then what?"

"Wrigley, Crowther, and Franklin will follow the bomber—or bombers—into the woods, tailing them until they're a safe distance away from the crowd. They'll immobilize and disarm the bombers. That's when you come in, secure the bio-agent, and we all go home to wait for Rainier to erupt, killing only thousands instead of the millions it might have been."

"Cheery outcome," said Tal.

"It is what it is," agreed Hawkins.

"One more thing you should know, Bannerman." Ziegfeld's face, gray with strain and grimed with perspiration, blurred in front of Tal's tired eyes. "This engineered virus, when activated by extreme heat, causes a full-blown, communicable disease. The long-term ramifications of that are dire, but there are short-term concerns as well."

Tal sighed. There would be.

"Even in a semi-dormant state, the virus in powder form, if inhaled, causes immediate respiratory distress, membrane bleeding, and a quick death. Goreham assures us that Intikam will have equipped the powder packs with a detonator designed to blow on impact. Sort of like a dead man's switch."

Dead man being the operative term. "Good to know," Tal said. "Thank you so much." He turned to Hawkins. "Do I get a gun?"

Hawkins sat back, crossing his arms over his chest. "Do you know how to use one?"

"You should see me with my Elite Rhino-Fire Blaster."

"Then by all means, we'd be happy to issue you a Nerf pistol on a par with your expertise."

"You could have just said no."

"I did." Hawkins scanned the table. "That's all, gentlemen. Let's get this show on the road."

Tal stepped out of the van and felt the sting of many stares upon him. Even with the robe swishing around his ankles, he felt naked. How do women do it—going out into the world without pants? Too much air flow around his privates was making him nervous. Well, more nervous.

Strapped to his boxers was a quasi-holster securing the containment vessel against his abdomen, making him indeed appear pregnant. The empathy training module he'd endured on his initiation into the CDC couldn't hold a candle to this. He might make a suggestion for the feedback box.

If he came out of this alive.

As strange a spectacle as he made with his robe, beard, and cardboard replica of the Ten Commandments, no one stared for long. There were too many other gawk-worthy wonders spread under the towering pines.

A party atmosphere prevailed. The road, and the enormous clearing on either side, was lined with cars and trucks parked haphazardly, tailgates open, lawn chairs out. Portable barbecues smoked and sizzled, the smell of roasting hotdogs threatening to bring up the meager contents of Tal's stomach.

The air thumped with a heavy bass beat, and a nightmarish mix of music blared—metal competing against blue-grass and hip-hop as if a prize for volume points were on offer. Enterprising folks stood behind card tables, hawking ball-caps and T-shirts with pithy volcanic slogans—"Me and Joe vs The Volcano" and "Just when you thought it was safe to go hiking"—along with vials of ash, pumice stones, and Rainier-shaped ashtrays. Buy two, get one free.

Tal was more accustomed to working behind a microscope than with a squirming mass of live humans. "Where do I go?" he asked Wrigley.

Wrigley pointed. "I want you to stay out on the fringes and keep an eye on anyone heading off into the trees. How's your earpiece? Can you hear me now?"

Tal was too stressed to appreciate any trace of humor that might be wrung from the worn-out joke. "I hear you," he said. "Am I coming through?"

"We got you," said a voice from the command center.

"Off you go, then." Wrigley gripped his hand in a firm shake. "You'll do great, Doctor."

Tal trudged over to hang with the outcasts, trying not to trip on his skirts. A whiskered man in a tattered gray watch cap lounged back on his elbows, sharing a bottle with a fat woman in a flowered sundress. She persistently brushed a non-existent strand of hair from her face while keeping up a rumbling conversation with herself in a low, gravelly voice. A yellow cat rested at her feet, licking its paws.

Beyond them, an old man with a scraggly beard and bald head paced along the edge of the crowd, quoting scripture. A sandwich board encased his scrawny body. In blood red letters, the back of it asked: ARE YOU READY? When the man about-faced to begin his return trip, Tal saw the front: DOOMSDAY IS HERE! THE END IS NEAR!

Wrigley hadn't been kidding about the fringe. As Tal gazed into the milling crowd, a squishy missile hit the side of his head and fell to the ground. He stooped to pick it up, and his earpiece crackled to life.

"A new piece of information just came in from Everglade. The powder will be packaged to look like a hacky sack."

Tal stared at the bag in his hand. Somewhat larger than a regular hacky sack, it bore the words: I KICKED RAINIER'S ASH. Another souvenir.

"Sorry Mister Moses," said the kid who came to collect it. "Pretty cool, right? It's filled with genuine ash."

"Yeah, super cool. Where'd you get it?"

The kid pointed to a woman bearing a wicker basket over her arm before snatching the sack and kicking it to a friend. The woman strolled through the crowd, handing out hacky sacks. Tal approached her.

"Want one?" she asked.

"Love one," he said, tucking the toy into a pocket of his voluminous gown. "Did you make these?"

"Heck no. A guy gave me fifty bucks to distribute them for some marketing campaign."

Clever. Shades of the Thomas Crown Affair. Plaster the area with decoys.

"Which guy?"

She shrugged. "He left."

Tal spoke to command, telling them what he'd discovered.

"Nice job, Bannerman. This just came in. The signal song is *Don't Fear The Reaper*."

"I don't know that one."

"Everyone knows *The Reaper*."

"Hum a few bars."

"Laaaa, la, la, la, la. Laaaa, la, la, la, la—"

"Not ringing a bell."

"Never mind, just watch the fringe. Wrigley and the others will follow the suspects and you follow *them*. At a distance. Copy?"

"I copy."

Ugh.

Someone belted out the last few bars of *Livin' On A Prayer* that would've made Bon Jovi eat a loaded pistol. There was a pause, followed by a squeal of feedback. Then a man spoke, his voice fraught with appeal.

"Ladies and gentlemen, please listen to this important announcement. Mt. Rainier is about to erupt. I repeat, the mountain is gonna blow. Please pack your things and leave in an orderly fashion. You are in danger here and you n—"

The voice broke off and a loud *thunk* resounded, as if the speaker had dropped the mike. After a flurry of rustling and curse words, a mellow tenor broke out singing *Grandma's Featherbed*. Tal watched as two men dragged a third between them, depositing him in a heap next to the woman in the sundress and her cat, who protested with a yowl.

Wanting—and yet fearing—to ask the man about the announcement he'd tried to make, Tal backed off. He couldn't afford to be distracted by conversation right now. John Denver signed off and a new song started up. Tal didn't know the words, but he found himself singing along by the third chorus. La, la, la, la, laaaaaa!

It was time. Tal's heart thudded so loud in his aching chest that he barely heard the voice in his ear.

"Package is on the move. I repeat, the pa—hold on, two packages moving out. We have a single white male with a backpack headed up from the north end of the clearing, and an older couple leaving the south side."

"I see them," said Tal.

Wrigley piped up. "I'll cover the single. Crowther and Franklin, you take the couple."

No response. "Crowther? Do you copy?"

Silence.

"Command, something's happened to Crowther and Franklin. I'm already on the single. Bannerman, you'll have to take the couple on your own."

"Oh no," Tal said. "Not without my Rhino-Fire Blaster."

A voice boomed from command. "Get moving, Bannerman, before you lose them."

Tal stared at the poster in front of him. DOOMSDAY IS HERE! THE END IS NEAR! He sank to his knees, burying his head in his hands. They were all going to die. The fast way—scalded by volcanic emissions, drowned by epic mud-flows—or the slower, more agonizing route—lesions, internal bleeding, and oxygen starvation. He thought of Bridget, dear Bridget. He could have married her and died blissfully unaware of all this.

"Bannerman, what's your position?" a voice demanded.

"Moses is praying!" someone in the crowd shouted.

Tal realized he was still on his knees, head bowed, and prayer was the most sensible thing he could be doing at this moment. He tore out his earpiece and turned his heart heavenward, pouring out his fears, pleading forgiveness for his cowardice, begging mercy for the people of the earth.

He heard a voice: "Get up, Talmadge, and get thee into the mountain. You can do this."

It was Wrigley, speaking from the dangling earpiece, but Tal thought it might have been inspired by a higher source. He took heart, lifting his head just as the man in the sandwich board made his turn at the end of his pace. The message flashed like a beacon: ARE YOU READY?

Tal squared his shoulders and hit the button that would carry his voice to Command.

"Agent Bannerman, reporting for duty."

It was a tough slog through slippery pine needles and tree roots, tripped up at every turn by the blasted robe. At least he'd drawn the line at the flimsy sandals they'd wanted him to wear. The fate of the world might swing on his choice to stick with a good athletic shoe.

A fluffy-tailed squirrel spiraled up the trunk of an alder tree, scolding him as he passed. He hadn't spotted the couple yet, but knew they were up there. His instructions were to let them get at least 600 yards away from the roadblock before revealing himself, and then try to talk them into turning over the hacky sack.

Yeah, right.

Long before reaching the 600 yard mark, a faint whiff of something floated in the thick-needled pines ahead of him—an odor he remembered from college. The couple had stopped for a smoke. He adopted the air of a casual hiker as he approached the log where they sat, passing a joint, and realized he'd never pull off the casual hiker charade dressed as he was.

But he was wrong.

"Hey, brother," said the man. "Pull up a stump, take a toke."

He wore a long robe of a dark gold hue, and did Tal one better by completing the effect with a pair of sandals. Three or four strings of beads looped his neck, a large silver peace sign hanging from one of them.

Tal's brain raced, burning rubber inside his head. Was it possible this was an innocent couple who'd coincidentally headed up the mountain on cue? He felt a weight lift, life and breath flooding into his lungs. Of course! They were in no way dressed for a hike to the top of Rainier. Wrigley, the trained professional, was tracking the one true bomber.

He eased himself down onto a fallen tree, waving away the burning twist of paper. "Nah, I'm cool," he said. The woman smiled at him, her eyes looking a thousand miles beyond, halfway to stoned. She wore a flower in her hair. A white petal daisy with a fat yellow center, the bloom of innocence.

They passed the time chatting until the joint burned down to the clip. Tal let out a loud, satisfied sigh.

"We should go back down now," he said.

"You go," said the woman. "We'll be along shortly."

A reluctant spear of doubt pierced Tal's certainty. Duty called for more probing.

"Did you folks pick up any souvenirs this afternoon?" he asked.

"We sure did," said the man. "I bought a T-shirt and Hetty got a vial of genuine volcanic ash."

"Not a hacky sack?"

The man's face turned hard. He opened his mouth to speak, but the woman laid a hand on his arm. "Is that the little beanbag thing you kick around?" she asked. "Yes, we got one from a lovely young girl."

"May I see it?"

The man stood. "No, you may not. We've tried to be subtle about it, son, but you're not taking the hint. Some folks like to light up after, but we like to have our little smoke beforehand. Get my drift? Now beat it."

A wave of heat washed over Tal's face. He felt like a fool.

"I'm sorry," he said, standing up. His glance fell upon a backpack behind the stump, its open mouth revealing a down jacket and sturdy pair of hiking boots, as well as the rounded corner of what looked like the hacky sack in question. A conviction that he was in the company of a ruthless pair of bio-terrorists descended upon him. He had to think fast.

Fixing his eyes on the man, Tal spoke in a clipped, no-nonsense voice. "Well done. I was sent to test your commitment to our cause, but I can see you mean to carry out your mission. In that case, I must tell you that the hacky sack is a dummy. I can now release the real bio-agent into your care."

He lifted his skirt to reveal the containment vessel strapped against his belly. He freed it from its holder and pressed the release button. The slight hiss of a vacuum seal escaped the vessel and Tal removed the inner canister, handling it with exaggerated caution.

"I applaud your courage and integrity," he said, handing over the capsule. "Do not, under any circumstances, open this until you've reached your position at the top and eruption is imminent." After a pause, he added, "I'll need to take the hacky sack in exchange."

The couple eyed him suspiciously, but Tal held his ground.

"Okay," said the man, retrieving the hacky sack. "But before you do..."

He tossed the bag of powder high into the late afternoon sky. It hung against the blue backdrop, frozen for a single instant, before beginning its plunge downward to meet the man's lifted foot. That impact would set off the detonator, exploding deadly powder in a radius wide enough to wipe out every happy camper at the roadblock party in choking, writhing agony. No one deserved that.

Not even the woman who'd butchered Bon Jovi.

Springing off the soles of his trusty sneakers, Tal leapt into the air, holding the containment vessel open to receive the falling bomb. He stretched his arms to meet the deadly package, but he overshot and the bag fell to the ground with a *plop*.

Tal rolled into a ball, squeezing his eyes shut and holding his breath. He counted off twenty seconds before he was forced to gasp down a tortured breath. He waited for the agonizing spasms, the blood pouring from his nose, and prepared to die. Ten seconds after that, he opened his eyes. The woman stood before him, an identical hacky sack in her hand, a taunting look on her face.

"Is this what you're so interested in?" she asked.

Tal sat up, swallowing. His throat was so tight it hurt. "Please don't do this," he pleaded. "Millions of innocent people will die."

"There's no such thing as an innocent person anymore," she said, her voice a harsh twang. "Every one of us has dirt on our hands, but at least we're willing to do something about it, something to stop the spread."

Now there's an ironic mind twist. Tal tried once more. "There are better ways—"

"Just zip it," said the woman.

The man picked up the containment vessel, hefting it in his hand. "What's your name, son?" he asked.

"Tal. My name is Tal."

"Say goodnight, Tal."

The man swung the vessel and everything went black.

A searing pain shot through his cheekbone and Tal shifted, coming fully awake. He'd been lying face down on a sharp stone and was relieved to find most of the pain receded when he sat up.

"I knew you'd be coming around soon. You did good, kid." It was Wrigley.

The sun was lower in the sky, but enough daylight still spilled through the swaying pine branches for Tal to see that the couple had vanished, leaving behind the containment vessel they'd pounded him with.

"They got away," he said dully.

"True," Wrigley replied. "But don't feel too bad about it. They left you a little something to remember them by."

He gestured toward the log. At its base lay a T-shirt and a tube-shaped vial of genuine ash, accompanied by a handwritten note.

Dear Tal,

Sorry to bump you like that. You seem almost redeemable, but we have a job to do and couldn't let you stand in our way. You have a liking for souvenirs, so we left you ours. Enjoy them in your last moments.

Boris and Natasha

"It's funny," said Wrigley, "even to the bitter end they're reluctant to use their real names."

"But we have to go after them! They've got the hacky sack. They have to be stopped."

"Oh, they'll be stopped all right. Which reminds me, we should be getting out of here. Rainier really is going to blow at any moment and we'll want to be many miles away when it does."

"But what about the virus? It will disseminate, wiping out the western United States before spreading around the rest of the world."

"I don't think it will," Wrigley said with maddening calm. "You see, the single guy with the backpack was the lead on the operation. Goes by the code name Hades. I took him down, applied a little pressure in all the right places, and it didn't take long for him to crack. He told us the hacky sacks were a harmless decoy to throw us off the real scent. Given the right motivation, Everglade confirmed it. The real bio-agent is in the vial of ash, left to you so generously by our escaping friends."

Tal winced, rubbing his forehead, "They didn't know?"

"They didn't know. Hades didn't trust them. He instructed them to mix in with the crowd, pick up a few souvenirs. He forced the vial of ash on them like a magician forces a card, while letting them think the lethal stuff was in the hacky sack the whole time. He marked it special for them. Instead of saying 'I kicked Rainier's *ash*' it says, 'I kicked Rai—"

"I get it, Wrigley. Thanks for putting me in the picture."

"Sure thing. That's enough slack time, buddy. Do what you came here to do. Put the deadly bio-agent in the containment vessel and let's make like the Red Sea and split."

"Hey Wrigley, will you pass the sugar?"

"No can do," said the agent, pulling it out of Tal's reach. "That stuff will kill you, Bannerman."

"Along with thirty-six thousand seven hundred and nineteen other white, crystalline substances known to man," Tal said. "Why can't you just let me poison myself in peace?"

He sighed and drank his coffee black and bitter.

He and Wrigley had been meeting every Thursday lunch hour for the past six weeks, steering things toward a certain conclusion. As they finished up and shook hands, Wrigley said, "I'm glad we'll be working together in the Seattle office. Homeland's lucky to be getting you."

"I'm looking forward to it too, though Ziegfeld gets a little cranky any time I bring it up."

"He hates that we found a loophole around your two-year obligation."

"Yeah, speaking of obligations, don't forget—the wedding's on Saturday."

"Not on your life, buddy. I'll be there."

"Great! Bridget can't wait to meet you."

Tal pulled up the hood of his raincoat and stepped out into a drizzling flurry of droplets so tiny they fluttered like snowflakes. It still terrified him, thinking about the events of that day last fall and how close they'd all come to being obliterated. But it made him realize one thing.

He could face a lot more than he gave himself credit for. He had coasted through life long enough, and now he'd better do what he came here to do. Bridget, the three kids, and the mortgage didn't scare him anymore.

But the mother-in-law? He shuddered—that was another matter entirely.

Thank you for reading *Rapid Pursuit*

If you enjoyed the book, I would love for you to leave a review to help other readers find and enjoy it, too. Thank you so much for taking the time to share your opinion.

If you haven't yet joined my readers' group, you're just a click away from VIP access to bonuses and updates.

Visit https://joslynchase.com or scan the QR code.

I'd love to welcome you aboard!

Scan here for more books by Joslyn Chase

ABOUT THE AUTHOR

Joslyn Chase is a prize-winning author of mysteries and thrillers. Any day where she can send readers to the edge of their seats, chewing their fingernails to the nub and prickling with suspense, is a good day in her book.

Joslyn's story, "Cold Hands, Warm Heart," was chosen by Amor Towles as one of the *Best Mystery Stories of the Year 2023* and "A Band of Scheming Women" was a finalist for the Derringer Award in 2025. The second book in the Riley Forte Suspense Thriller series, *Staccato Passage,* was chosen as a semi-finalist for the Adventure Writer's Grandmaster Award in 2025, as well.

Her short stories have appeared in *Alfred Hitchcock's Mystery Magazine, Malice Domestic's Mystery Most Devious, Thrill Ride Magazine, Fiction River, Mystery, Crime, and Mayhem, Mystery Magazine,* and *Pulphouse Fiction,* among others.

Known for her fast-paced suspense fiction, Joslyn's books are full of surprising twists and delectable turns. You will find her riveting novels most anywhere books are sold.

Her love for travel has led Joslyn to ride camels through the Nubian desert, fend off monkeys on the Rock of Gibraltar, and hike the Bavarian Alps. But she still believes that sometimes the best adventures come in getting the words on the page and in the thrill of reading a great story.

Join the growing group of readers who've discovered the thrill of Chase! Sign up for Joslyn's readers' group and get VIP access to great bonuses—like your free copy of *No Rest: 14 Tales of Chilling Suspense*—as well as updates and first crack at new releases.

Visit joslynchase.com to get started now!

bookbub.com/authors/joslyn-chase

facebook.com/joslynchasewriter

goodreads.com/author/show/16850235.Joslyn_Chase

linkedin.com/in/joslynchase/

pinterest.com/joslynchase/

youtube.com/@joslynchase5955/videos